QUICK TRIGGERS

EUGENE CUNNINGHAM

THORNDIKE
CHIVERS

This Large Print edition is published by Thorndike Press, Waterville, Maine, USA and by BBC Audiobooks Ltd, Bath, England.
Thorndike Press, a part of Gale, Cengage Learning.

The text of this Large Print edition is unabridged.
Other aspects of the book may vary from the original edition.
Set in 16 pt. Plantin.
Printed on permanent paper.

LIBRARY OF CONGRESS CATALOGING-IN-PUBLICATION DATA

Cunningham, Eugene, 1896-1957.
    Quick triggers / by Eugene Cunningham.
        p. cm. — (Thorndike Press large print western)
    ISBN-13: 978-1-4104-0514-2 (alk. paper)
    ISBN-10: 1-4104-0514-1 (alk. paper)
    1. Large type books. I. Title.
PS3505.U428Q85 2008
813'.52—dc22   2007046706

BRITISH LIBRARY CATALOGUING-IN-PUBLICATION DATA AVAILABLE

Published in 2008 in the U.S. by arrangement with Golden West Literary Agency.

Published in 2008 in the U.K. by arrangement with Golden West Literary Agency.

U.K. Hardcover: 978 1 405 64472 3 (Chivers Large Print)
U.K. Softcover: 978 1 405 64473 0 (Camden Large Print)

Printed in the United States of America
1 2 3 4 5 6 7 12 11 10 09 08

QUICK TRIGGERS

CHAPTER I

Poplar station was noisy and crowded, for it was payday in that section of The Territory. Twenty cow outfits, large and small, were in town. Men young and old and middle-aged crowded the long main street, the seven or eight cross-streets, yelling enthusiastically at acquaintances rarely met — or just yelling. Dance-halls, stores, saloons, gambling layouts, were ready for their customers.

For Poplar was a wide-open "hurrah" town, a young man's town, a salty town, a town as dangerous as any in The Territory for the man who could not use his head or fists or guns — particularly head and guns. . . .

The customers in the Horsehead Saloon — townsmen and transients alike — knew this so well that it never occurred to the most philosophical to voice the fact. They merely watched young Clay Borden playing stud, or mentioned him as they drank at the

Horsehead's long bar, and wondered if he would "last out." Five men were at the stud table with Clay — a big freight contractor, a storekeeper, two brown and shabby riders of the XLN outfit, and — Pecos Pawl.

Clay Borden, at twenty-four, with some reason considered himself a tolerably experienced young man. Ten years of saddle tramping in five states and across into Mexico had made him learned in many subjects found in no books whatever. But he looked no more than nineteen or twenty. He was perhaps five-seven — and slender. His blue eyes were wide and somehow incredibly innocent against the light bronze of his smooth skin.

Poplar Station inspected the almost girlish regularity of his features, ticketed him swiftly and turned to Pecos Pawl. For the two of them had played without stopping during the afternoon. Other men had played a few hands, but Clay and Pecos were fixtures. And Clay had won or lost smilingly, treating Pecos as if he were an ordinary hard-working rider, instead of the bad-tempered gunman Poplar Station knew him to be.

"Bet 'em!" Pecos snarled at Clay, after a squint at the three other stud hands remaining in the pot. "Your pair of aces is high.

8

Bet 'em — Baby-Face!"

Clay lifted his eyes quickly. He had learned on many a spread, in many a cow-camp, in twenty cow-towns like Poplar Station, not to show that he minded the nicknames that seemed bound to come with sight of his features. But this particular phrase always edged his quick and gifted tongue. However, now he controlled his expression. "High they are," he agreed, in a drawl a bit slower, softer, than usual. He studied Pecos's pair of kings, backed by the ten of clubs.

"All right, a pair of aces is quite something to figure, in stud. So — right into the face of that possible two pair or three of a kind, we bet you four round chips — *Funny-Face!* Oil up your old bones and pop your whip!"

About the table, men stiffened. For Pecos's yellow eyes flamed like an angry cat's. The watchers looked from the reckless boy to the grim, battered, and leathery face of the older man. They were ready to slide out of bullet range at the first twitch of Pecos's hands.

Then they saw what the gunman had possibly seen in the beginning. Accidentally — perhaps — Clay Borden's right hand had disappeared beneath the table. Those who knew Pecos's week-long record in Poplar stared narrowly at Clay's innocent blue eyes and easy grin. Their expressions were speculative. Pecos had been winning heavily at one game or another during his week here. He had blown the bulk of his winnings in saloons and dance-halls. He had added a notch to the tally on one of his matched .45s. A pretty tolerable gunfighter that notch represented, too. And now a beardless child from Nowhere was rubbing the killer's hair backward.

The XLN cowboy on Clay's left hesitated. He stared at the blue chips; peeped at his hole card and whistled dolefully. Then he pushed in all but two of his chips.

"I'll see one card, fellow," he told Clay. "But by rights, I had ought to be back at the XLN wagon, with my boots off, and a rag tied around my head and my both feet in hot water — real *hot* water!"

The storekeeper at his left, at the end of the table, shook his head and turned his jack-ten-four face down. "*Uh-uh! Uh-uh!* I been a damn fool long enough. Frostbite wins by a mile, gents. How do *I* know I'd catch two more jacks."

Pecos glared at Clay. Since they had sat down four hours before, the play had been a virtual duel between them. They had been the heavy winners. They had seesawed back and forth, their piles of chips about even in amount. Pecos picked up his whisky glass and emptied it. He was plainly irritated.

"There's your four chips — and I up you ten!"

Clay frowned a little as he studied Pecos's cards. His small, tanned left hand played uncertainly with his chips. Pecos's mouth curled unpleasantly. The other players had quit.

"That's a plumb wicked hand to bet into . . ." Clay muttered, just above his breath. "Old Snaggle-Tusk might accidentally *have* 'em. But then again, he mightn't. So —— There's the raise and I'm upping *you* twenty more! It's going to cost you about all an old man ought to risk, to see another card!"

The XLN puncher waved both hands. He was out — gone! He leaned back to watch the duel comfortably. Clay made a cigarette. Pecos snarled and shoved in two stacks of blues.

"Deal 'em! I'll show you a few, before I'm done with you!"

"Yip-yip-yip-yip!" Clay cried mournfully, and slapped the trey of hearts on Pecos's layout. "Excuse me! I'm getting so clumsy you wouldn't believe it! I meant to give you another ten. Well, let's see what Old Lady Luck has got for me!"

He slid the top card from the deck and faced it — and grunted like one punched amidships at sight of the nine of spades. He pulled his silken neckerchief up around his neck and shivered ostentatiously.

"Will somebody please ask Bar-keep for some more wood on the fire? This is the coldest day in June I can remember. Well, Grandpa! How you feeling? Could you be persuaded to check the bet?"

Pecos made an angry-dog noise in his throat. Clay nodded to the watchers, very solemnly.

"He says he won't check. Says he never did care much for checks except on his Sunday shirt! And he wouldn't even *dream* of checking on a Tuesday. Well, sir! You have got me so excited now, I am not responsible. In spite of the terrible shortage of aces we've noticed so far, I'm going to bet you — oh, about four stacks of blues!"

"Yeh? Well, sonny, there's the bet! And you better reach in your cradle and lick the glue off your chips. For if you aim to stick around in a grown man's game, she's going to cost — every last chip I got here and —"

He fished in his pocket and brought out three gold twenties. He shoved the whole pile violently toward the table's center. Clay groaned again and rubbed a smooth chin.

"You know," he confided to the watching men, "I really don't feel so good! My erysipelas is bothering me again! I thought maybe I'd scare him plumb out into the wilderness; out in that far region the poets tell about, where the owls marry into the chicken families — and here he does a thing like that! I don't know him real well . . . Could he, you-all reckon, be desperately striving to scare out my pretty aces? Or has he got something he's fond of, in the hole?"

He checked the chips and scowled.

"You're topping my last penny by forty dollars. If you'll drag the forty, I'll call you off the cross!"

"She goes as she lays! I been hearing a lot of loud, windy noises out of you. Now — put up or shut up!"

"I'll put up my blue cutting horse for the forty."

"That crowbait?" Pecos jeered. "Nothing stirring!"

Two twenties rang on the table from the end where the storekeeper was sitting. He grinned at Clay. "I saw that blue horse you rode in. I like his looks forty dollars' worth. Anyhow, this is too good to boggle down over forty dollars."

Then, meeting Pecos's baleful yellow eyes, he lost his grin and stared soberly enough at Pecos's hand.

"Kings! Three of 'em!" Pecos cried triumphantly. "And you got no more aces, for I see two throwed away by these fellows that pulled in their horns."

"Likely, *you* mistook that deuce of spades for an ace. I almost did. And I have got three aces. Count 'em — three!"

He was reaching for the chips when Pecos whipped up a .45 and rammed it almost into his face.

"Yeh? Well! A .45 beats three aces! Three aces like them. Gents! I seen two aces throwed away. He couldn't have three aces — honest!"

He leaned toward Clay:

"You ought to be killed — coming in here with your baby face and trying to run a sandy like that! I swear, I don't know why I don't plug you full of holes. But you can stick your hands up around your ears and drag it — fast. Clean out of this neck of the woods. If *I* see you again, nobody'll ever see you no more. Drag it!"

"A .45 does seem to make your three kings beat three aces," Clay said thoughtfully. "I reckon it would have made a pair of deuces plumb unbeatable. So ——"

He put his left hand to hatbrim in mock-salute. And the hat left his head in a snake-like forward dart. He twisted sideways and his right hand flashed to the Colt that swung butt-front on his left thigh. Pecos's pistol went off, but the bullet was wild. It plowed the ceiling. Clay's slug struck the gunman on the wrist and went on to put a hole in his shoulder. The second bullet struck Pecos on the point of the jaw. He fell face downward across the table.

Clay caught him by the shoulder and looked at him quickly, then shrugged. Pecos was merely nicked on the jaw, and the hole in his shoulder was too high to be dangerous. The XLN rider who had cut the cards for Clay's deal stood up.

"He was lying about that ace!" he told Clay. "I see the two of spades fall, too. He was just hunting an excuse — but it never seemed a judgmatical time for *me* to be telling him so!"

The storekeeper who had banked the game now got up off the floor, where he had hurled himself with the first shot. He paid Clay off and shook hands with him.

"Hope he catches blood poison!" he grunted in Clay's ear. "I'm certainly *grieved* you never hit him center!"

CHAPTER II

"I wonder how many good friends Pecos had here . . ." Clay Borden said to himself as he sat, after dark, in the You Bet Eating House. "That kind, lots of times, don't ever have many wet-weather *compadres* — but if they have got any at all, they're apt to be good. And me, I'm the pore strange lamb in the wolf pen. Any way I step, I'm likely to step the wrong way — and right down somebody's throat."

He saw nothing — which is to say, nobody — of dangerous aspect, in the restaurant. It was crowded, but few gave more than a passing glance to the smallish figure at a table in the corner. He was not a noticeable figure in that sort of gathering; his wide, gray hat, buttonless vest over blue cotton shirt, fringed shotgun leggings; even — or particularly — the Colt's .44 on his left thigh, were like the outfits of most of the punchers. A few, who had been in the

16

Horsehead during his row with Pecos, nudged their companions and indicated Clay.

He finished his third cup of coffee and went at stiff-legged horseman's gait up to pay for his meal. Somebody's elbow brushed his lightly, as he laid down his dollar before the fat woman who owned the place. Automatically, he turned with a thumb hooked in the waistband of his leggings, just over his Colt. Beside him was that friendly XLN puncher who had proclaimed Pecos Pawl a liar in the matter of the discarded ace.

"Better hightail!" the puncher muttered in his ear. "Pecos had some friends — hard cases. And more'n that — you're toting mucho dinero. Cut stick kind of non-publicly — but thorough!"

"Thanks! Thanks a lot!" Clay told him in the same tone, looking away with blank face. "But — who're these friends?"

He rolled a cigarette and glanced at the feeders who almost filled the room.

"They're — well — look out for a square-shouldered, black-eyed boy that's always grinning. Dink Badey's the name he's using around here. I —— But cutting stick's your bet."

Clay licked the edges of the cigarette paper and smoothed the cylinder; put it in

17

his mouth and got a match from his hat-band. He closed his eyes while he lit it, nor opened them until he had jerked out the little flame and broken the stick. He wanted no dazzle of retained vision to bother him. For it was very true that either friendship for Pecos, or the money sagging in his pockets, would furnish sufficient foundation for interest in him, here, tonight.

When he opened his eyes after that brief space, a square-shouldered and rather hand-some youngster was standing directly in front of him. Something clicked in Clay's memory with sight of this neatly dressed and smiling boy — for he was hardly more than that; twenty or twenty-one at the most. He remembered what grim old Long Al Kendrick, Bar B wagon boss, had said one night in a line camp over on the Diamond River.

"Frenchy Leonard? Yeh, a plumb bad egg and be damned if that's Spanish! Lit Taylor certainly must've took unto himself a col-lege education in gunfighting, to have beaten Frenchy Leonard to the leather and downed him over there at Los Alamos. But you listen to me, you damn' slick-ears that think you know lots:

"The dangerousest man, absolutely, that ever hit the Diamond River country and

18

shoved our stuff across into The Territory was that boy some called 'Smiling' and some named 'Fancy' because he was always slicked up and wore a grin nothing could rub off his face. Frenchy and him was side kickers, oncet. But they fell out over a Mex' gal in a *plazita* down the River, and if the gal hadn't run off with a *vaquero,* there'd been shooting. As it fell out, they busted up and never met again. My money'd have been on Smiling. For he's hell from the forks of the creek with his hardware. Frenchy was maybe a shade better with a long gun."

And here before him was Dink Badey, alias "Smiling," alias "Fancy." It was quite enough to make a young man in Clay Borden's position feel very, very thoughtful. For, according to Long Al's account, that smile he now wore meant nothing whatever. He could shoot down a man who had the drop on him and never once lose that gentle lip curving that showed even rows of white teeth. Clay pulled himself together.

"You're the young fellow that smoked up Pecos, huh?" the smiling gunman inquired. "They say you plumb fooled Pecos with the old hat trick. I never thought he'd fall for that."

"It's mighty hard to keep from dodging,"

19

Clay said carefully. "I've wondered, sometimes, if a fellow wouldn't jump back from a cigarette paper that was chunked at him."

He tried to put just the proper amount of scientific inquiry in his tone.

"Yeh, that's so — if a fellow's built to worry. Me, I never was. Born thataway I reckon. Nothing like that'd throw me off my balance a minute. If I was up against a man and he heaved a wagon at me, *I* would just shoot over or under or through it."

Clay had to wonder if this were just the matter-of-fact statement it sounded, or — a warning; a challenge. He knew he was pretty fast on the draw; pretty apt to throw his lead straight after the draw, regardless of side issues. But tales of Frenchy Leonard were still going around cow-camps and saloons, more than two years after his death. He had been "chain lightning and thirteen claps of thunder," the cowboys said. And here was a man Long Al called faster still.

"You got me interested," Badey said smilingly. Clay began to wonder if he grinned in his sleep. "Let's have a shot of whisky somewhere, and drink to better acquaintance."

They went out together. Smiling — Clay always thought of him by that name, afterward — kept on the outside of the wooden walk and moved at a silent, catlike gait which seemed habitual. They passed three or four saloons, then turned into a dingy place well up the main street, on the edge of Poplar's Mexican quarter.

There was a fair crowd in this saloon — and in the main a hard-looking bunch. The drinkers turned and, with sight of Smiling, they seemed to rather overdo their welcome. Or so Clay felt, and he was on edge tonight. He felt like a lobo wolf prowling about a barnyard.

"Hello, Smiling!" the bar-tender cried effusively. "First one's on the house. What'll it be? On the house, yessirree!"

"You just said it before I could," Smiling told him.

They drank, then Smiling looked at Clay and motioned toward a door that seemed to lead into a back room. Clay's face gave no sign of his ponderings. They were very quickly done, anyway. If he refused to leave the lighted bar-room it might very well mean a fight. And this was Smiling's hang-out, Smiling's crowd. If the young gunman had been no more than the usual hard case, still Clay would have hesitated. For — down Smiling and there would be plenty of others to swamp one man. So he nodded indifferently and seemed not to have hesitated at all.

The back room was a dingy little hole, with a pine table and five or six home-made, rawhide-bottomed chairs. The bar-tender came after them and stood in the doorway. To Clay, there was no alteration in the boy-gunman's face, but the man of drinks perhaps knew him better. He seemed to sense a difference.

"Can't I bring you-all some drinks — and some cigars?" he cried eagerly. "Business is easier talked over a bottle and a good cigar. And — and this is on me! Between friends!"

He hurried away. Smiling stared thoughtfully after him.

"Damn' mouthy fool," he grinned, evidently speaking of the bar-tender. "If I was sticking around much longer, I reckon I'd have to kill him. Seems like you have to kill some people, to learn 'em to keep their noses out of other folks' business."

When the bar-tender bustled in, to set a bottle and glasses and a box of pale, dry cigars upon the table, Smiling's hand went in a snaky movement toward the unbuttoned throat of his white shirt — and back again. The bar-tender squeaked like a frightened rabbit, and fled before the muzzle of that .45.

Smiling reholstered it under his arm with the same magically smooth, swift motion, reversed.

"Pecos was aiming to tie up with me!" he said abruptly to Clay. "But you put his tail in a sling. You got a couple of thousand, I reckon. I figure you win that much."

"Eleven hundred, about," Clay answered truthfully. "When I hit town I had nine dollars. This was my lucky day."

"Anyhow, you won't keep it long. None of us ever does. Whisky and women — and some more of the same. 'Houses and lots'; that's all it's good for. When you pass in your chips, you're a gone gosling. That's my idea. So nothing you take down under the grass roots with you is going to do you a bit of good. My motto's to grab everything I want right now — and my grab hook has proved right sharp, so far . . ."

He poured himself a drink and Clay followed suit, wondering what was to come; what idea lay behind that fixed smile and the black eyes with their suggestion of a reddish tinge.

"Throw in with me, fellow," Smiling proposed, when their drinks were down. "Take Pecos's place. I got an idea you're a better man than Pecos. He's too damn' old. Sulks around too much. You're more my style — you can laugh. Never see old Pecos laugh, and he's been on a job or two with me. We're rambling over farther into The Territory. Good pickings over there. And ——"

His smile widened a trifle as he paused; the black eyes narrowed in a sort of anticipation.

"And there's a girl," he went on softly.

Clay put both his hands on the table and leaned back. He whistled and seemed to consider; then leaned forward a trifle and folded his arms. He had no way of knowing how Smiling would take a refusal. He was ready for what he intended to make the fastest draw in his life, if gunplay became necessary. Chances were, he thought, that he hadn't a chance of matching speed with this boy — but he would try. It had never occurred to Clay in all his life to be afraid of another man.

"Now, now," he said, and his smile matched the other's. "I have got some chores of my own to do. It might be — even — you're not the only one thinking about a girl . . ."

"Girls would be bad medicine for you," Smiling told him. "I *sabe* that, if I don't know how I *sabe* it. Me, I can take my ladies like I take my whisky — take 'em or leave 'em alone. But I got a feeling that *you'd* be fool enough to cotton to one and want to marry her and settle down like a damn' nester — and all that *tonto* business. You better leave women alone."

Clay only grinned. But he was ready for action. Smiling surprised him, for he took no offense at his refusal. Instead, he poured himself another drink and sat staring at it.

"Going to be good pickings over west. A while back, like you maybe know, King Connell of the Los Alamos outfit was topdog. But John Powell of the Ladder P was about as hefty as the King. When the Governor whitewashed the books, for all the gunslicks and rustlers in The Territory, on condition they cut out fighting each other and buying each other's stuff from long ropers, Powell never come in. He sat back to see how everything worked out. He's a deep one, Big John Powell!"

"But they all calmed down, didn't they?" Clay objected frowningly. "That deputy sheriff, Lit Taylor, he downed Frenchy, and Frenchy's gang was whittled to pieces. Then Taylor, he married King Connell's daughter and started running the whole LA outfit over at Los Alamos. Since then the whole Territory has been more or less peaceful."

"Peaceful as a bunch of bulldogs that

don't know yet how long the whip is," Smiling drawedl. "But in two years they have come to figure they was unduly scared. John Powell wants to be the Whole Works in The Territory; wants to be the Big Casino clear across the table. And nobody's there to stop him. King Connell, he's went back to Ireland on one of his trips — and took Lit Taylor and Sudie May and the kid with him this time. You see — I know them all. Know them from the back!"

"You mean — it's going to be the old business, all over?"

"Fella!" Smiling assured him easily, "*it's going to be a heap more so!* For the other time, *I* wasn't mixed up into it any. I don't know what John Powell aims to do, but I know he owes me money and I'm hell on collecting what's due me. I'm going over and I'm going to see John Powell. I'm going to throw my white-handled .45s right up close to the Ladder P off ear . . .

"Old John, he'll say: 'Well, I be damned! If it ain't Smiling back again! He's come after what I owe him, of course! Reckon the boys over along the Diamond River never treated Smiling and his friends right. I better pay him up before he begins to cash in with that big old six-shooter!' He — will — that!"

There was no humor in his lip curling to match the rough humor of his description of John Powell. Clay was interested chiefly in getting away. He poured himself another drink and looked inquiringly at Smiling with bottle poised over the young killer's empty glass. Smiling nodded and Clay filled the glass. They looked each other squarely in the eyes and touched glasses.

"Salud' y pesetas," Clay grunted.

"To better acquaintance," Smiling replied.

They drank and Clay stood up.

"Thanks for the offer you made. But, like I told you, I've got some chores to finish up — and, too, I've got eleven hundred dollars."

Smiling's smile widened — somehow became sinister:

"The money won't bother you long. You won't keep it. You better forget about it and come along. I told you there was a girl. Maybe I'd give you an even break with her . . ."

"Even break!" Clay laughed. "What do you call an even break? A chance to shoot it out with you — and *you* packing the name of making Frenchy Leonard look like something out of the Old Folks' Home, at gunplay! Damn' if it looks even to me. Even break'd be letting the girl choose between

27

us. Who is she, anyhow? I don't know's I'd even look slaunch-ways at her!"

"John Powell's daughter. I never seen her, yet. But I see her picture once. She's been back to Philadelphia with John's old maid sister, going to some girls' school. She's been home a couple months now. She's pretty as a picture in a saloon!"

"I might drift over that way, later on. Now ____"

He shook his head and grunted his good-bye, then loafed out as if he had no such thought as was really in the forefront of his mind — of Smiling starting fast and furious gunplay. The men in the bar-room — several of them undoubtedly of the smiling killer's gang — looked curiously at him. But he walked under the shield of the boy in the back room. Had Smiling lifted a finger, Clay knew, there would be plenty to pull and kill without question. But, since he did not, none would take any initiative whatever in his presence. Then, behind him, he heard Smiling's voice.

"Turl! Jake Turl! Some of you tell Jake to come here!"

In the ten years since leaving Dallas County with a bunch of cowboys returning to Barred Diamond range, Clay had never held so much as two hundred dollars at one

28

time. He had gambled — everybody gambled in the cow-towns — which were the only towns he had seen except for one trip to Chicago. But fifty or sixty dollars was a big winning. And he had never been tempted to do any mavericking, or join the wilder of his fellows in shaking out a hungry loop in his skilled rope and heeling therewith salable horses.

Now, with his fortune in his leggings pockets, Clay was thinking pleasurably about his trip back to Dallas County. He pictured himself walking into the door of the Borden farmhouse and cascading gold pieces into his mother's apron. As he walked with a sort of instinctive, automatic caution, along the hell-roaring streets of Poplar Station, he was grinning to himself. His father had owed a thousand on the place ever since Clay could remember. He could show the grim old man that his wanderings had produced more than sticking at home could have done ——

He caught no more than a shadow of something coming out of the dark behind him and on his left. He reached for his pistol and began to turn, all in one lightning-fast motion. But he was too late. He went down with the pistol in his hand, under a savage hail of blows. He was unconscious before he fell flat on his face in the dirt of the sidewalk.

"*Git up!*" were the first words he heard. They came to him as from a tremendous distance. Vaguely, he wondered if they were addressed to him.

"*Git up!*" the command came clearer, nearer. "Put your hands up over your head, you damn' bar-louse! That's better! I would hate to waste a shell that could just as well kill a snake, on the likes of you. What was you taking off that drunk? His gun, huh? And he's —— By Godfrey! That's the young wolf that shot Pecos Pawl! Bum! When he comes to and finds out you was rolling him, The Territory won't be big enough for the two of you. And you know what that will mean!"

A hand gripped Clay's shoulder and shook him vigorously. Involuntarily, he groaned, then opened his eyes dizzily. When he could see anything plainly, he saw silhouetted against a window farther along the street a pair of boots. He tried three times to get up and managed to stagger to his feet with the help of the strong lifting grip.

"If I'd win what you win," his helper's voice said disapprovingly, "I would certainly pick me a better place than the street to sleep in. You young nitwit! I come along while this tinhorn sneak-thief was gitting ready to clean out your leggings and the seams of your clothes!"

Mechanically, Clay took back his .44, handed to him by the scolder. He felt in his pockets. A few silver dollars were in one.

But the winnings from the stud game were gone.

"He'd have got about fifteen dollars," he mumbled thickly. "For somebody else got to me first. I was knocked cold, from behind! Before he wandered up."

"My — stars! Come along to Irish Mike's. How much'd you lose?"

"Eleven hundred," Clay said dully, as they went toward the lighted saloon. "I was coming along and a fellow hopped out and cracked me. I had my pistol out, but not quick enough."

He had his drink at Irish Mike's bar, while his companion — the city marshal, it was — told all and sundry of the robbery. Clay's head ached from the heavy blows he had got. He was in a vile humor. Not only had his pocketbook been injured, but he had been pinked in a much more sensitive spot — his pride.

He had always believed that he could take care of himself in most situations a man might meet. And now, in the half-smiles he saw around him, he read amusement.

"This baby-faced kid" — he thought *they* were thinking, and whispering to one another — "he had a lucky break and gathered in a bunch of money, all right. But the hard cases took it off him like taking striped stick candy from a baby!"

He had another drink. His head was clearer, now. He answered the myriad questions put to him rather curtly. He saw — without paying any particular attention — the man who came through the front door and looked around — an ordinary sort of man.

"Anybody seen Turl lately?" the man asked of one of the interested group at Clay's elbow. "Jake Turl. Anybody seen him?"

Clay turned abruptly, so that he faced the man. Without thinking of what he did, he stared at the inquirer. For that name had set something moving in his head. Smiling had told him that the eleven hundred dollars wouldn't bother him long. "You won't keep it." Then Smiling had called from the back room:

"Turl! Jake Turl! Some of you tell Jake to come here!"

Now, there might not be the faintest connection with the robbery, in what Smiling had said about his losing the money swiftly; or between his calling for the man Turl, and the robbery.

But ——

"What do you want?" a voice called from the rear of the bar-room. "Flea bite you, huh?"

Clay was now perfectly in control of himself. He made no abrupt inquisitive turn to look at the man Turl. He yawned a little and looked at his empty glass; then he moved very deliberately until he could see the dusty rider. Turl was coming almost at a waddle, so curved were his legs.

He was thirty-five or thereabout; a hard-faced, stooping man of bullet head and bristling black hair and the small, grim, black eyes of an Indian. He looked like a breed — and like a salty customer to choose for a row. Nothing of the dude about him! Sweat-stained shirt; ancient and faded overalls, snagged here and there, one leg in, one leg out, of his boots; a wide cartridge belt with double row of shell loops and a black-handled Colt on his thigh in an open-topped holster — yes, he looked to be salty!

Clay turned back to the bar as Turl passed him going toward the man who wanted to see him. Then he turned slowly to the right and watched the pair from the corner of his eye.

Turl was standing six feet away, staring straight at Clay. And — what was his expression to be read as? Clay could have sworn that there was a mocking, malicious glint in the small black eyes; more mockery in the vague grin of his loose mouth.

That was all he needed.

He had been wondering what to do. Now, he had no more idea than before, but the interpretation he put on Turl's manner was like a spur. He moved across the intervening space and regarded the hard-faced older man very steadily. Turl's grin widened. It was as if he were admitting to Clay that all he suspected was true — and asking what he was going to do about it?

How prove it, to others?

One man, only, seemed to feel the tension or give any heed to Clay as he moved toward Turl. That was the sardonic city marshal. He stared frowningly at the pair of them, but hesitated.

Poplar Station was a place not much troubled by book law. City marshals were not apt to hunt trouble with such as Smiling's men.

So — he continued to hesitate.

"You know, Turl," Clay drawled, "I was

34

just thinking — about Smiling: How he as good as warned me that I couldn't hang onto my money. And how he called *you* to come get your powders — as I was walking out of the place, you know? Where's Smiling?"

"*Quién sabe?*" Turl said carelessly. He shrugged and grinned. "Rode out somewheres — right soon after *you* went out. Why?"

"Just wondered. Thought I'd ask him a question. But I can ask you, just as well. *What'd you do with my money?*"

There was a sound, in that hushed barroom, as if the long room had been a living creature — and had suddenly gasped. Even to Clay, concentrating on the man before him, it became clear that this Turl was one with a reputation. Which in no wise slowed him; merely made him a shade more careful.

"Money? Money? What do you think you're driving at?" Turl demanded, without losing that mocking grin. "You never give me no money. You give Smiling some? If you did, you'll have to see him about it."

"But, you see, *he* didn't slap me on the back of the head with a pistol — and take this money I'm talking about, out of my pocket."

The bar-room's second gasp was one so tense as to be agonized. But the watchers, listeners, were rooted to their places. For this was killing-talk! They went unceremoniously out of the line of possible lead. The bar-tender's moan and the scuff of his backward sliding feet were plain even in the noise of the others moving.

Clay understood it all — perfectly. These others were the ones misunderstanding. Clay thought that Turl must have a record; must be more than ordinary as a performer with that rather high-slung Colt. But he had one advantage and he was gambling that it would be enough — *he* knew exactly what he intended to do if Turl's hands went toward his gun.

"Are you saying that I knocked you in the head and stole your money?" Turl cried. He glowered fiercely at Clay's smooth, youthful face. "Why, I'll pistol-whip you ——"

"You won't pistol-whip anybody!" Clay told him flatly. "You hid in the dark and sneaked out behind me — like you had been told to do! But coyote tricks like that are your limit. You haven't got the sand to try anything in the open ——"

Then Turl drew! The black-handled Colt flashed out with a smooth, practiced speed that would have explained the bar-room's gaspings — if Clay had had time to consider the matter. It came out of the holster, a long-barreled .45 with the hammer back as the muzzle cleared holster top. Even though Clay had been the stage manager of this business and had known that Turl must fight as well as show his part in the robbery, and so had been expectant of the move, it was still almost too fast for him.

He wore only one Colt — Clay. It was slung on his left thigh, its butt to the front for a right-hand draw. But he was a two-handed shot and now he twisted his left hand to jerk out the .44. It came clear in a twist that leveled the muzzle at Turl's body and the hammer of the "doctored" weapon was back and fallen again as the muzzle jumped up.

He fired three shots, thumbing the smooth-filed hammer twinklingly. The first slug tore through Turl's heart. He was dead on his feet before the second shot hit him. His thumbs slipped on the hammer of his own weapon. A bullet burned Clay's side.

It had been that close. Clay had to step back to avoid the falling body. He stood, gun gripped hard, watching with narrow eyes.

"Fair?" he queried the city marshal, as he moved back to the place he had so swiftly vacated an instant before.

"He pulled first," the city marshal admitted. He was more than a little uneasy, by his expression and tone. "But — you deviled him into it! You never really meant that Jake Turl robbed you!"

"Was he so pure and high-minded a citizen you find that hard to believe?" Clay asked with lifted eyebrows. "Look in his pockets! Let's see what you can find."

He squatted with the marshal and while the officer went pocket by pocket about his task, Clay picked up Turl's Colt. He looked at it thoughtfully, then twirled it on a forefinger. The marshal looked up:

"He's got two hundred in gold . . . But that don't spell a thing — necessarily. Turl, he had his ways of getting money!"

"I — reckon," Clay said dryly, watching all ways at once.

The marshal spread out the little heap of twenties and tens. Clay poked at it with the muzzle of Turl's Colt. He separated one twenty from the pile. A man had come crowding up through the press, to stand beside the marshal. He grunted with sight of that gold piece.

It was that storekeeper who had loaned Clay forty dollars on his blue horse, to meet Pecos Pawl's last bet at the stud table.

"You see it, too?" Clay drawled, looking up sideways. "I looked at the twenties you pitched me, hard enough to know 'em. And that X-scratched one I will remember all my life. Mister Marshal, here's one twenty I had in my leggings! And ——"

He held Turl's Colt close to the officer's face. There was a large discoloration near the muzzle. The marshal said "rust" in a vague sort of tone.

Then he rubbed the stain with forefinger and looked at the finger.

"Blood," Clay corrected him grimly. "And — *por Dios!* Some of my hairs! Well!"

"Ebert — he's coroner — he'll have to look things over tomorrow," the marshal decided. For some reason or other he seemed a worried man. "I — I reckon you was right, young man, but —— But don't try to leave town until after the coroner's inquest . . ."

"Two hundred . . . Leaves me nine hundred short," Clay drawled.

CHAPTER III

"By rights," Judge Ebert said severely to Clay, scowling across steel-bowed glasses, "I'd ought to fine you the whole two hundred — brandishing a weapon the way you done. But I'm going to let you off lighter'n you deserve. You take that hundred, and you climb onto that blue billy goat of yours, and you git out of this town! And if you don't ever come back — that will be just about the *sagest* thing that you ever done!"

Clay said nothing. He counted out five twenties from the little pile on the counter before him and pushed them toward the coroner — who had so abruptly resumed his usual status of justice of the peace. The inquest had been held in a store next door to Irish Mike's saloon. There was evidence enough from responsible citizens to prove Turl's killing a justifiable homicide in Poplar Station.

In fact, the only note of disagreement

came from the witness who wanted to call it suicide.

Clay walked out with his remaining hundred. He got his horse from a livery corral and rode out. A boy came tearing up the street, quirting a lathered pony, shoulders and rump. He saw Clay and pulled up before him. The pony spread its legs and dropped its hammer head and relaxed with heaving sides.

The boy — he was a light-skinned Mexican — called Clay by name.

Then ——

"*Habla Ud. Español?*" he demanded. "Do you speak Spanish?"

Clay nodded, eyeing him curiously.

"Then — understand this — Smiling sends you word that he has heard of your killing of a good man. He was about to turn his horse last night and come back to prepare you for burial in the same grave that will hold Jake Turl. But he has *negocios* — affairs of so much urgency. He could not turn back. So, he bids me tell you that, no matter where you go — to sleep, or wake, or eat, or drink — you are marked. When he is ready, he will open a sack and your head will roll out of it!"

"I certainly do appreciate your riding so hard to tell me!" Clay cried earnestly — and

41

repeated it in Spanish. "Will you not take this and buy yourself something to wash from your throat the dust?"

But the boy slapped the silver dollar into the dust very scornfully. He whirled his little horse and, with a wild yell, spurred back down the street. Clay grinned and jogged after him. He was heading for the interior of The Territory. He was a stubborn young man and, as he had said in Irish Mike's, recovery of Turl's share of the robbery had left him nine hundred dollars short. He felt that he had a bone to pick with Smiling. He laughed suddenly. For it occurred to him that, had he remarked this in Poplar Station, he could have hired a doorkeeper and stood in a tent, collecting a dollar a head from those who would have been interested to see him. Amusement faded quickly!

He began to give some grave consideration to the matter of hunting Smiling.

He looked down at his low-swung pistol and said very solemnly aloud:

"I have got to do more practicing with old Betsy Ann. Lots!"

It was a lovely morning and there were few horses with smoother gaits than Azulero, the bluish cutting horse. Clay rode along the yellow sandy tracks southward, Gurney-bound, watching the country to right and left and dead ahead with merely mechanical alertness. There was a dome-like hill up to which the trail led and the cloud shadows played on its northern face like the shadows of swooping birds. Clay sang softly to the rhythm of the jogging hoofs; the ancient song of the *vaqueros:*

Una mujer por amor;
Una botella de vino;
Una canción que cantar
Y mucho dinero en mi camino!
Un buen machete en mi mano;
Un buen juego que jugar;
Ni por fraile o rey úfano,
Deseo yo cambiar!

A woman to love;
A bottle of wine;
A song to sing
And much money in my road!
A good knife in my hand;
A good game to play;
Nor with friar or haughty king,
Desire I to change!

He rounded the hill, whistling softly — and rammed the hooks to Azulero so viciously that the blue horse vented himself of a sudden sound, half-squeal, half-groan.

43

Clay lay flat over the horn — wasting no time even in snatching for a weapon — as Azulero shot forward to leap a dry watercourse and make for an arroyo that opened on the right of the trail, in the base of the hill.

The greasewood and mesquite on the other side of the trail from Poplar Station, where it curved here to round the hill, was suddenly aflame with rifle-fire. But Clay's abrupt movement had disconcerted the assassins. They had been too deliberate; had counted too much on being perfectly concealed, and having all the time they wanted to get sure aim and loose their volley. So as he fled up the slope toward the arroyo's mouth, he heard the rattle of Winchesters, but never the hum of a close-missing shot.

The ambushers altered aim as flashingly as possible. Lead banged on the rocky walls close behind him, with their second and subsequent shots. But he was inside his shelter. He flung himself out of the saddle — Azulero stopping as if shot. He snatched out his saddle gun and looked flashingly around him. There was a big rock on the tip of the arroyo bank, eight feet above the floor. Behind that a man commanded the arroyo and the hillside also. Clay led Azulero farther along, to shelter behind a turn in the water-course. Then he scrabbled up the arroyo bank and got behind the huge boulder.

He was barely in time. The same big-crowned hat which had lifted above a greasewood top in time to warn Clay of the ambush now showed at the base of the hill where its wearer was snaking forward to enter the arroyo mouth. Clay watched tensely, waiting for companions of this *sombrero grande.* They were coming, too! They made little noise, but they made some; and the close-growing greasewood waved as in a gentle breeze when their bodies brushed the shrubs.

"Now, if they're figuring on coming into the arroyo, I had better wait a while," Clay told himself. "They'll be right under me — *muy pronto* — and right underground just as quick . . . But — no, Big Hat aims to Injun up the hill and shoot down at the pore, misguided *Americano* that's looking down the arroyo bed."

So he waited no longer. He could see the tip of the big sombrero crown and he allowed for the hat's size, in aiming. He drove two lightning shots at the sheltering brush, well below the hat crown. The bullets shredded the leaves — and that was all. There was neither sound nor movement from the greasewood. Either the man of the hat had been instantly killed, or he was biting the sand trying to get below the lead.

"Donde está el saco por mi cabeza?" Clay yelled gibingly. "Where's the sack for my head?"

They yelled at him furiously. Then from behind their cover of brush they sent lead ringing against his boulder. He watched the lifting puffs of smoke and picked the rifleman with the poorest shelter. With his shot a Mexican jumped up — "as from a hot stove," Clay thought grimly. More grimly, he drove two shots into the figure before it could disappear, watched the man drop his Winchester and sprawl half-sideways, half-forward, back upon the greasewood.

The battle progressed spasmodically between Clay and the remaining bushwhackers. Then, from behind him, a rifle woke ringing echoes. Again and again it sounded, with the metallic ripple of spreading reports bouncing back from the hills. Bullets glanced off the boulder above Clay's head. One ricocheted off, ripped the back of his vest and shirt, and seared a long course from the point of his right shoulder almost to the left hip bone, before digging into the ground.

He threw himself toward the arroyo edge

and dropped over the bank. The men waiting beyond the arroyo mouth blazed away as if they had expected the movement. He had all the rock splinters and buzz of bullets that he could digest, for a hectic moment. He hugged the floor of the arroyo and was for a time out of range. They began yelling — a sort of fierce, mocking chant. He turned his head a little to the side, the better to hear.

"Here is the sack for your head! Come and see it!" they were inviting him.

His mouth corners lifted a shade. They had him pretty thoroughly bottled up, all right. That rifleman who had gone around and up the hill had the advantage of him.

He yelled at them and they checked their fire to listen. He told them that before they put Clay Borden's head in any sack, they would know that there were teeth to bite in that head!

He had a brief glimpse of the Mexican uphill, slipping from one boulder to another. Clay thought it was the boy who had brought Smiling's message and so contemptuously slapped the silver dollar into the dust of Poplar's street. Clay half-lifted his carbine, but the boy was out of sight in a twinkling. He was working his way down the slope to get where he could open fire into the arroyo depths.

So, for a moment or two, there was a hush. And Clay's eyes narrowed, abruptly, as he rammed shells into his Winchester. To him came the pelting *thuddah-thud-thuddah-thud* of horses at a racing gallop. He moved instantly to hurl bullets toward the Mexicans outside of the arroyo. For if these men coming so fast were re-enforcements for the bushwhackers, his ball of twine was rolled up! If, on the other hand, the galloping ones were not men of Smiling Badey, he wanted the hunters for his head to have no opportunity to get away.

In some respects Clay Borden was a vindictive soul. So he and the bushwhackers made so much noise, between them, that if the Mexicans had not heard the horses at the time Clay caught the drumming thud of their hoofs, they would not hear them now, with the reports of the rifles in their ears.

"Yaaaiiiaaah!" a sudden fierce yell came to Clay, and again: *"Yaaaiiiaaah!"*

It split the ragged bellow of the rifle-fire like a knife through smoke. Then the firing took on a deeper note. A Mexican bobbed up suddenly in Clay's vision, jumping from under a green crown of greasewood, running for the arroyo. Clay knocked him spinning with a .44 that caught him in the shoulder; then sent dust jumping from his shirt just above his belt.

"Yaaaiiiaaah!" the unseen ones yelled again.

Clay rolled over, reminded abruptly of that boy on the hill. He was barely in time, for the muzzle of a carbine was pushing over that arroyo bank not twenty feet away. Behind it was the pale, fierce face of the young messenger. Flat on his back, Clay fired two shots before he put the carbine to his shoulder. Then he sat up and blazed away. The slim, fierce youth had jerked his head with the splatter of dust rising in his face from those two close misses. He came sliding down; limply, like a slipping sack. He lay still on the floor of the arroyo, his big .45-70 beyond him.

Outside, the firing stopped abruptly. Someone was yelling out there in an oddly accented sort of English. But the matter of the speech was plain — it was now safe for the holed-up one to come out. Clay turned from the dead messenger and went that way. Two men, each holding a carbine, stood at the mouth of the arroyo.

One was a six-footer, slim and sinewy, with about him the supple grace of a great cat; and a man about thirty, with lean, brown face and sea-blue eyes that twinkled, now, in a way to match that gentle smile that curved thin lips under a spike-pointed mustache. He was very much the cowboy dandy, with his flannel shirt of silken blue, his tight trousers of hand-woven woolen, his stitched and inlaid boots, new, gray Stetson and pearl-handled, silver-and-gold-mounted .44 Colt.

The other man was round of face and body; yellow-haired and blue-eyed; threatening to burst the seams of his brown duck pants and jumper. His boots were rusty and runover of heels; his twin Colts were as the factory and the weather had made them. But, somehow, Clay had no doubt that the fat man — no less than his elegant, efficient companion — was a Hand!

"Por Dios!" cried the tall man. "She's one nice row, no? We're hear them shooting and so we're riding like the hell and we're help them to git sick! Hey, Lum?"

The fat man only nodded and continued to stare at Clay while he rolled a cigarette. The tall man was looking the same way, with black head on one side a trifle. Clay gave them his sincere thanks for the rescue.

"They just about had the axe hanging over my neck. One had sneaked uphill and I couldn't whang away at him without leaving myself open for these hairpins with the sack, down here."

"Well — them sack; she's go empty, now! Smiling, she's lose one hand in this game. And lose some good men, too . . ."

Clay stared at him. How did these strangers know what that sack had been intended to hold? The turquoise eyes twinkled the more brightly; the shadowy smile on the thin mouth deepened. It seemed to Clay that his thoughts were read . . .

"You're Clay Borden, *no es verdad?* You're — have them letter from Smoky Cole, w'at's sheriff in Gurney, huh?"

"Uh-uh. Never did have a letter from him," Clay denied, his eyes narrowing slightly. "The old sidewinder is my mother's half-brother, but I never laid eyes on him in my life; never got a letter. What makes you think I did — if that's a fair question?"

"Me, I'm Carlos José de Guerra y Morales, señor, w'at the fellow in these damn' Territory they're call 'Chihuahua Joe.' And now I'm introduce my *amigo:* This, señor, she's Lum Luckett. We're come from Texas and we're riding through them Diamond River country and we're looking for you. For we're think mabbe you're ride with us to Gurney."

Clay had acknowledged the introductions by shaking his head with a puzzled face. Now he stared frowningly from the tall,

51

handsome Chihuahua Joe to the round-faced and silent fat man.

But — why would his uncle be writing him a letter? Why had this efficient pair gone to the Bar B to ask him to ride with them?

"Well, I'm certainly pleased to meet you both! Particularly right now. For I don't know when you could have fitted in sweeter!" he told them, with a sudden grin. "But you're certainly talking trigonometry, so far as I can figure from listening to you. Trigonometry or maybe Greek or some dead language like that."

Chihuahua Joe grinned suddenly in his turn. But to Clay came the assurance, very abruptly, that here was a man who in one way resembled Smiling Badey: Chihuahua Joe Morales could smile and fight; smile and kill; smile and face what seemed to be certain death. The difference would be that Chihuahua would be the kind to stick by his friends — as Smiling had no record of doing; that Chihuahua would be on the side of honesty, even if he fought fire with fire.

"W'y, if them triggernometry, she's mean to work your trigger, then me, I'm not say no!" he drawled. "And if you're mean by dead language that I'm speak about them men w'at will never smile again, after we're see them — *bueno*. She's truth that I'm talk

52

them triggernometry and dead language. But — here, you're read this letter!"

Clay took the crumpled paper which Chihuahua fished from his shirt pocket. It was penciled on ruled tablet paper:

Dear Frend Chewawa:

I take my pen in hande to rite yu these few lines. Trusting yu are the same. I am in a jackpot. If yu can come back to Gurney rite now same will be mutch apreciated, for rite now frend Chewawa it is like the olde days again and steeling and killing where ever I turn. It is too mutch like the olde days when Frenchy Leonard's gang was helling around and we had to finish him.

King Connell is gone to Irland to visit his folks and he taken Lit Taylor and Sudie May and the baby with him so I can not get Lit for Deputy and frend Chewawa I am sore in need of some deputies that have filed off their front sights and throwed their both spurrs away. So if yu can serve again same will be mutch apreciated. I have rote my nephew too. His name is Clay Borden and he is riding for the Bar B on the Diamond River. I have never seen him but from what I hear the other day he is

53

a good saltie boy and will make a fine Deputy.

Respy yrs

S. Cole, Sheriff

Clay looked thoughtfully at the two who were watching him. So, the old times of which he had spoken to Smiling were back. "It's going to be more so!" Smiling had said with the grin that masked perfect sincerity. And his uncle wanted him to serve as a deputy — along with two such as these Bearers of Winchesters. Well, he thought, he had been heading that way, he had come to pick a crow with Smiling Badey.

"I left the Bar B after — well, a little bit of trouble with one of the boys," he said cautiously, and marked how they grinned quickly; grinned as if they already knew a great deal about that trouble with Windy Winters and his two tough friends. "Reckon I must've missed Uncle Smoky's letter that way. I'll head on towards Gurney with you-all. But ——"

He stopped. He was picturing Smiling and the way he had said so knowingly that Clay wouldn't keep his money long enough to make any difference. He could hear the veiled mockery in the killer's voice. And he began to dislike Smiling more violently than he had ever before disliked a man — more, even, than Windy Winters.

"But I don't know about being a deputy . . . I — we'll see." He was thinking that wearing a deputy's star might handicap him in the matter of collecting nine hundred dollars from Smiling.

That was important. It must be looked into before he pinned on a star and bound himself to obey Smoky Cole or anyone else.

"We're miss you on them Bar B," Chihuahua told him. "But them range boss, Long Al Kendrick, she's tell us you're smoke them fellows and you're leave for a while. In Poplar Station, we're hear about them fiine time you have — and about Smiling, w'at will open one sack and watch your head roll out."

"We found it very interesting," Lum Luckett said gravely. Then a flashing grin came. "So we split the breeze on your trail. Chihuahua has an unusual sort of instinct — he is prone to term it a nose for trouble ____"

"*Por Dios!* I'm smell trouble today, too!" Chihuahua cried.

Clay stared from one to the other of these oddly assorted trailmates. Longest, he regarded the fat man. Then:

"You — you wouldn't be *The*

55

Schoolma'am?" he inquired hesitantly. "It's not possible, but ——"

Chihuahua whooped ecstatically and banged a hand upon Lum Luckett's thick shoulder.

"*Yaaaiiiaaah!* And me, I'm not say one word, Lum! But these fellow, she's know you right off. W'en you open up your mouth, Lum, we're see them li'l' bitsy red schoolhouse!"

"Daggonit!" Lum said sourly. "It's as Chihuahua says. My father was a frontier editor and schoolmaster and he drilled me in English until I can't speak in an ordinary, colloquial fashion unless I carefully choose each word — and life is too short for that sort of expression. I've broken horses and punched cattle — to use a colloquialism, for I never actually poked a cow — but I'll never hear the last of that 'Schoolma'am' nickname."

Clay laughed. Somehow, he was very cheerful. The trail ahead promised to be a pleasant trip. At first sight he liked these two as well as he had ever liked men.

"Let's hightail it, then!" he said.

"But first ——"

Chihuahua was moving toward a Mexican and after a moment of staring, Clay and Lum followed his example and helped

56

gather rifles and pistols. These divided and lashed behind their saddles, the trio mounted and rode on toward that salty village on the Rowdy River's Lower Fork; toward Anthony.

Jogging into the huddle of 'dobes something after noon, they found a half-breed storekeeper. Apparently he knew Chihuahua well, but that knowledge seemed only to make him more careful about what he said and did in Chihuahua's presence. He asked about Chihuahua's health and Chihuahua beamed upon him:

"Me, I'm feel damn' fine. W'at the hell! I'm wish for to drink the w'isky and dance and shoot the pistol. Oh — *valgame dios!* Me, I'm feel like them fighting cock, Miguel Rafael Rodolfo Schwingle. How is business, my old, dear friend? If we're wish to buy them Colt, them Smith and Wesson, them Remington six-shooter; them Winchester rifle and carbine, you're sell 'em, no?"

"Very dear," the half-breed sighed, his green eyes narrowing. "Oh, very dear! For it is a matter of the hardest, old friend, to get the pistol, the carbine, the rifle, here to Anthony. You would not believe! So the prices — oh, very high!"

Chihuahua expressed himself as very

much saddened by the news. Schwingle elaborated upon the difficulties. He quoted prices — twice those asked anywhere else — for pistols and long guns. Chihuahua smiled gently. He and Lum went outside. When they came back in and put down their burdens, Schwingle's fat, yellowish face seemed to fold up as amazedly he pursed his thick lips.

"Is it not lovely?" Chihuahua cried enthusiastically in Spanish. "I told you that my heart is big — swollen with happiness — about to burst with pure joy. Why? Because, my old, we found these beautiful, so-hard-to-be-obtained pistols and rifles and carbines, beside the trail. Now — we will sell them to you!"

"Not to me!" Schwingle denied, speaking also in Spanish. "I have no need for them. Besides — how do I know ——"

Then his green eyes dropped, for into Chihuahua's eyes had jumped a flare — like light on blue ice. He mumbled, Schwingle. And he seemed to be looking around, hunting very furtively for something. Which gave Clay an idea.

He had never before been in Anthony. But he had come with Bar B trail herds a time or two as far as Porto, twenty miles southeast. It occurred to him that Schwingle was well and unfavorably known to Chihuahua — who seemed acquainted with everyone — everything! — of importance about the whole Territory.

Chihuahua, Clay thought, was merely amusing himself by this cat-and-mouse play with the storekeeper. Also, recalling what he did of the rustlers' town, Porto, he wondered if Anthony was any better. Poplar Station was a salty camp, but by comparison with Porto, Poplar Station was downright peaceful.

So he slid backward as Schwingle's eyes wavered. He stopped in the doorway cut in a three-foot-thick 'dobe wall. There were three men down at the corner of the store building. They were sweat-stained and dusty men, stubbled with beard, long of hair.

They were looking at the three horses — Chihuahua's calico, Lum's hammer-headed zebra dun, Clay's blue — which stood at Schwingle's hitchrack. As Clay watched them from the dusky embrasure of the door, they turned his way, but gave no sign of seeing him. Instead, they looked at each other and seemed to arrive at a decision without need of words. They whirled and went out of sight around the corner.

"Ho-ho!" said Clay underbreath and looked at Schwingle.

The storekeeper was not watching him. Chihuahua was sufficient to engross the half-breed's attention. Clay stepped outside, went softly down the dirt walk and looked around the corner. The three men were not in sight. So he drifted to the back of the store, going along the side wall. He peered around that corner and saw the last man just stepping into the back door. He followed, after a quick glance around. At the door, he stopped and listened. He heard the mumble of Chihuahua's mock-serious argument with the stubborn, nervous Schwingle.

The argument went on. Chihuahua was evidently enjoying himself. For he pleaded and argued about the sale of the weapons.

Then a strange voice cut in:

"You're making a hell of a lot of noise!" this voice remarked snarlingly.

Clay looked through the door then, showing no more of his face than was necessary. The three men stood well apart in the dusky rear half of the store, among bales and boxes of merchandise. It seemed to Clay that each held a gun at hip level.

He slid inside with no more noise than a snake might have made — to see if this were true.

"First man makes a move toward a six-shooter, I'll six-shooter him!" the trio's spokesman grunted sinisterly.

"Me, I'm never dream to make them move!"

Chihuahua's silky drawl was the more deadly-furious for being so repressed.

"And w'at you call this?" he inquired. "One robbery?"

"They got Pedro Alarcon's rifle," Schwingle told the stranger who had done the talking. "Got Manuelito's old .45-70, too. I figure they wiped out the whole bunch."

"The hell they did!" snarled the tall man. "Speak up, Greaser! Where'd you get them guns? Better talk, else I'll blow you ——"

"Take her slow and easy!" Clay advised. "No! Don't try looking around or you'll collect a slug in the nose! And if you make a sudden, funny move, we'll six-shooter *you!* I reckon maybe it'd be better if you'd just drop that hogleg. Let her flop! Same for you other two! Move speedy, children! Speedy, or else ——"

"Shoot and be damned!" the tall man snarled — but without looking around, or getting much conviction into his tone. "I'll get this friend of yours before you get me. We'll plug 'em both!"

"Friends of mine?" Clay repeated in amazed tone. "Go on and plug 'em. They're

61

nothing to me. But I have got a bone to pick with you-all. Now drop your guns or —— "

There sounded in the stillness a sharp click of pistol hammer going back. The two with the tall man waited for no more.

Two pistols made dull thudding sounds on the planks of the floor. The tall man hesitated.

Clay began softly to count. There was a third rap of pistol striking floor.

Chihuahua looked narrowly at them. He began to whistle softly. Then he turned sidewise and regarded the pallid Schwingle. He took a long step toward the counter behind which the storekeeper was penned. He slapped the fat jowls resoundingly, then, still whistling, loafed over to pick up the fallen pistol of the trio's leader. Lum Luckett had already moved to get the gun dropped by the man on the leader's right.

"Now, w'at will we do with them, Clay?"

"Fella!" the tall leader gritted, "you want to remember one thing — hard! When Smiling hears about this —— "

"Oh, so you're Smiling's little playmates!" Clay cried. "Then let me make you used to some gentlemen you ought to know: This handsome man here is Chihuahua Joe. You must have heard of him. He's deputy sheriff under Smoky Cole. And the heavyset gentleman there is Mister Luckett. Funny! But *he's* a deputy sheriff under Smoky Cole, too! As for me — well, you can call me Mister Borden. And — you know, damn' if I'm not one of Smoky Cole's deputies, too! Did you ever hear of such a pe-cu-liar thing?"

Then his voice altered abruptly.

"You-all climb onto your horses and you hightail out of this inside two minutes. We'll come hunting you, then — with shotguns. It'll be a new deal, and we'll aim to blow some windows in you!"

"All right!" the tall man snarled. "We'll be
——"

"Listen, Yates!" one of the other men cried swiftly. "Remember ——"

"We're moving," the tall Yates said grimly. "But we'll be seeing you. All of you. And when we do ——"

Then the three of them marched stiffly. Lum Luckett followed.

Chihuahua, with the three pistols the men had left without remark, strolled back to the counter, humming softly:

The lady looked down from her window;
Don Francisco he strummed his guitar.
The lady tossed out of her window
A flower — that yet grew in a jar.

Don Francisco caught the fair blossom
On the tip of his Castilian nose ——

"Now," said Chihuahua to Schwingle, "about these rifles and pistols . . . The price I will not increase because of — anything which has occurred. But now — is it not truth? — I have found three more pistols! I have for them not any use. So — for thirty dollars each you may have them, also. Is that not a fair enough arrangement, Clay, my soft-walking friend?"

"*Seguro!* Let him have 'em for that. Ninety dollars for the three. He's shown us an interesting time today!"

"I will not buy! I will not be threatened. When it is known that you have acted so ——"

Chihuahua's brown hand flashed up and caught the open collar of Schwingle's cotton shirt. His right hand snapped to the back of his neck and brought out a glittering bowie knife of ten sinister inches in blade length. Straight at the palsied storekeeper's throat it darted and Schwingle made a guttural, tinny sound — like the squawk of a hen that sees the hawk swooping.

Then Chihuahua was staring dreamily at six inches of collar point, severed from the shirt. Schwingle cried out that he would pay.

As they rode away from Anthony, grinning, pockets heavier, Clay grew curious about the three men they had driven away.

"Eb Yates," Chihuahua grunted. "He's killed plenty. But now ——"

CHAPTER IV

They could have ridden for two days across the width of the Ladder P. But by coming upon a trail that Chihuahua knew, just outside Porto, they made no more than a day's steady jogging of the distance to the foothills of the Diablos, beyond which lay Gurney. Their course left the great 'dobe house of the cattle king miles to the east. Clay, staring off that way at the misty blue heights of the Diablos' northern buttresses, wondered if Smiling were on the Ladder P. And he found himself wondering about that daughter of John Powell, of whom Smiling had spoken.

Chihuahua had an idea. One Jed Wyndham had a small nester-style outfit in a bend of the Rowdy on the very edge of the Ladder P range. He was a sour, suspicious, and very salty soul, by Chihuahua's account. He had been suspected of the very common practice of the day and place — of owning and using a flexible iron; one which could be stretched to make any brand look like something else. Chihuahua wanted to call on Wyndham while they were in that neighborhood.

"But she's better if Old Jed sees just me and Lum, Clay. You're ride on for Gurney. We're cut across them Diablos and find you close to Gurney before the sun, she's down."

Clay nodded. He agreed that three men were more conspicuous than two, in this business. He rode on into the south, crossing dry arroyos, beginning to climb high rolls that swept up toward the Diablos' feet. And he rode around a tiny hill to be jerked out of his thoughts by a woman's screams. He stiffened in the saddle, staring right and left. Then he spurred Azulero into a gallop and continued around the little hill into a valley.

A riderless buckskin horse was running away, with a girl racing frantically after it, and a tall gaunt steer charging behind her, hardly twenty yards away.

The girl looked back over her shoulder at the steer. Clay had one glimpse of her face, ghastly white above the vivid blue of her shirt. There was no shelter ahead for her. Nothing but bare floor of this valley for a hundred yards and the big longhorn was coming like a race-horse, head down and a little sideways, so that one two-footed horn was like a scoop, ready to flirt upward.

She stumbled as he watched, but got up quickly from her knees, to turn and face the black death that came down on her like a tornado. She screamed at it thinly and waved her hands. But this brute was accustomed to holding his own with everything which moved on the range — except a cowboy on a horse. He seemed to hurtle down upon her faster as she tried to wave it away.

Clay, coming toward the steer in a drumming rush, took his hand away from his pistol butt. A shot from the saddle at this speed was not sure enough. There was no time to rope it. It was too close to the girl. No time to dive out of the saddle and bulldog it. A big fellow like that might drag him over a hundred yards of ground before he could throw it.

He came up on its flank when it was no more than three yards from where the girl stood rooted, her hands moving now in a futile little gesture.

"Run!" Clay yelled frantically to her. "Run like hell!"

Then he bent from the saddle and snatched the steer's tail. He jerked upward and whipped a turn around the saddle horn as if he were taking his *"dale vuelta"* with a rope. Azulero whirled off at right angles and dug in his hoofs cunningly. Almost at the girl's moveless feet the steer came crashing down with a great panting groan. Clay, letting go his *dale,* jerked his pistol and, with the roar of it, the black steer's lifting head dropped back to the grass, a bullet through the brain.

Clay jumped off. He caught the girl as she turned away, took a step forward and began to sag. She hung limp in his arms, a pliant weight, the small, pale oval of her face upturned upon his sleeve, and one blue-black, shimmering lock of hair across her cheek. Clay's disjointed mutterings to her produced not so much as a flicker of an eyelid, and he stood as transfixed as she had been before the steer, holding her, fairly gaping down at her. And after the passing of some thirty seconds — which seemed an age — he found his near-panic wearing off. Actually, it became rather pleasant to hold her so.

"Now what do you do when a woman faints?" he asked himself. "Bucket of water flung in their faces — but I've got no water — so ——"

The long-lashed eyelids fluttered now and

lifted. Clay looked down. Her eyes were neither black nor brown, but some dusky shade between the two. But they were glaring up at him fearfully, as if still the image of the charging black death hung before them. Clay talked to her soothingly, without knowing what he said. She relaxed and shook her head a little. It made that lock of hair bob fascinatingly. Clay watched and became conscious with a start that she had spoken to him.

"What?" he said quickly. "Oh, he's dead. I shot him. You're all right now. I'll catch up your horse in a minute. You're all right. Nothing to worry you."

"I thought he had me!' she breathed. "But — I'm all right now. If you'll let me go — I can stand now."

He turned her loose so abruptly that she almost fell, and he had to catch her again. He knew that his face was flaming red. But — so was hers! Gorgeously flushed, clear to the base of the smooth throat. And for the first time he asked himself who she could be. Was it —— Could this be the girl Smiling had spoken of? He asked her if she were John Powell's daughter.

"Helen Powell — yes. But — I don't seem to know you. You don't ride for my father?"

"No. I'm from over on the Diamond

River. I'm a deputy of Smoky Cole's. But I heard about you coming home from school."

"A deputy! You're one of the — the —— You're serving under Smoky Cole at Gurney?"

"Is there a law against it being so?" he inquired, puzzled. For if he had said that he was a champion horse-thief, he thought that her tone would not have been different.

"I'll go catch your horse," he said formally. But as he turned toward Azulero he glanced mechanically at the dead steer — and stopped short, frowning. Barred Double Diamond and — if top and bottom of that brand had been burned on at the same time, Clay Borden admitted frankly that *he* would be damned. Superficially, it was a smooth brand. But not to an expert's eye. Not — at — all.

"Your father's steer?" he inquired. "One of his brands. Is, huh? Well, he ——"

He turned back to Azulero. What he had started to say was that, almost, John Powell had swapped a daughter for a steer. That it would have been a kind of rough justice if this theft of which Clay suspected the Ladder P owner had worked to bring about the messy killing of Helen Powell.

He swung into the saddle and galloped off

71

after the girl's runaway buckskin. He found it within a half-mile, grazing with the reins looped about a forefoot. He led it back to where she sat on the ground staring at the steer's carcass.

"What made you ask about that steer?" she demanded, when he reined in beside her. She was watching him steadily. "I know it wasn't altogether because it so nearly killed me. Your voice was perfect. But I happened to see your eyes. I don't know anything about this cattle country. I haven't been down here since my mother died, when I was four. But — I *think* I can read a man's eyes, even if I can't read a cattle brand. Why did you ask?"

"Because I wanted to know" he told her, in a surprised tone. "Couldn't you read that burning inquisitiveness in my eyes?"

"You're not telling me the truth!" she charged, after a long stare into his smiling face. "I owe you my life and yet — I have the feeling that you are not friendly. That the steer there means something to you —— Oh, I don't know exactly what I feel. I can't express my intuition clearly."

"You're using a lot of jointed words on me," he said — and grinned. "I'm just a pore cowboy, and I know I done wrong ——"

She had been staring past his shoulder for a brief space. Now she looked at him directly, and her dusky eyes, the twist of her scarlet mouth, were unreadable.

"Whatever it is you want to know, you can ask my father," she said softly. "There he comes."

Clay turned with real curiosity to see the lord of this cattle empire. Something of John Powell's repute had traveled the long miles to the Diamond River. Once or twice a Ladder P animal had showed in a Bar B roundup. But he had no knowledge of Powell's description.

He was prepared for almost anything but what he saw — Smiling Badey riding with the Ladder P owner. He stiffened and, with sight of his tense face, Helen Powell made a gasping sound and her widened eyes turned from him to the men approaching, then turned back in time to see his hand go down to curl about the butt of his Colt.

Clay kneed the blue horse around and faced the riders. He saw that Smiling's hands were not upon his Colts, then glanced at the huge, tight-mouthed man beside him. John Powell was as shabby of ancient Stetson, snagged flannel shirt, patched overalls and rusty boots, as the poorest cowboy Clay had ever seen. But instinctively Clay sensed the iron in him, and knew that here was a Power in The Territory. Suddenly, he thought of what Smiling had said in Poplar Station. And ——

"If King Connell, big as he was, ever bested John Powell, then King Connell was Somebody!" he thought.

"Hi, fellow!" Smiling greeted him and drew rein to grin at the girl.

This might have been the most casual meeting between two men slightly acquainted. But Clay had seen the shine in Smiling's dark eyes before they turned to Helen Powell.

"I don't want to hear any more pretty speeches out of *you,* young man!" the girl said emphatically, to Smiling. "You were miles away, I suppose, when that black brute scared Dixie away and left me afoot. He came charging down to kill me and if it hadn't been for this young man — and whatever amazing thing it was he did — I'd be dead, now!"

Smiling's grin was unaltered. But he turned and looked Clay up and down, as if re-examining a specimen of some sort. He seemed to ignore the fact that Clay had never released his grip upon his pistol.

"Hear you had some trouble in Poplar," he drawled.

"Nothing to talk about — now," Clay denied, with a shrug.

"How'd you happen to ride over this way? Thought you had a lot of important business to take care of — and a girl, too, you said."

"I got a word," Clay said gravely. "I was asked to come over and take a job. Since it was an uncle asking — well, relations ought to stick together if they can, I always said."

"And who is your uncle?"

"Smoky Cole. Maybe you've heard of him. He's sheriff at Gurney and — well, I suppose I'm just the same as a deputy sheriff, even if I haven't been sworn in."

John Powell pushed his tall horse to the front, blanketing Smiling, but not so much that Clay could not keep watch upon the gunman's hands. He looked inscrutably at Clay.

"What's your name?" he demanded. "What are you doing on Ladder P range?"

Helen Powell's smooth face flushed. She drove the spur into her buckskin's flanks and came alongside her father's stirrup in a jump.

"He's on our range because he heard me scream!" she told her father. "No matter what his name is, and even if he is one of those Gurney deputy sheriffs, the fact

75

remains that the favor was from him to us."

"Be still," was all John Powell said to her, nor did he lift his grim voice a note. He was staring steadily at Clay. "I'm waiting," he said evenly.

Clay was still watching Smiling's hands.

"My name? Why, it's Clay Borden, and I'm on your range because I heard your daughter scream, just as she told you. And if I happened to be built that way, you could certainly make me sorry I heard her."

"Deputy under Smoky Cole, huh?" said Powell. "Going to help Smoky clean up things, I suppose? Well, you can high-tail! And when you get to Gurney, tell Smoky Cole for me that John Powell says he had better stay off the Ladder P range and keep his spying deputies off, too. I don't need any officers around. It seems odd to me that you should be so handy to hear my daughter scream. Spying for a chance to get in some funny work, likely!"

Involuntarily, Helen Powell's eyes went to the carcass of the dead steer on which the Barred Twin Diamond brand showed. John Powell, who seemed to see everything without the necessity of watching, turned slowly. He stared at the brand, then at his daughter, and last at Clay, who watched him from the corner of an eye while still facing the silent boy killer.

"What is peculiar about that steer?" the girl asked her father abruptly. "What is even — oh, interesting?"

"Oh!" said John Powell, in his even emotionless voice. "Oh, so he's interested in one of my brands . . . Odd, hey, Smiling?"

"You have got to kill some people" — thus Smiling, as on that night in Poplar Station Clay remembered, when the bartender had been so officious — "to learn them to keep their noses out of other folks' business."

"What do *you* see, that's peculiar, about that steer?" the Ladder P owner inquired of the calm-faced Clay.

"Peculiar? Who? Me?" cried Clay, in grieved accents. "It was your daughter who used the word. But that Barred Double Diamond is a new iron to me."

"It's one of the twenty-odd I own," John Powell said quietly. "You'll find it registered in Gurney. But you'll also find that I don't fancy inquisitive folk studying my brands and acting as if they found something — *odd* about them."

"Of course, you wouldn't!" Clay agreed heartily. A devil of perversity, of audacity, was riding him. "Certainly, you wouldn't. That's a pretty hide," he went on, further tweaking Saint Peter's white whiskers.

"Make a nice overcoat. Sell it to me for two dollars?"

John Powell ignored the question. He turned to Smiling.

"Let's go," he said.

Smiling hesitated almost visibly. Clay's thin mouth corners climbed.

"Smiling," he said in a lazy drawl, "I can hit a running quail from a horse with a .44. I reckon I can hit a man, don't *you?*"

Smiling turned his horse. John Powell followed. Just for an instant Clay and the girl sat alone, looking each other in the face. Her horse wanted to go with the others, but she held it in. She watched until thirty yards separated Smiling and her father from them.

"What is it about that steer?" she asked softly.

Clay made no answer. His left hand was twisted now, openly resting on the butt of his pistol. He was watching the pair ride off, alert if Smiling should whirl suddenly with a pistol in his hand. What answer was there that he could give her, anyway! Should he tell her that the animal had been originally branded — Double Triangle, perhaps? That the brand had been deliberately and feloniously altered to this Barred Double Diamond? That he suspected her father of actually stealing cattle, or at least purchasing cattle stolen by others?

"A fine way to make a hit with a girl!" he said to himself sardonically. "Likely to throw her arms around my neck and thank me as soon as I tell her that."

She was watching him steadily. With his hesitation she suddenly jerked her small chin up. Dark eyes, scarlet mouth, hardened.

"If you're trying to think of some story unfavorable to my father," she flashed, "you can save yourself the effort. I thank you for what you did. Nor do I believe that you came here to spy — not at first, anyway."

"Don't thank me," he said airily, with a flick of the hand. "I'd have done as much for any Mexican girl. Now, your father's calling. Go on with them."

He rammed the steel to Azulero and was gone at the gallop to regain the trail he had left at the sound of her scream. But when he came to the little hill, he half-turned in the saddle — he could not help it. She was still sitting there looking after him, but when she saw his head movement, she roweled the buckskin and charged after John Powell and Smiling.

"She's certainly a hot-tempered proposition!" Clay decided as he rode on. "But pretty! My Lord — pretty! If *I* had seen her picture, the way Smiling says he saw it, I would have ridden, not across The Territory, but across the United States, to see her."

He made a brown paper cigarette and lit it with a match from his hatband. He scowled blackly as he smoked. For thought of Smiling brought to mind another angle of this girl proposition.

"They certainly have got mighty friendly! — 'Smiling' and 'Helen.' He has got a reputation — it seems to me I have heard — for heeling the ladies. They do say he gets them so they come when he whistles!"

He pondered Smiling's lack of belligerence back there. But he held no illusion concerning the smiling young killer. Smiling was merely more sensible than he had given him credit for being: for he appreciated that a difference of one-sixteenth of a second between two gun-drawings means one dead man and one live man. That grain of advantage, in this encounter just passed, had been all with Clay. Smiling had merely seen that. But Clay knew very well that next time the breaks might be even, or in Smiling's favor.

"And that time it'll be shoot on sight! It can't be anything else," he told himself. "For he's a real gunman. A gunman from who laid the chunk!"

The encounter on the Ladder P had so

delayed him that it was dusk when he began to climb the foothills of the Diablos, beyond which lay Gurney, the county seat. Chihuahua and Lum would probably be waiting for him, somewhere along the trail now. Unless they — also delayed — had thought him ahead of them and pressed on into town.

The trail was steep, but quite passable. The darkness thickened as he climbed along a shelf which had on the right a deep cañon, on the left the sheer side of the mountain.

He heard a scratching and a snuffling behind a great boulder on his left, at the mouth of the narrow arroyo. He recognized it automatically and slid the Winchester carbine from its scabbard and tightened his knee-grip on Azulero. For almost every horse goes wild at bear-smell. Then came a deep-toned *"Wooooh!"* from behind the boulder. Azulero jogged on quietly. The high yap of a coyote was like an echo of the bear's snort. The coyote — apparently — disturbed a mountain lion, for a shrill scream rang out. Then all three animals seemed joined in battle to the death, with diabolical howlings and growlings. Clay grinned — and shoved his carbine back into the scabbard. "Too much menagerie," he called. "Overplayed your hand. If you two had just stuck to being bears, I would have been fit to tie."

"Ay de mi!" Chihuahua said sadly, standing up. "She's these damn' Lum. All time act like one damn' schoolboy."

"Tut-tut!" Lum reproved him. "Whose juvenile notion was it, to imitate the bear? My contribution was not only small, but ____"

"You're maybe see Smiling, hah?" Chihuahua grinned. "Them Jed Wyndham, w'at's one lobo, she's tell Lum and me how Smiling's holed up on them Ladder P. Jed, she's say Smiling and John Powell — they're thick like — oh, two thorns of one *cholla* cactus. But we're have camp made, Clay. She's no good to ride for Gurney, before them moon, she's rise."

Clay turned Azulero from the trail and followed the two back into a narrow cañon. Supper was ready for him, and he found that he was very ready for supper. They ate and lolled on the hard, stony ground, with cigarettes and tin cups of black coffee.

"Why, yes, I did run into Smiling," Clay drawled, over his second cup of coffee. "Ye-es, you might say I ran into him and —— Do you know, I'm beginning to think that fellow is not fond of me . . ."

"No!" Chihuahua cried incredulously. His blue eyes were very narrow as he regarded

Clay. "Me, I'm *so* damn' surprised for to hear you say that!"

Clay began an account of the afternoon's adventure. But he began with the arrival on the scene of John Powell and Smiling. True, he spoke of the burned brand on the black steer, but quite failed to mention his shooting of the steer.

"And then," he finished, "I rode on down here, to where the bear was *woooohing* behind the rock and — this is certainly fine coffee, Lum. I hope you made plenty!"

Chihuahua stared dreamily toward the serrate crest of a mountain, over which the moon might soon be expected to rise. At last he turned to Lum Luckett and shook his head gloomily.

"Lum," he drawled, "She's — oh! so damn' funny! Me, I'm listen, and I'm listen, until my both ears, she's stre-etch. I'm have one very funny feeling: I'm feel like I'm not hear — oh, everything. How is she by you, Lum?"

"Why, there was a certain atmosphere," Lum admitted, "as of hurriedly rearranging a record. Too, as our young friend remarked this and that incident of the encounter, I found myself meditating upon his presence there, on Ladder P range. Clay, we're not criticizing you — far from it! It's just that one or two minor points of your narrative aren't crystal-clear to us. We're — confident that you can explain these. So ——"

For a fat man, his movements were amazingly fast. So it came about that he was sitting upon Clay's chest before that young man guessed Lum intended to move.

"Hey! You're spilling my java!" Clay protested, struggling furiously. But Chihuahua wriggled to lie across Clay's knees. He laughed softly.

"You're not worry too much about them java," he said ominously, and he pulled off Clay's boots.

With a small sprig of greasewood, he began to tickle the soles of Clay's feet.

"Now," Chihuahua invited the writhing captive, "you're *please* to tell some more of them story. We're worry like hell, Clay. You're tell *so* much about Smiling, but nothing about them daughter of John Powell."

"Let me up, then, and I'll tell you," Clay yielded.

So, this time, he told everything — or almost everything. For he made no allusion to such things as the pliant weight of Helen Powell lying in the hollow of his arm; the small lovely oval of her face, upturned upon his sleeve; nor did he see fit to mention that disturbing, blue-black, shimmering lock of hair which had lain across her cheek. Why should Chihuahua and Lum be interested in such things, anyway?

"Oh — oh!" said Chihuahua softly, at the end. "Me, I'm think John Powell and Smiling, they're know damn' well you're know how Jed Wyndham's Triangle Bar black steer, she's come to wear them Double Bar Diamond iron and so —— Huh! them moon, she's up. We're ride now for Gurney."

As they jogged on over the mountain trail, Chihuahua slipped up into the lead, with Winchester across his arm. Clay and Lum followed him in single file and to them came the sound of his soft whistling. He seemed — for some reason, or no reason at all — very happy.

An hour, two hours, passed uneventfully. Then Chihuahua turned in the saddle and remarked that it was no more than five miles, now, to the county seat. With which information he faced front again. Staring past the tall, swaggering figure on the calico, Clay saw how the trail seemed to end in the moonlight.

Chihuahua reined in. He seemed to be listening. Clay and Lum rode up behind him. Then he saw that the trail did not end here, but merely went to the left, around the side of the mountain.

"Now, I'm wonder ——" Chihuahua said slowly.

Then he pushed on around the elbow in the trail, moving very slowly. From somewhere across the cañon, not more than fifty yards away, a rifle *whanged!* suddenly.

The leaden slug slapped viciously against the rock ahead of the calico's nose. Chihuahua came out of the saddle like a cat. Clay and Lum Luckett were scarcely slower. Squatting there in the trail, they rained bullets around that area in which the flash had shown. The concealed bushwhacker kept up his end of the battle for a minute or two — but for no longer. Even with the ringing of the rifle reports in their ears, they could hear faintly the crackling of brush across the cañon to tell that he was retreating.

"He is certainly breaking down the timber in no uncertain fashion," Lum commented dryly. "But his intentions were first-rate. And — his orders."

Chihuahua swung up again. He turned with flash of teeth beneath dark mustache.

"She's damn' bad medicine," he observed, "to look *too* close at them black steer, on Ladder P range. If you're spell them dry gulcher yonder, she's spell P-o-w-e-l-l!"

86

CHAPTER V

Gurney had but a single sandy main street. At one end was the hotel of Mrs. Sheehan. At the other end of the street was the square, two-story 'dobe which was the courthouse, jail, and sheriff's office, all in one. On both sides of the street between these two boundaries were divers stores, saloons, residences, dance-halls, saloons, gambling-halls, and saloons.

Chihuahua led the way. As he remarked, this was his old stamping-ground and he had several times worn the badge of a deputy sheriff.

There was nobody in the sheriff's office but one Bib Alder, a youthful, rather surly, deputy. He seemed much swelled with his importance. He had two horse-thieves upstairs in the jail, he said, awaiting trial. Smoky Cole was somewhere in town — or, at least, he had said nothing to Alder about going out of town, three hours or more before. Shorty Wiggins, the one-legged jailer, was home.

"Might not be back till morning," Bib Alder said.

They put their horses in the corral behind the building and hung their saddles in a back room. Then they drifted out, hunting Smoky.

Most of the stores were closed, but the saloons were wide-open; well patronized, too. There were men from a half-dozen outfits, large and small, so Chihuahua informed his companions. In the Palace, now owned by a gambler named Ritt Rales, seven men of Powell's Ladder P were drinking, but of Smoky Cole they found no trace. Nobody had seen him within two hours. Neither Chihuahua nor Clay recognized any known men of Smiling's anywhere about town. So the three got into a poker game in the Last Chance with two young Wagon Wheel riders and a pair of local tinhorns.

It was an interesting game — for Chihuahua won the deal and, before riffling the cards, he reached absently to the back of his neck and produced the bowie knife which had so impressed Schwingle at Anthony. This he placed hilt-up on the table by the simple process of driving the point into the soft pine wood. Thereafter, he looked long and steadily at each tinhorn in turn, with meditative blue eyes. Throughout the game, these two fairly leaned backward in their efforts to prove straightness of conduct; to keep everything but the faces of the cards in plain sight for any who might look. It was made very clear to Clay that Chihuahua had no little reputation in The Territory.

Towards eleven, there entered a short, thick-set man, red and cheerful of face, with twinkling pale blue eyes.

"Hiyah, Chihuahua!" he cried. "Back again, huh? Smoky *says* he thought you was coming."

He sat down and bought chips in the game. Chihuahua introduced him to Clay and Lum as one Halliday, a leading storekeeper of Gurney. Halliday grinned.

"Hell," he said easily, "I bet I have shot off most as many cartridges around this country as I ever sold. I swear, I'm nothing but a depot for outfitting posses."

Thereafter he devoted himself to poker, and the Halliday version of the game was a fast and shifty campaign. He stood pat on a pair of jacks — his openers. He stood pat, again, the next hand, and was caught by Clay on a pair of queens. He raised one of the tinhorns to the roof, soon after, on an

ace-high spade-flush — and collected pro-
fusely.

Midnight passed and still Smoky had not
shown up. Chihuahua yawned and proposed
that they go back to the sheriff's office. Halliday went out with them. Jail and office
alike were dark, but the office door was
open. Chihuahua stepped inside and groped
for the kerosene wall lamp. He struck a
match and, with its flare, they heard his
violent, wholesouled oath, and the shatter
of glass breaking on the floor.

"*Por dios!* She's hot!" he exclaimed, refer-
ring to the lamp chimney. "Me, I'm think
that's damn' funny!" he muttered, after a
moment.

He touched match-flame to lamp-wick.
The room appeared flashingly and they
stiffened. Sprawling upon the floor, tied in
a helpless bundle and gagged with his own
bandanna, with his hair matted by drying
blood, lay the youthful Bib Alder. To Chihuahua and Clay came, apparently at the
same moment, identical thoughts. They
glanced at the roped deputy, then into the
dusky corners of the square office, and
finally at the door opening into the jail corridor.

That door was open some six inches. They
slid across to it with pistols drawn, and

listened. Chihuahua drew the door further open and reached inside. Then he struck another match and lit a lamp. From the corridor a stair climbed, with a sort of watchhouse at its head. They left Halliday and Lum to loose Alder while they raced up to the jail. The cells were empty.

"Jail delivery, huh?" Clay grunted, as they turned back downstairs.

Bib Alder leaned against the table and put gentle fingers to his bloody head. He knew nothing. He had heard no alarming sound; he had seen nothing; he had merely turned his back to the street door for an instant, felt a crashing blow on the head and then

---

"When I come to, I was lying there on the floor, hog-tied like a slick ear!"

"Who were those horse-thieves?" Clay asked of Halliday.

The storekeeper shrugged wide shoulders.

"Nobody to signify! They *called* themselves the Ettison brothers. But I reckon they have not been too economical in names, the last few years. They lifted the six top horses of the town, a couple of months back. So Smoky, he took after them. Found them holed up over on Squaw Creek three weeks ago and brought 'em in."

"No dear bosom friends of theirs around

that you know about?" Clay frowned.

The storekeeper shook his head.

"I was thinking about that, too," he answered softly. "No, I just do'no' anybody that would feel it a bounden duty to help the Ettisons. They was kind of foreigners to this part of the country, you see."

"I wish Uncle Smoky was here!" Clay said irritably. "But meanwhile — suppose we take a ramble around and see what we can see?"

It was hardly probable that whoever had helped the brothers Ettison in their escape from Smoky Cole's jail would be hanging around the lighted part of the county seat; or if they were, they were not apt to be identifiable as jail deliverers. So, outside the sheriff's office, they stood looking up and down the street. Alder stood moodily beside them.

"They come on horseback, of course," Clay mused. "Now, where, do you reckon, would they have kept the horses? Behind the jail?"

They adjourned in a body to the corral where their own animals were — where they still were, to Clay's great relief. They nosed around in the darkness until Chihuahua bethought himself of an old, half-ruined corral on the very edge of town, sixty yards away.

An ideal place, he thought, for such as the jail deliverers to use. They went towards this old corral — and they went "loose-holstered."

Of the corral there remained only part of a six-foot 'dobe wall on each side of a gaping opening which had been the main gate. The gate had been formed by two upright cottonwood logs, nearly fifteen feet tall, with a third log laid across their tops for brace.

All evening, the moon had been intermittently obscured by floating clouds, and so it was now. They had one glimpse of the gate, then their path was almost pitchy dark as the drifting clouds blanketed the moon. Chihuahua went like a great shadow to the gate. The others, coming softly behind him, could barely see him — and could not hear him at all; but they heard very clearly the grunt with which he recoiled from the corral gateway and all but backed into them. There was the sharp sound of creaking leather as Clay, Lum, and Halliday pulled out their six-shooters — Bib Alder had carried his all the way out here. Then the moon came out for a moment.

They saw Chihuahua standing, pistol in

hand, with face all but against the boot of a man who hung by a short rope from the crossbar of the corral gate; a man swathed by many turns of binding rope. Two yards on Chihuahua's right was another, shorter figure, which had been drawn up nearer the crossbar. The choking rope had slipped to the back of his neck, forcing his head forward. So this short man seemed to regard them broodingly, with chin upon his breast.

"The Ettison brothers!" Halliday said metallically. "Dead enough to skin!"

"Por dios!" Chihuahua remarked calmly. "Me, I'm never before have one dead man kick me in them eye."

He stepped back a pace and regarded the two hanging men thoughtfully, with a kind of unmoved, professional interest.

Then Clay saw on the gate-frame at his left something grayish-white and roughly rectangular. It was the side of a pasteboard box, with large letters printed upon it. He went over and pulled it down. The others grouped behind him. He read slowly:

NOTISE
Theeves and Theeves
Frendes take warnin
we are tyrd of steelin

" 'Crooked county officers,' " Halliday quoted — as if to himself. " 'Old-Timer Committee' . . . Huh! That's funny! I would've said *I* stack up as an old-timer around here and I have heard not one word about the organizing of any such committee. 'Crooked county officers!' Well, far be it from me to deny that many a true word can be written on the side of a cardboard box and nailed to a corral gate!

"Simon Dee, now — our well-knowed county attorney — he's the kind of man you could trust with your life — if you'd made your will and was ready to cash in, anyhow. Sye Stubbins, our dashing city marshal — at least, if he ain't dashing, I'm damned if I know just what he is! — is a gentleman that has to be mighty careful about where he sleeps. Curled up inside a coil of rope lets him be most natural. But the district attorney, he's at Arno. Smoky Cole's sheriff — and tax collector and assessor, too, so ____"

"So, what?" Clay asked, frowning at the storekeeper. "What are you driving at?"

"Oh! Damn' if *I* know!" Halliday confessed. "Wonder where Smoky can be. He's not fond of having his prisoners taken out of his jail and handed dancing lessons, this way."

"By Gemini!" Clay grunted. "Reckon this lynching and Uncle Smoky not being in town *could* be hooked up?"

"Can happen! We're better leave these fellows for them coroner's jury, huh?" Chihuahua asked Clay — though why he should have turned to this young man, a virtual stranger in Gurney, Halliday by token of his stare did not understand.

"We'd better make another stab at finding Smoky," Clay said slowly.

They moved back toward the sheriff's office. Clay, staring absently around, pondering the lynching of the two luckless horse-thieves, chanced to look through the moonlight in the direction of the corral behind the jail. He stopped short, hand on his pistol. Something wriggled like a great snake across the ground.

"Look at that!" he cried to the others. Then he moved toward that object, which had stopped its crawling progress.

In a half-dozen steps he could see that it was a man. Two steps more and he could hear the wheezing half-groans of the prone figure. He broke into a trot, until he could squat on the ground beside the man. It was a tall, gaunt figure in rough flannel shirt, waist overalls and punchers' boots. So much Clay saw in a flashing glance — and saw, too, that the man's pistol holsters were empty. Then Chihuahua and Halliday cried a name together:

"Smoky Cole!"

The sheriff's seamed face showed ghastly pale under its weathered tan, in the light of the yellow oil lamp in the sheriff's office. In a corner old Dr. Brown put away bandages and instruments in a battered leather case. He turned to face the grim, silent group about Smoky's cot.

"I would say," he remarked thoughtfully, "that from now on my old and valued friend Smoky must be more careful. Quite so! Even a cat has only nine lives and, on this theory, it is my opinion that Smoky can only be killed once or twice more. Even with his constitution, I doubt if he will be good for much, except office work, inside the year. That gang which jumped him came very near to doing a complete job. Quite so, indeed!"

Reference to a "gang" was apparently complimentary. Smoky had not yet regained consciousness. He was a very mass of stab-wounds and bruises. The doctor, Clay thought, merely presumed that no one or two men could have inflicted so much injury on the gaunt, muscular old sheriff, and so implied that Smoky must have run foul of at least a half-dozen.

"One of you boys had better sit by him all night. I'll look in again, first thing in the morning. But, unless complications set in, such as the jail catching fire or the roof falling in, or a herd of steers stampeding through the office here, he'll recover. Smoky's a sheriff out of the Old Rock."

When he had gone, they looked at one another. Chihuahua lounged full length, propped on one elbow like a huge cat, on the floor against the wall. Lum Luckett swung a thick leg from where he sat on the battered pine table. Halliday sat in Smoky's own kitchen chair, propped back against the wall, his heels hooked in a rung. Clay leaned against the wall near Smoky's body, staring broodingly at the sheriff's still face.

The tales current about this famous old peace officer had certainly been borne out in this, their first meeting! No ordinary man would have survived such an attack as Smoky had evidently suffered. The doctor's head appeared in the doorway again. He was the coroner of the county.

"I'll empanel a jury, first thing in the morning. We'll have a look at those Ettisons. No use waking anybody this time of the morning. If the Ettisons were dead when you found them, it certainly won't hurt them to hang a while longer!"

He vanished. Silence again gripped the office, broken only by the sheriff's stertorous breathing.

Clay, it was, who saw the flutter of Smoky's eyelids. He leaned at the side of the cot. Smoky's small blue eyes were glassy, staring straight upward. The first word distinguishable was not printable. Apparently, Smoky was voicing his opinion of the ancestry of those who had ganged him! Chihuahua grinned amusedly.

"Yeh, she's alive!" he cried. "She's them same damn' Smoky!"

He came over, in his hand the sovereign remedy of the cow-country. Deftly he inserted the neck of a flask between Smoky's lips and let the whisky trickle down the sheriff's throat. Smoky's eyes blinked rapidly; again his lips moved, when the bottle had been taken away. Again Clay listened; again the words meant nothing to him. But Chihuahua nodded, grinning.

"She's say, them w'isky come from the Antelope Saloon," he explained. "Smoky, she's maybe not them scholar but — *por Dios!* she's one gentleman — and one damn' fine judge for good w'isky. She's never drink the w'isky from the Antelope — only from them Palace."

"Gang jumped me — tolled me down — edge of town," Smoky whispered huskily.

"Know who they were?" Clay asked eagerly.

Almost imperceptibly Smoky shook his head. He was staring hard at Clay. He seemed to be trying to keep his thoughts straight, trying to concentrate.

"You Nettie's boy?" he asked faintly.

Clay nodded.

"Clay Borden," he said. "And here's Chihuahua and another good Texas man — Lum Luckett. If it's all right with you, we're your deputies."

"Fine!" Smoky breathed. "Halliday! You're a county commissioner — you swear 'em in — for me. Where's Bib Alder?"

But Alder had vanished with the coming of the doctor.

When the very slight formality attendant upon swearing in the three as deputies was finished, Smoky closed his eyes again. His face, Clay thought, was very peaceful.

Clay kept watch beside Smoky while the others found cots in the back room and went to sleep — all but Halliday, who went home. The remainder of the night dragged endlessly. With the pale light of dawn, Clay rose to blow out the kerosene lamp. He turned to see Smoky's eyes fastened upon him. The old sheriff made the slightest beckoning motion. He spoke almost in a whisper:

"Want that you should be chief deputy. Tell Bib Alder!"

When the others came into the office, Smoky was again lying with eyes closed. Alder appeared. He was revealed in daylight as a young man in early twenties, with small, deep-set black eyes and a heavy, bulldoggish face, none too intelligent.

He looked the fighter, not the thinker.

"He come out of it?" he inquired, with a jerk of head toward Smoky Cole.

Clay nodded.

"For a minute or two. Seems a gang jumped him on the edge of town. Wouldn't surprise me if that gang was the same that hung the two prisoners. Do' 'no' why I should feel that way, but I do. Had breakfast? Well, then, if you'll watch here, we'll eat. I reckon the coroner's inquest will be held pretty soon."

"We're eat in them hotel of Mrs. Sheehan," Chihuahua said. "She's one fi-i-ine lady and her fried chicken and biscuits —— Come and see."

They filed into the big dining-room of the hotel. Mrs. Sheehan, vast of girth, red and belligerent of face, kindly of snapping Irish-blue eyes, looking up; flung both hands high.

"The Bad Penny in person! Chihuahua Joe himself."

She picked up one of the teacups from the table, for Chihuahua rushed at her with hands outstretched.

"Don't you! Don't you, now! None of your monkey business, or I'll set Merle Sheehan on you. Tell me: How's Smoky?"

"Oh!" Chihuahua said, stopping. "So you're know about Smoky . . ."

"Know about it! Why wouldn't I? Who else stuffs the wagging mouths of the useless cowhands around here? Of course I know about it. Anyway, it's all over town — how a Mexican boy tolled Smoky to the edge of town to stop a fight and how he walked straight into a gang that had knives and clubs.

"And they lynched those two tough Ettisons . . . You know, there's something funny about that business, and that 'Old-Timer Committee.' Nobody'd kick a lot about two horse-thieves doing the cottonwood prance. Me least of all! For they lifted Black Colum right out of my corral. But manhandling Smoky Cole, to get to lynch the Ettisons —

that's what sticks in my craw. I'd love to put my hands on those *old-timers* that ganged Smoky!"

There was a shuffle of feet in the entry-hall behind the trio. Mrs. Sheehan looked that way and the broad, red face stiffened subtly; the blue eyes narrowed.

"Well!" she muttered. "Big Casino himself and — yeh. The girl."

Clay moved quickly around the table. He took a seat on that side which permitted him to face the door. Chihuahua glanced at the pair in the doorway, then turned his sea-blue eyes sadly upon Lum. Lum sighed, glanced at John Powell and the girl, then regarded Clay steadily.

" 'How do I love thee?
Let me count the ways!
I love thee to the heights
My soul can reach,
When reaching out of sight ——' "

"W'y, Clay's never tell me that!" Chihuahua said reproachfully. "W'y *is* that, Clay?"

"Will you two damn' fools kindly go to hell!" Clay inquired, in a low, deadly voice.

For whether Helen Powell's face had turned fiery red because she had overheard Lum Luckett's quotation, or because ——

But he could find no other reason explaining the violent deepening of her color. Then, behind John Powell and his daughter, he saw a smiling face — and promptly he forgot the girl.

Dimly, almost automatically, he heard from where Chihuahua and Lum sat on his left a faint and furtive creaking, as of well-oiled leather touched beneath the table. He shot at the two a darting glance and saw how they had slightly shifted their positions.

John Powell ignored the three at the small table. Helen did more than ignore them, despite her flaming cheeks. Clay thought it was easy to see that *she* had no knowledge of the existence of three such men! When the other party had been seated and were eating, Clay found that he could not keep his eyes away from them. John Powell meant nothing to him. But about Smiling and the girl, and the way they talked and smiled at each other, there was something that drew his angry eyes again and again.

At last, he could bear it no longer. He set down his coffee cup with a wordless, impatient sound. Chihuahua looked knowingly at Lum Luckett, who shook his head sadly. Then Chihuahua leaned to inspect Clay's cup.

"W'y, you're not ready to go, already,

Clay?" he cried, in a loud, surprised voice. "W'y, she's half-full — your cup — and these coffee of Mrs. Sheehan, there's not so good anywhere else in these whole Territory! You're better drink plenty, Clay. For we are ride to catch the big thief, and them middle-size, in-between thief, and them boy w'at wish to be the killer with so many notches on his guns — notches for them Mexicans w'at she's shoot in the back — there's no coffee like these coffee of Mrs. Sheehan, Clay! No, no, no!"

Clay snarled underbreath, but to avoid more of their loud talk he drained the cup. Then he stood up, and Chihuahua and Lum rose with him. All looked thoughtfully at Smiling and hitched forward their pistols a mere convenient trifle before going out.

Shoulder to shoulder they walked down the street to the house where the doctor had his office.

The doctor was just coming outside in his rôle of coroner. They accompanied him to the old corral where a jury was already gathered about the gate. Formalities were few and procedure swift, for the essential facts of this lynching seemed to the jurymen most obvious.

"Strangulation," the largest juryman said oracularly and looked around to note the effect of the word. He spat impressively.

Chihuahua whispered to Lum and Clay that this juryman had once spent a week in Chicago and had never been the same man since. Nothing underneath the sun could surprise him, or leave him at a loss for answer or opinion.

"That certainly what it looks like," the other jurymen agreed, one by one. "Uh — strangulation." They spat, too. "And by the hands of some party known to somebody, but not to us, but leaving their sign."

"All right to cut them down, Doc?" the leading juryman inquired of the coroner. "And go get a drink?"

Returning along the street, the doctor remarked to Clay and the others that Smoky was not doing so well as he had hoped. He said that Smoky had fallen into a coma.

"But you found no fracture?" Lum asked the doctor. "Merely concussion and the weakness attendant upon multiple wounds?"

"What?" the old doctor grunted, staring at this amazing cowboy. "Multiple ——"

"You're not worry, Doc!" Chihuahua said soothingly. "She's *The Schoolma'am* and them words, they are tumble w'en she's open up his mouth. She's bad — Smoky? But we're make four deputy — *pues,* we're make more: we're make somebody get ver' sick . . . Who will be chief deputy, Clay? Not them Bib Alder?"

"Uncle Smoky told me this morning he wanted me to take the chief deputy's star," Clay said, without much interest. "Don't suppose it makes much difference which of us is it — us three, that is."

"Ha! She's suit me fine if you're chief deputy," Chihuahua grinned. "For them chief deputy, *she's* the man w'at will fight them county commissioners all time. They're say — them commissioners: '*Porque* the hell you're not keep these county ni-i-ice and clean, like them kitchen floor?' Them chief deputy *she's* say: '*Porque se. Quién sabe? Segur' Miguel!'* "

Back in the sheriff's office, Chihuahua pawed through a drawer in the table. He straightened, scowling, with three deputy sheriff badges in his hand.

"Now, I'm wondering w'ere's them chief deputy star?" he muttered. "Smoky, she's always keep them badge in this drawer."

"Well, it makes no never mind, now!" Clay said indifferently.

He took one of the badges and pinned it to his breast, then moved doorward.

"Let's squander around town awhile. See if we can find out anything about our mysterious Old-Timer Committee."

But all their "squandering" produced no more evidence than they had owned since finding the committee's notice. None in town knew — or would admit knowing — anything whatever about the stranglers' organization. Nor could they discover anyone who had heard the beat of horses' hoofs the night before, in the vicinity of the jail.

They stood silently outside of the Palace Saloon, their last inquiries proved unavailing. Clay stared unseeingly toward the sheriff's office. Chihuahua and Lum Luckett were looking the other way, toward Mrs. Sheehan's hotel. It came even to the preoccupied Clay that Chihuahua had stiffened suddenly — and queerly. Mechanically, he turned and looked in the same direction.

Four men were walking toward them. The first to catch Clay's eye was that tall, dark Eb Yates, who had been so anxious to kill Chihuahua and Lum in Schwingle's store in Anthony. With him were the same two smaller men who had backed him, there at Anthony. The fourth man was — Smiling.

Clay watched their approach with a sense of inner calmness that surprised even himself. Strange how much older, maturer, he felt now, than upon that night in Poplar Station. Perhaps it was because then he had been merely a drifter, blowing like a tumbleweed before the vagrant winds of circumstance. Now he had a definite job, a definite place, in Gurney.

"Chief Deputy . . . Acting Sheriff . . ." he said mentally.

However, his calmness did not make him any the less alert. Four dangerous men were coming. What they might intend to do was unpredictable. But, almost certainly, it would be swift and violent!

Smiling and his companions came abreast and stopped. Yates's black-stubbled face was expressionless. One might have believed that never before had he set eyes upon the trio. The short, stocky, tow-haired boy at his elbow regarded them with faded blue eyes almost cowlike in their lack of any interest at all. The slender, foxy-faced redhead let his twinkling green eyes rove from Chihuahua to Lum, to Clay, then back again. But never did his gaze lift above their chins; never could any of them look straight into his eyes. Smiling wore his habitual grin.

"Hello!" he said cheerfully. "Hear Smoky kind of run into an accident, and that leaves you upholding the Law west of the Rowdy."

Clay nodded, as if the subject were of small interest. Just what, he wondered, was the little killer's game here?

Smiling turned his grin from one to the other of them.

"Who's chief deputy?" he inquired. "You, Chihuahua?"

"No-o, Smoky, she's tell Clay to take them chief deputy star and make them bad men hard to find; to help them to get sick," Chihuahua explained blandly.

"I — see," Smiling nodded. "Yeh, I see. So long!"

"*Pues,* me, I'm think you're *see* all right," Chihuahua nodded, with sardonic flash of teeth beneath black mustache. "Or, if you're not see, right now, you're see plenty, in just one little w'ile. You're — not let your foot slip, Smiling, old friend?"

CHAPTER VI

Clay watched the four of them out of sight. When he turned back to address a remark to Lum and Chihuahua, only Lum stood beside him. Lum, by his expression, was as surprised as Clay upon discovering Chihuahua's disappearance. But Clay, looking hard at him, had his earnest doubts. Still, it made no difference. Chihuahua had a way of turning up at the proper time!

"Lum," he said thoughtfully, "you've been a deputy before . . . I wish you'd drift down to the office and see if you can kind of dig into things there, and find out what Smoky had on his docket when he got smacked. Then we'll have something to go on. With that gang in town — in the country, for that matter! — there'll certainly be plenty turning up, any minute, to keep an ordinary sheriff's office busy. But if Smoky had work on hand, we'll have to get after that first; right away."

As he stood alone there before the Palace, a dusty rider came charging down the street, raking his lathered horse. He pulled to a halt before Clay and inquired croakingly for John Powell. The chunky gray he rode was branded Ladder P. He was a lithe young daredevil, this rider, and Clay wondered what could be the urgent message he bore to his boss. He inquired. The cowboy's eyes narrowed a trifle as he stared at Clay. Then he seemed to lose his suspicions. He shrugged impatiently. But he was full of news, too long bottled up. Clay thought the boy would have talked, right then, to a Chinaman.

"Oh, nothing much," he grunted sardonically. "That damn' old loafer wolf, Jed Wyndham, and them two long-coupled boys of his'n, they run into some of our men late yesterday. When the smoke had blowed away, Frisky Wyndham was eating daisies and Durrell — he was our wagon boss — and three more of our boys was crossing Jordan River along with Frisky. Jed and his other boy got off — and so did two of our bunch."

He grinned without humor.

"But I reckon them Wyndham's won't get *too* far. I sent one boy fogging it to gather the hands from the Bosque Verde Ranch and the other to pull our crowd from the San Simon. The old man and me, we'll cut across and meet the boys north of the Diablos and easy head them Wyndhams off from the east bank of the Rowdy. Then — all we'll need is a cottonwood with the right kind of limb!"

"What's the quarrel between the Wyndhams and the Ladder P?" Clay inquired, keeping his tone most innocent, most casual.

"What the hell *you* so inquisitive about?" the Ladder P man demanded — perhaps conscious, now, that he had too freely spoken that which was on his mind.

"Why, because I want to know," Clay replied simply. "You see — I'm acting sheriff of the county . . ."

"Sheriff?" The cowboy's brown face set like stone. "Sheriff! Then you can go plumb to hell!"

In all matters requiring flashing action — and for which he had no precedent — Clay was a young man who acted almost wholly on impulse. So it was now, when he whipped out his pistol and took a long step to the cowboy's stirrup:

"When *I* go to hell, young fellow," he informed the Ladder P man quietly, "quite some few Ladder P men will be along to keep me company! It's just because there's been so damn much of this Ladder P-Triangle Bar rowing and killing that I'm acting sheriff now! Fellow, when *I* ask you a question about shooting that's been done in my bailiwick, I want an answer, and not talk about geography!"

"What's all this?" John Powell wanted to know, from the sidewalk behind Clay.

The cowboy — and he seemed quite relieved, somehow — told his tale again. John Powell listened, with no sign of emotion except the faint tightening of his already tight mouth. Utterly, completely, he ignored the acting sheriff of the county. But Clay did not intend to be easily ignored. Of John Powell he asked the same question he had put to the cowboy. Powell seemed not to hear.

He stood there — a big, inscrutable figure, staring at the shabby buildings across the street as if he could see through them, and away to that spot on the Ladder P range where this battle had occurred.

Clay studied him. He remembered what Smiling had said that night in Poplar Station: John Powell wanted to be Big Casino of the whole Territory. Now, with the belligerent King Connell and his even more belligerent son-in-law, Lit Taylor, in Ireland,

Powell had a very open trail toward whatever goal he sought. It came to Clay that, directly or indirectly, John Powell was the man responsible for the bulk of the trouble The Territory was knowing; for the recurrence of the old, lawless, bloody days, when men said:

"There's no law runs west of the Rowdy."

He saw that any battle to keep the peace in the locality must be a battle with John Powell. There would be skirmishes, of course, with lesser lights. But many of these had been set ablaze by John Powell's ruthless activities. Yes, the big fight would be with Powell. It must be. And Powell would be a handful for any opponent.

"All right," he told Powell. "I have my own ways of finding out things . . . You'd be surprised — I mean *will* be surprised! I'll — snoop around a li'l' bit, in places where I can find out the *truth!*"

"Snoopers have a way of dying very, very young in this country," Powell observed evenly.

But now he was not ignoring Clay Borden! He was complimenting that young man with close and studious attention.

Clay slipped his .44 back into the holster and moved off, grinning. He wanted to find Chihuahua and set in motion a small, simple, but effective plan that had flashed into his mind. He looked into the Palace, but did not find the breed's tall figure. In the Antelope, a few doors farther down the street, there was quite a crowd. He had to go inside to see if Chihuahua were there. Halfway down the long bar-room, he heard a faintly familiar voice, a youthful voice, a loud voice, a voice somewhat thickened by liquor:

"— Smoky says he wants them to be deputies," the voice was proclaiming to the bar-room crowd. "Well, that's all right with me. They can *be* deputies. But, you want to know whose white-haired boy is going to tell them new fellows where, and how high, to step? Old — Man — Alder's! You can put your last *peso* on that! Yessir!"

Among those drinkers closely surrounding the vocal Bib were some who seemed to be hunting amusement. One such was a long and lean and rawboned individual with a craggy nose and a blue silk patch over one eye. As this man turned to grin covertly at others, Clay kept catching tantalizing glimpses of something that twinkled on his breast.

"But what'll you do, Bib, if them fellows, they don't lift up their hoofs when you tell 'em to?" inquired the man of the patch.

"For a kid, you're pretty good with the hog-legs, but —— Are you good enough?"

"Good enough?" Bib Alder repeated, staring sullenly around him like a none-too-bright young bulldog. "Say! them fellows'll think so — right quick after they start something. They start a row with me and they'll be in fine shape to tell folks they *tried* hard, but they — couldn't — quite — get there!"

An inoffensive-looking townsman, on the far side of the bar-room, was in the act of lifting a tin cup toward his mouth. Alder chanced to be staring blankly in that direction. Abruptly, he grinned.

"See that there cup of Thompson's? Well, *watch me!*"

Clay saw the boy's elbow move. The men about him gave back suddenly. Up came Alder's pistol and, with the roar of it, the tin cup jumped from Thompson's hand, spraying him with whisky. He made the thin, squealing sound of a frightened rabbit and dived under the nearest table. The men around him scattered without ceremony.

Clay moved up on the grinning deputy, who stood with pistol still in his hand, pointing with left forefinger at the half-frightened, half-furious, Thompson.

"Give me that pistol!" Clay said grimly.

He twisted it from the deputy's hand before Bib Alder understood what was intended. Bib gaped at him stupidly. The tall man with the blue patch over his eye was staring also, his grim mouth hanging ludicrously half-open. Clay saw that the twinkling object on the tall man's chest was a star, with the black-lettered legend *City Marshal.* So this was Sye Stubbins! He remembered how Halliday had remarked that Stubbins could sleep comfortably only in an extremely circular position. But for the moment he dismissed the marshal from his mind.

"I'll just take your badge, too," he informed Alder, and with his left hand unpinned it deftly from Alder's shirt.

It had all happened far too rapidly for the late-deputy. Like one dazed by a blow, he rolled his eyes toward the city marshal. Then abruptly the bulldog face turned deep red. Clay had rammed Alder's pistol into the waistband of his trousers. He had seen that Alder wore but one pistol and had not considered the possibility of any other weapon. Alder's hand went flashing to his shirt bosom, to reappear with a bowie knife.

"Why — I'll cut your damn' heart out!" he bellowed.

The blow which struck diagonally at Clay

would have cut his target almost in two, with better aim. As it was, it went by Clay's chin so nearly that he felt the fanning wind of the blow. Automatically, his right fist whipped up from belt level. He hit Bib Alder under the chin. It was too fast a blow to land full force. But it snapped Alder's head back and kept him from striking again with the knife.

Clay jabbed him swiftly in the face with his left, then set his feet and hurled every ounce of his hard-knit weight behind a right hook. It connected squarely with the angle of the boy's jaw. Alder sagged; the men standing behind him gave hastily back. Clay stepped in then, swinging furiously — right-left, right-left — to Alder's almost unprotected face and body. Bib Alder went down to strike the back of his head on the brass bar-rail and lie in a limp huddle.

Clay looked about him quickly. He saw that Sye Stubbins was gathering his ideas. The marshal seemed to be on the verge of remark. The best defense being attack, Clay stepped savagely toward the official.

"What the hell are you wearing a badge for?" he demanded. "Letting this nitwit shoot off his pistol in a crowded bar-room! And you hee-hawing like a damn' burro because he came so close to killing a man.

119

Shut up!" he snarled. For the marshal was spluttering furiously. "In about a minute, Mex' — and that's just exactly half a minute, English — you'll have me provoked into giving you free board for the night in the County Hotel."

Glaring at the marshal, he unpinned his own deputy star and replaced it with the badge he had taken from Alder's shirt — and which bore the legend *Chief Deputy Sheriff.* Evidently, Bib Alder had slipped it from Smoky Cole's table drawer, with the arrival of the new deputies and sight of Smoky's injuries.

"Well, well!" Smiling remarked, from behind Clay. "Still making loud noises, are you?"

Clay turned slowly. Close behind Smiling stood the tall, sinister Eb Yates, with the stocky, tow-haired youngster and the foxy-faced redhead. And, if there were a friendly face within the range of his vision, Clay failed to see it. Tense faces he saw dimly; expectant faces; and some that grinned — that was all.

He met Smiling's red-flecked eyes steadily. While half his brain was busy with calculation of his chances against this flashing gunman, the other half was wondering why the sight of Smiling should bring thought of

Helen Powell; why sight of the gunman, and thought of the girl, should rouse in him the grim fury that he knew now gripped him.

But that, after all, was not important. What mattered was that between him and Smiling there now crept a thin, red haze. If this were to be the showdown — good enough! He had the feeling that regardless of how quickly Smiling might draw; no matter how many shots he might get in; *he* could not be killed until he had emptied his pistol into the killer. When the last shot was fired, there would be two of them sprawling there on the rough planks of the Antelope's floor; not one.

"You have kind of overplayed your hand," Smiling said. "I hear you've been making talk about shooting me on sight."

As if the sentence were a signal, Eb Yates, the towhead, and the red-haired man moved to right and left of their leader. So Clay, standing with back to the bar, now was ringed in by the semicircle they made.

"Well?" he demanded. "What about it?"

"*What about it?* You poor fool! You poor damn fool! Because I've let you go, three–four times, you thought you could get away with it? Well, now ——"

"*Sí? Sí?*" an eager voice inquired from just to the left of the half-circle ringing Clay in.

121

"You're please tell us about 'now'! Me, I'm interest' like the hell, to know w'at *is* it you're do, now! But, w'at is it you're do, me, I'm wish that you're do him. For I'm get so *goddam* tired to hold these shotgun, Smiling, old friend!"

Chihuahua, with the magically noiseless movement peculiar to himself, had come unseen along the inner side of the long bar. Now he leaned both elbows upon its top. He had the bar-tender's sawed-off shotgun in his hand and the gaping twin muzzles were trained upon Eb Yates and Smiling. The corners of his thin mouth were lifted beneath the points of the black mustache in a smile gently expectant.

Clay shook his head slightly, as if to clear the red haze from before his eyes. Then he looked at Smiling.

"You-all had certainly better drag it!" he said quietly. "For, if you're in town fifteen minutes from now, you'd better be forted up! We'll be coming after you and we'll *gather* you, if it takes every honest man in this town! We'll gather you — hands up, or tails down!"

Smiling looked at him a full thirty seconds. The red flecks were shining in his black eyes. Then his grin widened:

"We was going anyhow. See you later! Yessir, that we will . . ."

As the four of them moved toward the door, Chihuahua came like a huge cat in one smooth jump to the bar-top. There he squatted with the shotgun upon his knees, watching. Clay, also, watched them closely, one hand upon the butt of his own pistol, the other upon that taken from Bib Alder — who had got up and now stood back in the crowd which had been watching the encounter. Smiling did not look back.

CHAPTER VII

Chihuahua squatted against the wall in his favorite position, a cigarette between his fingers, sea-blue eyes staring dreamily at the faded ceiling. Lum Luckett was "seizing" a frayed place on his quirt with waxed thread got from the cowboys' bootmaker next door to Halliday's general store. Clay stood at the table which served the office as desk. He thumbed a small stack of reward notices which Lum had sorted out. The circulars lay on top of the latest edition of that interesting and invaluable book issued yearly in Austin, Texas — *A List of Fugitives from Justice.* But he found nothing of immediate interest in the reward notices, and his mind drifted to matters of more current dates.

"What's it? Council of war?" Halliday inquired from the doorway. "If she is, do I come in, or stay out?"

From Chihuahua's corner came the sound

of amused laughter.

"Them fellow Halliday, she's ask! She's see plenty trouble, Clay, and all time see 'em through the smoke! W'en Lit Taylor and me, we're deputies for Smoky, them Halliday, she's fight two–three time with us. W'en Curt Thompson, she's act as sheriff and me, I'm one deputy — same thing. *Bang! Bang!* will go them pistol and — *Mira!* there will pop up them Halliday!"

"What's the trouble between the Wyndhams and John Powell?" Clay asked of the storekeeper.

"Oh, nothing much," Halliday shrugged sardonically. "John Powell, he aims to be the Big Casino of the whole damn' Territory. Anybody that gets into his trail is going to get tromped on — or so Powell figures. Jed Wyndham is a mighty salty cuss — honest, too — or reasonable honest, anyhow. He settled over there on Hell Creek with a little bunch of cattle, on range John Powell had always used.

"Well, so long as there was plenty water in the creek, Jed never kicked about Ladder P stock watering there. But when there was nothing but a few water holes left, he naturally begun to chase off Ladder P cows. Then, when the Ladder P hands took to shooting at him and his two boys, Jed

Wyndham showed 'em the other cheek, all right! But the cheek was facing the Ladder P over the stock of Jed's Winchester!

"He claims they stole him blind and I reckon that's just about the way of it. Him and them two boys was over on Ladder P range three–four months ago and they recovered — that's what Jed Wyndham called it, anyhow — fifty head of long yearlings that Jed claims had been Triangle Bar stock, but was burned into three–four other brands.

"John Powell, he come to town and swore out a warrant against Jed for cattle stealing. Smoky sent word to Jed to come in and make bond, and it so happened that the day Jed come in John Powell was in town, too. Reckon, if Jed hadn't had such a cargo on board, he'd've done more'n ruin a *hat* for Powell. He's been out on bond ever since. I'm one of his bondsmen. There has been promiscuous shooting and squabbling along Hell Creek ever since. If the Ladder P crowd comes up with 'em this time — well, I reckon Jed Wyndham won't never come to trial. They'll be too many for him and Ollie. But he'll down plenty before they rub out *his* chalk mark!"

"Will they come up with them, do you reckon?" Clay inquired of the silent Chihuahua.

"Me, I'm think no," Chihuahua grunted, judicially deliberate. "She's broken country — ver' rough. Jed Wyndham, she's know every trail between these Diablos and Diamond River High Bluffs."

"Reckon you could find them and talk them into coming to Gurney?" Clay asked. "They're certainly going to be killed — and do a lot of killing themselves — if they stay on the dodge along the Rowdy. But, if we can bring them into town, we can kind of ride herd on them until — well, until we kind of get things straightened out and talk John Powell into being satisfied with standing just a little bit shorter in the deck than Big Casino."

Chihuahua stood up, nodding. He got his silver-trimmed saddle and bridle from a corner of the office and tucked the deadly carbine under his arm. He halted in the back door, on his way to the corral.

"She's maybe take two–three day, to find them fellow. But, me, I'm bring 'em in. She's one damn' good idea. Jed Wyndham, she's one damn' fine fellow, and me, I will not be pleased to have them Ladder P hand dry-gulch him. So, if we're see them Ladder P crowd w'ile we're come back" — he grinned sinisterly — "well, *we're* help them to get sick!"

"John Powell's gone," Halliday remarked softly. "Rode out with that cowboy that come bringing the news."

Clay wanted to ask what had become of Helen. From Halliday's remark one might think that Powell had left her in town. But he would not display so much interest in her, before Halliday and Lum Luckett. Lum finished binding his quirt. He held it up and inspected it critically, then turned round and very innocent eyes upon the store-keeper:

"Continue, sir. Surely you have the word he expects! Where can he locate the young lady?"

"Oh! Well, she's staying with the Kene-dys," Halliday grinned. "Bill Kenedy and me, we're partners in several things and Bill has got a daughter about Helen's age — Barbara — a mighty pretty gal, too, Barbara is."

Clay had loafed over to the door. He stared idly up the street. At sight of three men, gathered together, he became alert, indeed. He did not recognize the big frock-coated man, who was talking earnestly — to judge by his gestures. He looked much like a lawyer. But the other two were the gaunt city marshal Sye Stubbins and young Bib

128

Alder, who had so recently been a deputy sheriff.

"I'm going to drift around a while," Clay told Halliday and Lum.

He wondered if Stubbins and Alder had been seeking legal advice. If they had, he guessed from the portly man's earnest gestures that they had received it! He watched the pair move off, leaving the frock-coated man to stand looking after them, rubbing his hands in a way that reminded Clay vividly of a cat licking its lips after eating a dickybird.

Halliday came over and stood in the doorway beside Clay. He remarked the portly gentleman, and made a gagging sound, deep in his thick throat.

"Simon Dee — the thieving, psalm-whining scalawag!" he said thoughtfully. "Now, what kind of dirty deal, between mayhem and murder, has he got planned? See'm rubbing his greasy paws? That's a certain sign. You know, Borden, I see him and Smiling in his office, with heads together thicker'n even thieves, this morning. And Sye Stubbins and your ex-playmate, Bib Alder, they filed in and made it four-handed, whilst I was eagle-eyeing 'em."

"Inter-est-ing!" Clay drawled, with sincerity. "Yes-siree! I would be the last cow-chaser around here to go denying it even in a whisper! I can somehow read my own palm, too, and I figure that meeting having something to do with my fortune — or misfortune, maybe . . ."

He pondered the matter, when Halliday had moved back inside. That notice of the "Old-Timer Committee" had remarked upon crooked county officials, and Halliday — who knew everything worth knowing about local politics — had agreed with that remark. Now, here was the most notorious rustler and killer in a huge scope of country hobnobbing with Dee, the county attorney, and Stubbins, the city marshal — and with young Bib Alder, who, but for the arrival of himself and Chihuahua and Lum, would now be acting sheriff . . . What was it all about?

He went slowly toward town, mulling the problem. His appointment as chief deputy had patently displeased certain ones among the Powers here. Alder *might* be honest, but, if so, he was thick with a very suspicious bunch. Clay found it a tangle. He considered John Powell, who did not like Smoky and his deputies; Smiling, who was apparently so close to the Ladder P owner. It seemed to Clay that Powell must plan to use Smiling in the advancement of his ambitions to be "Big Casino" of The Territory. But Smiling's talk, that night in Poplar, had indicated that the grinning young killer intended to use Powell!

"You are the sheriff, señor?" a Mexican boy inquired of him, sliding from a doorway he was passing. "The county attorney asks for you. He wishes to have talk with the sheriff where none can overhear. So he begs you to come with me to see him. He is in a private house near the hotel of the fat señora of the hard fists."

This *was* interesting, Clay told himself. He wondered what the "thieving, psalm-whining" Dee had to say to him. Some crooked proposal to make? It was by no means unlikely! Well, Dee would have to expose his hand to some extent, just to discuss the business. He grinned to himself. When Dee did ——

He nodded to the boy and went with him along the street toward the hotel of Mrs. Sheehan's. Glancing idly across at the dance-hall now run by Ritt Rales — the gambler who also operated the Palace Saloon and gambling-hall — he saw Bib Alder come out with a Winchester under his arm and go up the street toward the hotel. He also caught a glimpse, in the doorway of the dance-hall, of the tall, gaunt figure of

Sye Stubbins. But only for an instant. Stubbins pulled back inside. Alder turned off the main street at the next corner.

"Where does he reckon he's going with that carbine?" Clay muttered, then shrugged.

After all, what Bib Alder did when moving away from him was not of direct importance. It might chance to become so, but that could take care of itself for the time being. Then a girl came out of the dance-hall and stood on the side-walk, looking across at Clay. Her face was ghastly-white under the rouge on the cheeks. The pallor was plain even from across the street. She stared at Clay as if he were a ghost. One hand lifted from her side to the level of her breast; the fingers moved in a vague, clawing gesture.

It amused Clay. He wondered if someone had been telling her what man-eaters the new deputies were — he in particular. He grinned and lifted his hand in a cheerful salute to her. The result was not at all what he had expected. Her mouth dropped half-open. For an instant she gaped at him. Then:

"*Oh — my — God!*" she said in a queer, harsh, almost-croaking voice. "You — you ____"

"Della!" an even voice called from inside

the dance-hall. "Della! You come in here!"

She flung up an arm to cover her eyes and stumbled, rather than walked, back inside the door. Clay saw the flash of a black sleeve as she stepped over the threshold. She vanished as if jerked inside. He shrugged. It was a queer way to act, he thought.

"You might figure she could see something downright awful about me!" he muttered, and grinned to himself.

He walked on. The Mexican boy, his guide, had disappeared for the moment. But now he came around a corner opposite Mrs. Sheehan's. He beckoned Clay on, then dodged back out of sight. Clay went, but it suddenly seemed odd to him that this end of the street should be so quiet, so vacant of its usual traffic.

He was given but an instant to consider the emptiness of the street at this end. For Mrs. Sheehan appeared, at the end of the hotel porch nearest Clay. She leaned over the porch-rail and lifted a thick arm to beckon Clay imperatively. Without knowing it, he followed the ordinary habit of Gurney when Mrs. Sheehan beckoned and went toward her.

When he stood beside the porch, looking up, he became conscious of a girl behind the big Irishwoman. For one flashing, heart-jumping space, he wondered if it were Helen Powell. Then he saw that it was not. This was a girl somewhat larger; a very pretty, very cheerful, yellow-haired girl, with the widest of starry blue eyes; a shapely girl, as lovely as Helen Powell had seemed to him — or, almost as lovely.

"Barbara," Mrs. Sheehan said, "this-here's Mister Clay Borden. He's acting sheriff, the boy is, the Lord have mercy on him!"

Clay mumbled that he was pleased; he was happy; he was downright delighted to meet Miss Barbara Kenedy. The girl watched him with her yellow head on one side and an odd smile on her red mouth.

"I'm glad to know you, too," she said quickly, her voice shaking a little. "For — you see — I've heard so much about you . . ."

Mrs. Sheehan, with a wordless grunt, withdrew inside the hotel. Clay stared yearningly after her. He didn't want to be left alone with this girl. There was something about her manner, her small smile, that worried him. It gave him the impression that Barbara Kenedy knew something about him; something that he didn't want her or anyone else to know. What that could be was beyond him to decide, but he felt that way, anyhow. Very heartily, he wished that her path had not crossed his own this morning.

"That — that's fine!" he said energetically. "Yes'm, it certainly is. I have got to be going. I ——"

"You must come to our house soon," she said. "Oh, not to see me! Unless you want to . . . But I guess *you* won't be interested in blondes when you hear who's the brunette I have visiting me."

"Yes'm! No'm! I mean ——"

Clay stopped short angrily. Now what the devil had Helen Powell told her? Or had Helen told her anything? She might just be guessing at things; just bedeviling him. Girls were that way. He remembered his own sisters.

"*What* do you mean?" she demanded. Then: "Well, never mind. But you'll come to see us?"

"Oh, yes!" Clay assured her. "Yes, indeed!"

Mentally he crossed his fingers. Any time *he* showed up at the Kenedy gate, he thought, it would be because he had been dragged there by somebody's saddle rope!

"Well, I have got to be going," he told her again. "I have got to see a man."

"I saw our fat and noble county attorney giving advice to two men just a minute ago," she said. "Do you want to know what Sanctimonious Simon was telling these two men? Not all, of course, but the part I overheard?"

Now the wide, blue eyes were serious. Grudgingly, Clay began to revise his opinion of her. She might have sense after all — *some* sense, anyway. He nodded his interest.

"As I walked up behind them, Simon was saying to Sye Stubbins and Bib Alder, in his customary address-the-jury manner:

" '— You do that! The law will support you. You're senior. Everybody knows it; and *his* action was entirely illegal. So, you do as I've said and, regardless of what may occur, don't worry.'

"Then he said something to the marshal, so low that I couldn't hear. Our friend Sye seemed pleased by whatever it was, for he laughed in that — that ghastly way of his. It always reminds me of a one-eyed hyena, the way he opens his mouth and shakes his shoulders, but doesn't make a sound. So, if *I* were Acting Sheriff Clay Borden, *I* should be very careful about whom I saw in Gurney — and particularly about the way, and the place, in which I saw them!"

"Oh, maybe it'll serve, if I'm just careful to see *them* before they see *me!*"

Clay grinned at her now. His embarrassment in her presence had vanished. Under that pretty blonde hair of hers *was* a set of brains!

"I certainly appreciate you telling me all this. I reckon I'll have to uncross my fingers, now, and say all over again that I'll be coming to your house."

"Helen will be glad to see you — or I *suppose* she will."

"Now, that's certainly fine! And *you* will, too?"

"Oh, anything that makes Helen happy makes me happy, too," she assured him. Her tone was malicious.

"Well, thanks a lot! I'll be seeing you. *Hasta la vista!*"

So Helen Powell would be glad to see him, would she? Clay grinned sardonically to himself. Yes, she would! Barbara Kenedy was simply running true to form — to feminine form — he told himself sagely, out of the knowledge he had of his own sisters. So engrossing was his reflection that almost he forgot his business with "Sanctimonious Simon" Dee, the county attorney.

Suddenly recalling this, he looked about for the Mexican boy who was supposed to be his guide. He found him across the street, once more peering around the corner of a building. He crossed over, in obedience to the boy's beckoning crooked finger. He was thinking of Dee — but the picture he had of the girl on her buckskin, so friendly with Smiling Badey, kept getting between him and his errand. He was all but oblivious to movement on the street at his left — toward town.

So, when a figure stepped out of a doorway fifty yards down the street, Clay, catching the movement out of the corner of his eye, hardly heeded it. But with the *staccato* of rifle-fire he jerked about. Bullets were being hailed at him by Bib Alder, who stood in midstreet.

Clay went into action with the abrupt speed of a startled wolf. He jumped toward the wall of the building behind which the Mexican boy — a bit of the machinery of this trap, doubtless — had been lurking. He flattened himself against the wall, the long-barreled .44 out in a flashing, mechanical, draw. How he had escaped being shot to pieces by Alder's first unheralded burst of lead, he could not understand. Then something struck his right foot with numbing force. Other slugs kicked up dust fountains in the street; *rat-tatting* against the weathered store-front.

Clay opened fire with his pistol. By a great

effort of will, he dismissed all thought of those whining bullets, to take careful aim at Alder. He held low and snapped back the hammer of the big single-action again and again, as rapidly as his thumb could move. Five shots he slammed at Alder. Then he drew a long breath and shook his head. His ears still rang with the reports. Alder lay face-down in the street, his Winchester under him.

Clay looked at Alder, then down at his numb right foot. There was no blood. He frowned bewilderedly until he saw that the bullet had torn the heel from his boot. Quickly, he pushed the empty shells from his Colt, reloaded it, then hobbled up toward the fallen man. Before he reached Alder, the deputy moved. Clay halted instantly, his .44 leaping up to cover Alder. The ex-deputy lifted himself to an elbow in the street. Painfully, he raised his head until he was staring straight at Clay.

"Keep your hands off that gun!" Clay warned him grimly. "Bushwhackers are something I have got not the least use for. I would as soon kill one as do anything I can think of."

The street was now becoming crowded again. Men and women — the latter "girls" from Ritt Rales's dance-hall — came crowding around Clay and the sprawling Alder.

"Put that gun away!" a harsh voice commanded from behind Clay. "Don't you shoot at him again."

Clay turned, although he had already guessed it was the marshal. Stubbins was standing with pistol in his hand and it was trained directly at Clay.

As apparent as the heavy six-shooter in the marshal's hand was the hostile temper of a good many in this crowd. Clay began to have the idea that Alder's Winchester-work had not only been well-planned, but had been well-published; that this audience had been waiting for Alder to kill him. The thought in no way calmed his temper. But before he could make answer, the old doctor-coroner came pushing through the crowd.

Without a word, he knelt beside Alder. He made a swift and practiced examination, then looked up at Clay with a tiny twist of his clean-shaven mouth.

"Hole in the shoulder; glancing wound across the temple; broken leg —— One might think you couldn't make up your mind *what* you wanted to do!"

"Oh, my intentions were good," Clay denied grimly. "But the son of a dog opened up on me with that Winchester before I really knew he was in the neighborhood. Fifty yards is a pretty long range for a pistol, 'specially when the other party has already slammed five shots at you — and you know his friend, the city marshal, is in a doorway somewhere hunting a chance to six-shooter you in the back."

He regarded the marshal very grimly.

"The reason I don't pistol-whip you out of town right now is because that would be too easy on you. I'm waiting. If you had a friend, even a well-wisher, and he knew what *I* know, he would tell you that you had better practice howling in a whisper around Gurney right now!"

The marshal's eye roved down to the pistol in Clay's hand. Upon his face was an expression of utmost calculation. Clay read him as if he had been Long Primer print. A corner of his thin mouth lifted.

"Not being quite a damn' fool, I loaded it before I walked up on this two-for-a-nickel dry-gulcher here," he observed casually.

The marshal's eye batted rapidly at the announcement.

"Well, I don't care if you are a deputy sheriff, you can't come this shooting and lording it over the town. Don't you think you have heard the last of it."

Clay regarded him grimly, but what he

would have said was interrupted by a thudding of hoofs beyond the hotel.

A bareheaded man on a lathered, wild-eyed horse whirled around the corner and jerked to a stop on the edge of the crowd. The horse's head dropped to his knees; he stood trembling for a split-second, then crumpled like something made of paper. His rider tried to jump clear, but only sprawled in the street. His face was a haggard, dusty mask. He glared around him with red-veined eyes. Then Clay noticed that his red flannel shirt bore two shades of color . . . Around a gaping hole in the shoulder it was almost black — and wet.

"Stage — shot up — by five men — this side Porto!" the man croaked. "Driver killed — one passenger, too — got me — shoulder — five thousand bullion — and money took. I ——" Then he could hold up no longer. His face dropped into the dust of the street.

CHAPTER VIII

"Chihuahua is without doubt the nonpareil of trackers; a freak," Lum Luckett said slowly, staring around upon the scene of the robbery. "But even a *lusus naturae* could hardly discover more than you and I have, here."

Clay said nothing. They had come pounding up from Gurney along the road to Porto. Here was the empty stage before them. The bloodstains were still upon the seat, to tell where the driver had slid over dead, while his seatmate — that shotgun messenger who had ridden into Gurney — had fallen backward under robber-lead. Apparently, nobody else had been here since the robbery. They could still see tracks in the dust of the road beside the stage wheels, where the passengers had stood with hands in air. Near the front wheel a thin, reddish film like goldbeaters' skin bound together particles of the dust.

Clay guessed that the surviving passengers had taken horses of the team to ride back to Porto. Evidently, they had borne with them the bodies of the dead passenger and the driver.

Clay and Lum found where five horses had stood behind the boulders at one side of the trail. It was an ideal spot for an ambush. The stage, pulling a long grade up to the boulders, must have been moving almost at a walk by the time it reached the robbers. Four of these had stepped out into the road while the fifth held the horses of the others. Their job done, the robbers had returned to the horses and ridden hell-bent toward the Rowdy and its deep cañon.

Lum made a cigarette and lit it, gazing dreamily into the distance.

"Smiling Badey and his three henchmen departed from our midst," Lum drawled. "A stage was robbed by several men shortly thereafter. Could coincidence explain these facts? I — wonder, Clay! If only I could believe that somewhere ahead of us Smiling carries the loot from this robbery — and that we can overtake him . . ."

"I wish Chihuahua was along," Clay nodded. "But I'm damned if I'm going to take time to ride to Porto or anywhere else to rake up more help. I reckon it's not sensible for the two of us to go trailing five hard cases ——"

"In a long and tolerably grammatical twenty-five years," Lum said thoughtfully, "I recall very few occasions when any competent authority commended my intelligence. So — if that descendant of Bucephalus will carry me —— *Lead on, Macduff!*"

"I didn't know you straddled anything with such a handle," Clay told him, grinning, "and the name is probably *Nitwit,* not *Macduff.* But I'm willing to waive little things like that. *I* never was noted for brains, either. Let's go!"

They rode off eastward over rough ground, crossing the rises that were the foothills of the Diablos.

"*Can* this be Smiling and Company that we're trailing?" Lum drawled presently.

"It's the showdown!" Clay said grimly. *"The showdown."*

He was hardly answering Lum. Rather, he voiced the thought that mention of Smiling's name roused in him. Staring at the rugged country ahead, he could almost *see* the slender figure on a galloping horse; the mocking face, with lips that always smiled, turned over-shoulder so that red-flecked black eyes stared at him.

And he found himself fiercely eager to

close up the distance between! He leaned forward in the saddle. Azulero, feeling the pressure of Clay's knees, put a little more power, a trifle more speed, into his lope. Clay rode like a man with the loop of a lariat about him and its end in the tugging hand of a woman . . . Then he caught himself and checked his growing speed. They must not kill their horses, for this might be a long, grim chase.

A little ashamed, he looked back at Lum, who rode but a little behind.

"Queer!" Clay meditated aloud. "A man goes along, not hunting trouble, then there comes a day — all of a sudden, likely — when he knows that, no matter how big the world is, it hasn't got enough room for him and another man — It was like that over on the Diamond River on the Bar B, with that Windy Winters you and Chihuahua heard something about. Now — it's come to that again. There's not room in the world for Smiling Badey and me at the same time."

Lum Luckett looked this slender young man shrewdly up and down, from well-shaped, Stetsoned head and hard-set face, to quick, deft, brown hands, almost as if they were meeting for the first time. Very slightly then he nodded to himself.

"Is it — the girl who's caused this?" His

voice was very even.

"No, it's not," Clay answered slowly, but with conviction. "I thought of that, too, but it's not the girl; or not altogether. It's just simply that Smiling Badey and Clay Borden are two different kinds of men. The kind that have *got* to lock horns like two range bulls, when they meet. If there wasn't a girl within a thousand miles of us, still we'd tangle ropes. Most men get along with Smiling by letting him do just as he damn' pleases. Well, it happens *I* am not so built that I'll always step back out of anybody's trail!"

They made camp at early dusk. Their tiny cooking fire was built against a cliff so that the smoke lifted, almost invisible against the gray rock. When they had eaten, they moved camp a mile, spread their blankets behind some boulders and staked the horses out. They were up before dawn. Breakfast was a very brief meal.

On the rocky ground the trail they followed grew increasingly hard to see. In mid-morning, they lost it entirely. They were stubbornly averse to turning back, so they tried to put themselves in the others' place; tried to think as the robbers had thought; and pick a forward path as the fugitives had picked it.

Noon, and they had found no further trace of the men they sought. Then Clay's roaming eyes discovered a tiny wisp of gray smoke that seemed to curl out of some cañon invisible from where they sat their horses. It was so close that instinctively he lowered his voice to a whisper in speaking of it to Lum.

They looked at each other with mouths tightened grimly. Then, abruptly, they grinned, hitched up their shell belts and moved as quietly as the horses could walk toward the rim of that invisible cañon.

Presently they were on its edge, looking into a wide, stony chasm a hundred feet deep, its floor splotched with clumps of greasewood, mesquite, and cactus. The smoke which had guided them was vanished now. So, lying on their bellies on the cañon's lip, they searched in the brush below for the fire-makers.

At about the same time Clay and Lum made out horses stamping in a pocket of the cañon wall, two or three hundred yards away. And at about the same time they located the camp, the owners of the camp discovered them! Or so it seemed. From the shelter of some brush and boulders in the middle of the cañon there rang the flat, vicious report of a rifle.

The lead slug splattered on the wall below Clay and Lum. Another rifle *whanged!* some thirty yards to the right of the first; then came still a third shot from the rifleman's left. Clay and Lum pulled back hurriedly, for all three of those shots had come uncomfortably near. They found shelter behind boulders from which they could rain lead down at the three men firing from the cañon-bottom. Ten or twelve shots had been fired without noticeable effect, when Clay suddenly stiffened and peered more earnestly down at the greenery which partially hid the first man to fire. He cupped hand at mouth:

"Chihuahua!" he yelled. "Oh-h, Chihuahua!"

Again and again he must hail, to make himself heard above the rattle of the concealed men's firing, before there came an answering hail in Chihuahua's familiar voice.

Ten minutes later, they stood together in the cañon-bottom, grinning. Lum Luckett commented sadly to Clay upon Chihuahua's increasing years and failing eyesight. Chihuahua whooped indignantly and fell upon Lum. But now Jed Wyndham, enormously tall, but narrow and stoop-shouldered, with fierce, bitter-lined face and grizzled hair,

149

came out of the little pocket where the horses were. Behind him was his son — almost his twin, in appearance and economy of speech.

Clay and Lum shook hands with the Wyndhams. The old man stared long at Clay. His bristling brows drew together in a black frown above his great beak nose, as he studied Clay's slender five-seven, his wide, innocent blue eyes, his smooth, lightly tanned skin and the almost girlish regularity of his features.

"Changed my mind," he said abruptly to Chihuahua — and spat emphatically. "Ain't going to Gurney."

Chihuahua stared in bewilderment for an instant, then his sea-blue eyes roved to Clay. He threw back his head and burst into laughter.

"Oh-ho! So that's the dog w'at's bite you! You're think Clay, she's too much baby in his face, w'at? Well, *amigo mio*, me, I'm see these baby-face slap them leather and if I'm tell you that Clay, she's almost as good a gunman as Smiling — if she's not so good — you're take my word?"

Jed Wyndham stared again at Clay, evidently impressed by Chihuahua's endorsement. The breed's remark, its apparent sincerity, had amazed Clay. He had never thought that his speed on the draw, such as it was, had impressed this tall, most competent, gunman.

"Well, I'll see about it," Jed Wyndham conceded grudgingly. "How'd you boys happen to be nosing around, up here?"

Briefly, Clay explained. Chihuahua tugged at the spike points of his mustache and stared broodingly across the cañon. At last he nodded — as if answer had come to a private question. He looked at Clay.

"If them robbers, they're Smiling and his friends, they're head now for Gurney. *Segur' Miguel!* She's them damn' good idea. For who, in Gurney, will ask Smiling if *she's* them robber, hah? Come on! Smiling, she's know them trail ver' well, but me, I'm know still better. I'm know them short cuts. Maybe we're catch up with them and then — *por dios! We're* help Smiling to get sick!"

He jumped across to his calico horse and swung up without touching stirrups. All of them, including the two silent Wyndhams, were infected by his fierce eagerness. They climbed out of the cañon and fell in behind him. By narrow, almost impassable, trails or by no trails at all, they followed him through half the afternoon.

At last he reined in, on the crest of a hogback, to stare fiercely down a long, moderately level, slope. Instantly he whirled, with a fierce yell of triumph:

"*Yaaaiiiah!* You're see, hah?"

For a half-mile away, just dropping over another hogback, five men rode at a trot.

Chihuahua rammed the hooks to his calico and sent it squattering down that slope at breakneck speed. The others poured after him, their quirts swinging, their heels raking the horses' sides, their carbines jumping out of scabbards. So they came, in a mad, reckless rush of wild-eyed horses, to the foot of the incline. When next they glimpsed the men ahead, they were hardly half so far away. But the thunder of hoofs behind them jerked the fugitives' heads about. Instantly there began a wild race. For a while the advantage seemed to lie with the pursuers. Step by step, they closed up on the others.

Then one man whirled his horse around, and a rifle was lifting in his hand. Smoke began to puff from the mouth of his gun like jets of steam from an engine exhaust pipe. Chihuahua, now stirrup-to-stirrup with Clay, was yelling something frantically. At last, giving over the attempt to make himself heard, he roweled the calico viciously.

The paint horse leaped ahead in a sudden

spurt that left Azulero behind. Chihuahua waved at Clay and the others to stay back. Twenty, thirty, fifty yards, Chihuahua rode. Then he lifted himself in the stirrups and the calico fairly sat down upon its tail. Chihuahua came out of the saddle like a cat alighting from a branch. He ran a half-dozen gigantic steps ahead, carbine in hand. When he halted, he seemed to breathe deeply and gently for an instant. Almost negligently, the carbine lifted in his hands. It came to his shoulder as deliberately as if he were merely shooting at a mark.

Then — the sound of his shots was like the rattle of a stick upon a slatted fence. So rapidly did he fire that all the shots together made one long rippling sound. The rifleman ahead — who had been kicking up dust all around Chihuahua, seemingly unable to get a real range — jerked in the saddle as if someone had struck him. He stopped shooting and clawed desperately at his saddle horn. The long gun slipped from his hand and, as Chihuahua's firing continued, he slid sideways, snatched desperately at the saddle horn again; almost pulled himself erect. Then he let go and came like a sack to the ground.

The others of the party had galloped on. But, apparently, they had been watching over their shoulders. Now, they halted in a tight little group. They seemed uncertain whether to come back or go on. Clay, Lum, and the Wyndhams yelled savagely and surged up to Chihuahua. He had whirled and run back to his horse. This advance seemed to decide those doubtful ones ahead. They jerked their horses' heads around once more and popped over the crest of the hogback. Clay was terribly eager to look at the man on the ground. Was it — *could* it be — Smiling?

But it was only Gratt, that stupid towhead of Smiling's pack. They searched him and the pockets of his saddle, working very swiftly and finding nothing. Then they swung up and drove on up the trail, where the thunder of racing hoofs of the fugitives had dimmed to a faraway and tiny rumble.

Off the beaten path the hoofbeats turned, into the rocky wilderness of the *malpais*. Presently, Chihuahua reined in his calico. The trail had vanished like the riders making it. He counseled heading for Gurney by short cuts he knew, in the effort to beat the others to the county seat.

When at dusk they came wearily into town, it was without having come upon any trace of their quarry. They unsaddled and turned their sweaty horses into the jail corral. Then, with grim, long glances, one at another, they hitched up shell belts, looked to the hang of their pistols, and moved stiffly out to the street, going to "round up the town."

The Palace hitchrack held many drowsing horses. But not the sweaty, panting animals they sought. They looked inside. Ritt Rales was near the door, at the front end of the bar. He was a handsome man of middle height, this gambler-saloon-keeper, with curling black hair and hazel eyes and smooth, pink face. He stood with several prominent citizens: Halliday; Harrel, the grizzled cowman-banker; huge, slow-spoken Powers, the blacksmith; Merle Sheehan of the hotel; the gnarled freight-contractor, Comanche Smith; little Bill Francis, the cattle buyer; and two or three others.

Clay's party pulled in to the bar in response to Halliday's greeting and invitation. Clay fingered his glass absently as he searched the room and the noisy crowd for his men. A minute or two passed, then a door opened and a man came from one of the poker rooms partitioned off at the barroom's rear. He was one of the tinhorns of the gambling-hall adjoining the Palace. He turned back and, in one of those little lulls that come sometimes in crowded places,

Clay heard him speak to someone in the poker room.

"No, I'm cleaned, Smiling," he said. "Going to eat, now."

Clay let go of the whisky glass as if Carrie Nation had breathed on his neck. He went straight back to look into the door of that poker room. Smiling was in there with Eb Yates, Prather the slinking redhead, and a couple of nondescript saloon loafers. Smiling blew smoke rings, his hand cupped on the table to stop the cards being dealt by one of the loafers. He lowered his eyes from regard of the smoke and his grin widened.

"Run, Prather! Run, Yates! The Law's come west of the Rowdy!"

"When did you — all of you — hit town?" Clay demanded evenly.

"Couple hours back — maybe three. A hell of a dealer *you* turned out to be, Horton! Deuces and treys all there is in the deck? How-come the Boy Sheriff's so interested?" he demanded, looking up again at Clay.

"You figure they have been here that long, Horton?" Clay asked the dealer. "You say so too, Wallis? Think about it hard . . ."

"I reckon," said Horton, looking up blankly from his hand. "Since around four o'clock, seems to me. We been playing since then."

"I saw them come in about four," Ritt Rales said from behind Clay. His expression was one of faint bewilderment. "So did several others here. They'd been out to my ranch to look at some horses. Went out yesterday. Does it — matter?"

"Where's Gratt, Smiling?" Clay asked softly, watching.

"Gratt? Now, how the hell do I know? How-come you're so nosey, anyhow? Whose business is it where Gratt went off to yesterday? And what time I come to town today — or any other day?"

"It's the business of the sheriff's office," Clay said grimly. "Business that probably ought to've been attended to a good while back. Of course, if it had been, you wouldn't be sitting here, now."

Smiling's face was none the less a deadly mask because of the set smile on his mouth. Clay had stepped inside the room and had his back to the wall. Smiling stared at him, the red flecks seemed to dance and glow in his black eyes. Outside, the crowd about the door appeared to collectively hold its breath.

"Better speak up, Smiling — without so much auguring," old Harrel of the Stockman's Bank said quietly from behind Rales.

"It's the sheriff talking and he's got right smart backing from honest, peaceful folks, here in Gurney. Folks that're sick of things like — stage-robberies and murders."

A door opened noiselessly, behind the men at the poker table.

A tall, sinewy figure seemed to *flow* into and fill it.

"Oh, Smiling, she's speak up like them ni-ice boy. *Segur' Miguel!*" Chihuahua drawled soothingly. "*No es verdad,* Smiling?"

"Gratt hightailed yesterday," Smiling said easily. "Said he had a hen on — a fat hen. Now, what's it all about?"

Clay, without taking his eyes from Smiling, told of the trailing of the stage-robbers — and his certainty that the robbers could not have beat his party into town by more than brief minutes. Rale asked if that did not automatically clear Smiling.

"Where are your horses?" Clay snapped at the grinning killer.

"Hitchrack on the side. But *they* won't talk!"

Clay moved over to the side door. He recognized Smiling's saddle on a bay. But the horse showed no signs of having been ridden hard. Nor did any other horse at the rack. So they had changed mounts some-where. He stared absently along that vacant lot and stiffened with sight of a squat, mis-shapen figure that was swaying back and forth at the corner of the next building — just across the vacant lot from the Palace.

"Bronzalez . . . That crippled beggar's not *blind*, anyhow. And he knows Smiling. He was bragging about knowing him, just the other day. He might have noticed 'em ride up . . ."

He turned after a moment of staring at the rocking beggar. Ritt Rales stood at his elbow. As Clay regarded him, Rales moved to cross the bar-room and speak casually to a couple of men. Then he looked thoughtfully at Clay and, seeming to come to some decision, made a slight beckoning motion. Clay frowned, then went over. Rales looked him straight in the eye.

"Aren't you jumping Smiling more or less because of his reputation?" he demanded. "And because Gratt was with the robber-outfit and you had seen him, riding out of town with Smiling?"

Clay studied him shrewdly. He had no doubt, whatever, that Rales and his satellites had lied freely, indeed, to make an alibi for Smiling. This seemed to be further effort to cover Smiling's trail. So he answered carefully, not denying the gambler's accusation, but not showing his suspicion of Rales, either. They argued mildly for three or four minutes. Then from outside came the report of a pistol. Clay whirled and ran across the bar-room to the side door. He looked out past the hitchrack and instantly missed the figure of the beggar Bronzalez, which had been rocking like a chained bear in the pale light from the windows of the general store behind him. But only for an instant did he miss Bronzalez. For there was a huddled figure on the ground.

He was followed quickly by Chihuahua and Lum and others of the Palace's customers, as he ran across the lot to where the beggar lay face downward with a Colt near his limp, outflung hand. Clay stared dourly. As surely as he knew his own name, he knew that it was his long stare at this poor, flawed creature which had been responsible for the beggar's death. Rales had guessed his thought; and had sensed the danger in Bronzalez's testimony. That talk at the bar had been intended only to hold Clay while Palace killers removed the danger.

"My notion is," a man in the gathering crowd said dogmatically, "he found a gun somebody'd dropped and he monkeyed with it and shot hisself. Didn't nobody happen to see him?"

Clay had the same thought. But questioning discovered nobody who had more than heard the shot and turned to see him dead. It had been easy for the assassin to move through the darkness of the vacant lot, fire his shot, throw the pistol down and vanish into the darkness once more.

Nor was there any evidence to connect Rales with the affair. But Clay made a mental promise to the pallid, handsome gambler; a promise to put a noose about his neck.

CHAPTER IX

"Ritt Rales is standing in with Smiling!" Clay said grimly, the next morning in the sheriff's office.

Lum and Chihuahua looked at him quickly and narrowly. For he had said nothing to them concerning his suspicions of the suave saloonkeeper.

"No more doubt about that than there is that Smiling and Yates and Prather and that extra man stuck up the stage. Just pure luck it was Gratt you killed. If it'd been the extra man, we couldn't have been sure."

He shrugged.

"Well, I got Rales on my List of Hairpins to Watch. Wonder what Smiling did with the loot from that stage? If we could only find that!"

"*Por dios,* me, I'm think she must eat 'em!" Chihuahua scowled. "Lum and me, we're search them saddle pockets on every horse. We're find — not one *chiquito* thing."

"Now that Smiling and Company have produced their certificate of character," Lum drawled, "it *would* be a joy forever to deliver a slap in the face by locating the loot from the stage."

"I'm just in the humor to take another kind of slap at Smiling," Clay told them in a flat, hard tone.

Chihuahua and Lum regarded each other quickly, then turned to Clay more quickly still. Chihuahua shook his head.

"Clay, you're one fine boy," he said, as if he but meditated aloud. "You're not sing so nice, like me. You're not know them fine, big word, like Lum. For wrangling them ladies, even, you're not so much. But, still, *we're* like you — Lum and me. And we're *not* like it w'en we're have to follow you to them Boot Hill! Smiling, she's one little bit faster on them draw than you, Clay. *Sí* — one day faster! You're wait and practice some more, before you're start to slap leather with Smiling — unless you *have* to."

"Go to hell!" Clay snarled, and went slouching out of the office.

Outside, the yellow sunlight of early morning flooded the little county seat, filming the old gray-brown 'dobes with pale gilt. The rugged heights of the Diablos that walled in the town were smoky-green and

163

infinitely peaceful. Peace! That was it. Gurney was like a graveyard; dreamily quiet as a little burying-ground Clay remembered, back of that tiny, white Methodist church, in the cedar brakes west of Dallas.

But this atmosphere of sleepy peace was deceptive. Gurney was like a powder keg, with somewhere out of sight the glowing end of a fuse creeping toward the explosive.

The quiet main street, with the horses drowsing with heads almost to knees at the hitchracks; with sunbonneted women coming out of, or going into, the stores; with cowboys and traders and townsmen moving slowly up and down — in the twinkling of an eye, that street could become a battleground, the still summer air quivering with the roar of pistols and rifles. In the past, the sand of that street had been splotched leprously with red. It might well be blotched so again, considering all the forces that moved here, now.

The extra man . . . The extra man . . . That phrase kept running in Clay's mind. Who *was* that extra man who had assisted in the stage-robbery? Had he come in with Smiling, Yates, and Prather? Was he in Gurney now? Clay could identify no one man who seemed to be intimate with the trio. Investigations, the night before, by Clay, Chihuahua, and Lum, had not discovered anyone who seemed to fit the rôle of the other stage-robber.

Far up the street he saw the tall, dark figure of Sye Stubbins. Sight of the marshal reminded Clay of that message from the county attorney which had led him into the rifle-fire of Bib Alder. It occurred to Clay that he would like a word or two with "Sanctimonious Simon." Dee, he knew, had an office in a dingy 'dobe building. He went there, but the place was empty. He drifted, in search of the official.

Passing a big 'dobe which sat well back behind a white picket fence, almost opposite the hotel of Mrs. Sheehan, he was hailed by Halliday from the veranda.

Clay went in and up the walk to be propelled by Halliday's thick, imperative arm around to the wing of the veranda. There Barbara Kenedy and Helen Powell sat with a dishpanful of doughnuts on a small table beside them.

"Now, this-here's a boy," Halliday said oracularly, "that has seen right smart. He has rambled and trambled between This and That and, likely, he has seen the elephant and heard the owl. But there's one thing he's a complete and teetotal ignoramus about: and that's the doughnuts that wear the B K brand of Barbara Kenedy. Finish up your education, Clay!"

"*He* didn't come for doughnuts! Not he!" Barbara said scornfully to Halliday. She looked at the ceiling; lifted her voice: "Miss Powell! Miss Powell! Someone to see you!"

"How do you do, Mr. Borden," Helen said frostily — and immediately looked out over the hills — and far away, Clay told himself.

"Do you really want to know?" Clay returned her frigid tone. "Thanks for the doughnuts, Miss Kenedy."

"Doughnuts?" Barbara inquired, looking up from the search she was making, for something or other. "Oh — yes! Of course! Now, where did that dratted thing get to? I suppose I left it inside ——"

She got up with a small, impatient sound and vanished in the direction of the house door. Halliday loosed the mate to that impatient sound and disappeared. Clay grinned inwardly and took another doughnut. He looked thoughtfully at the heiress of the Ladder P — and sat down beside her, turning to face her.

"I have never been so far East as Philadelphia," he said, with the slow indirection of the cowboy. "Nice people up in Pennsylvania? All just alike? I — have wondered . . ."

"Of course they're not!" she said impa-

166

tiently, after a suspicious stare at him, then away. "Not just alike! There are all sorts in Philadelphia, the same as anywhere else. Don't be silly!"

"Then, if I happen to cut the trail of some Philadelphia folks," he said — seeming to be working out some puzzle in his mind — "and there happened to be several in the party, there'd be some different from others. So —— Why! It might be, even, that I'd run into one that wouldn't have such a terrible dislike for a deputy sheriff! Just think of that — and how different that would be from — now!"

"Why should I like deputy sheriffs in general, or — you in particular?" she countered very calmly — and faced him. But he was trained to note small things; such as clenched hands. "Why should I, when the — profession has the reputation of killing off men in The Territory who don't salaam to the sheriff? Why — I shouldn't be surprised if *you* had killed men!"

"Neither would I!" Clay admitted dryly. "I'm not cut out to be a John Wesley Hardin, but I saw my first trouble through smoke before I was fifteen. But — I had kind of hoped ——"

She turned, as his brown face set like a bronze casting of *A Man Alert.* Smiling had come with his usual catlike, noiseless step, around the elbow of the veranda.

"Thought I smelled doughnuts!" he said easily. "So I stopped in to beg a couple. How's everything, Helen?"

He ignored Clay utterly as he ate his doughnuts and talked easily to the girl. Then he took two more of the golden rings and grinned a little more widely as he turned away.

"I'll be seeing you!" he said.

"I was hoping" — Clay picked up his talk again — "that I could sort of start even with you. Start as a mightily ordinary specimen of leather-pounder who finds himself sitting in the middle of a tough job. For — the first day I saw you I liked you. And being more or less human, I wondered if it would be possible for you to like me. Do you *have* to figure that people out here are not like those in Philadelphia? Have to believe that we're all cut from one bolt, I mean? Couldn't you force yourself to think there just might be a sheriff that wasn't a lowdown bush-whacker?"

She sat silent as if she had not heard. Clay's face hardened. He got up, a dough-nut in each hand forgotten. She stared straight ahead and with a quick, angry shoulder motion, he turned and walked fast away. Just beyond the Kenedy gate he was pounced upon by Chihuahua and Lum. If he had not been thinking of Helen Powell, he would have guessed that their manhandling of him now was a kind of reaction from strain.

"Doughnuts!" they cried in chorus. They snatched the articles from his hands and beamed upon him as they ate.

"It is one of the most abstruse problems I have ever considered," Lum said in a muffled voice. "Shall we *let* him marry a girl who can make doughnuts like these, or should we see that he married her? He is so young, Chihuahua, to enter upon the duties and responsibilities of the marital relation."

"Maybe-so she's handle them marrying all right if she's have much, much good advice from us, no?" Chihuahua inquired.

Then he slid backward like a great cat, away from the foot Clay tried to hook about his ankle. Lum seized Clay from behind and marched him forward. Chihuahua walked backward, with the last of his doughnut in his mouth, gesturing like a preacher, his head, his shoulders, his eyebrows and mustache all eloquent, as he discussed the advisability of permitting Clay to marry — in a voice audible for no more than a hundred yards.

They overtook three more-or-less prominent citizens, who marched along to enjoy the free entertainment. So, the six of them came abreast the long 'dobe wall which was the street boundary of the Union Corral. Clay chanced to see a head lift above the wall, then drop back. As he stared, other heads appeared flashingly — also the barrels of rifles.

"*Bushwhackers!*" he yelled. "In the Union!"

Lum let go of Clay's arm and snatched out his pistol. Clay and Chihuahua were drawing their Colts with no less speed. They loosed their volley as a line of fire ran like a smoldering fuse along the wall, then they jumped for the nearest door.

One of the townsmen gave the grunt of a pole-axed bull and dropped with convulsed face, shot through the head. Clay, nearest him, let go a shot at the ambushed men, then stooped to see if the fallen man were dead. He straightened swiftly and jumped for the doorway from which the others were now raining lead at the corral wall. He felt a tiny plucking, as of childish fingers, on his shirt. As he sprang into shelter, he saw Lum's Stetson leave his head; saw one of the townsmen shift pistol from right hand to left and look down at a punctured forearm.

"Just hold those illegitimates a minute!" Clay snarled.

He ran the length of the store and out the back door, then along the rear wall to the corner. He charged across the street, thinking to take these bushwhackers from the rear. He made the end wall of the corral apparently without being noticed. It was a cold minute when he ventured to lift his bare head above the wall top. For he did not know but that, inside, someone waited with rifle poised for his head to appear as target.

Looking over the wall, he glimpsed several men on the inside of the wall, firing busily. He had to lift his arm awkwardly high to bring a pistol to bear on them. With the roar of it, he saw a man stagger.

Then they whirled, all of them, to throw such a hail of bullets at him that he was for an instant blinded by the dust the glancing lead raised from the wall top. He dropped down again and with eyes dust-filled waited helplessly for ten seconds. When he could see a little, he ran along the wall toward the rear of the corral and peered cautiously around the corner.

Then he inched along the back wall, heading for the rear gate. There was a pound of running feet behind him and he whirled.

"If prizes were awarded for the apotheosis

of imbecility," Lum Luckett snarled at him, "you wouldn't have a competitor! Perhaps you're suffering from delusions of grandeur and multiple identity?"

"Me, I'm think so, too!" Chihuahua cried. "Only I'm not know them words!"

The three of them pushed on to the rear gate and looked carefully through. But there was only silence and emptiness now, in all that big enclosed space. Crawling from one bit of cover to another — from wagon to a haystack, then to the corner of a 'dobe shed — they went quickly and alertly. Then Pat Sanchez himself came cautiously out of the shed which had sheltered him.

"They are gone, señores!" he said. "Some-one shot at them from over the end wall of my corral. They fired back and then — fear-ing that they would be flanked, perhaps — they ran away. I heard their feet."

"Who were they?" Clay demanded. He was answered only by a shrug and the prompt reply of any Mexican who cannot, or will not, answer a question —

Quién sabe?

And, though they scattered to look for these vanished assassins, they discovered nothing until Chihuahua found in the alley, almost at the back door of the Palace, one of the hangers-on of the saloon, groaning,

172

both hands clasped over the bullet-hole in his abdomen.

They bent over him as he writhed. They asked who had shot him? Who had been with him? Who had planned the ambush?

Men crowded out of the Palace, some whom they knew to be respectable and honest men, but more of the stripe of Smiling, Ritt Rales, Yates, and Prather. The dying man rolled his eyes round the circle of tense faces. He looked at Clay and his lips moved thickly:

"I'm gone! We — damn' near got you! It was ——"

Then he stopped short. The pale lips set stubbornly. He closed his eyes — and Clay was sure the thing that halted him was sight of Smiling's face. He died a little later without once reopening his lips. So the ambush-tally was one citizen dead — the man who had been killed with the first volley on the sidewalk; one wounded through the shoulder — the man who had spun about in the doorway ahead of Clay, shot by a bullet which had miraculously passed Clay to hit him; one dead saloon loafer.

And nobody had seen Smiling, Yates, Prather, and whatever others had been with them, running from the corral to take cover in the Palace. For that was the way Clay,

Chihuahua, and Lum pictured it to themselves.

Looking everywhere that afternoon for Dee, the county attorney, Clay came at last to the dance-hall of Ritt Rales. At a table in a corner of the otherwise empty room, he found that girl, Della, who had been jerked inside by — Clay suspected — none other than Rales himself.

He moved on impulse to sit down across from her. She had great china-blue eyes that seemed strangely childish in her worn, wise face. Clay grinned at her.

"Hello!" she said apathetically. "Glad Bib never got you. And — the others — this morning. Have a drink?"

"How!" he grunted, over his glass.

"Didn't used to like this stuff," she gasped, snatching at her chaser. "The other girls — that was in El Paso — used to tell me I'd find sarsaparilla wouldn't keep me from remembering the things that, pretty soon, I'd want to forget about. God knows they was right!"

"Who's been manhandling you?" Clay demanded abruptly. For there were several bluish smudges at the base of the still-round, still-smooth, still-pretty throat.

"Smiling was drunker'n a *lord* last night. He about wrecked me. And Ritt wouldn't let me run from him like I started to. Talk about wild animals! Kid, I've been here a year. Before that, I was in the Variety in El Paso. If there's any kind of a drunk *I* do'no' all about, it's a three-legged one! But the kind that'll keep grinning, no matter how drunk or how mad or how wild he gets ——"

She broke off with a small shrug, hand at the low neck of her dress, touching the bruises.

"Or a fellow who can walk off with a doughnut in each hand, grinning, to line up a sneaking ambush," Clay said grimly, out of his memories, with sardonic twist to his mouth.

"You —— It *was* Smiling in the corral, then?" she breathed, staring tensely into his face. "I — guessed that!"

"Who's this other man that's running with Smiling, and Yates and Prather, now?" Clay asked, keeping his voice indifferent.

Della — as she had said — knew much about men. Not only drunken men, but sober ones; even about men when, for instance, they were man-hunting . . . The rouged lips stretched in a mirthless smile. But those wide, babyish blue eyes were not smiling.

"*Wouldn't* you like to know! Wouldn't you

give a pretty to know! For you're guessing. Because you know five men stuck up the stage, you figure that one of the men met Smiling and Company outside town. But it's all suspicion. Nothing you can prove on Smiling. No sign of the loot. So — our young sheriff says to himself: Has this extra man, maybe, got the stuff? And where is he?"

Clay eyed her inscrutably. But inwardly he paid tribute to the shrewdness of her logic. Apart from that, he felt a sudden pity for her. Plenty of girls liked this life; they were typical dance-hall floozies at heart. But Della, obviously, did not like it. He folded his arms and stared straight at her.

"Suppose I was to hand you a ticket to Fort Worth, with a note to a lady I know that runs a big restaurant? Would hashslinging — and an easy mind — suit you better than this layout?"

She studied him with infinite calculation, then nodded:

"If I get out of this with a whole skin! *I* know what you want from me — the name of that extra man. All right! I'm going to play with you. Ritt'd just about cut my heart out with a quirt — and enjoy doing it — if he guessed it. But — that extra man never rode back with Smiling and Yates and

176

Prather. But pretty soon, he ——"

Abruptly, her expression altered. Her chin came up; the lids dropped over her blue eyes; her red mouth curled viciously.

"Why don't you go ask somebody that knows all those things? A pore dance-hall girl couldn't tell you all that!"

"Della!" Ritt Rales called from somewhere out of sight in the rear. "Where the devil's my —" the rest of the sentence was a mere muttering. "Come here and help me."

She got up and went to Rales, and Clay understood — or hoped he understood! — the flashing alteration of her manner. Presently, she and Rales appeared from the back room. Rales nodded blankly to Clay and busied himself behind the dance-hall bar. Della sat down at the table again. On her cheekbone were the dull red prints of fingers. She dabbed at them with a balled handkerchief and sat in sullen silence.

"Hell of a lot of company *you* are!" Clay told her disgustedly. He got up and loafed over to the door and outside.

A horseman was coming into the county seat from the southeast, the direction of Fort Lowe. Coming closer, he revealed himself as an ordinary sort of cowboy, if one efficient, self-sure, in an old and battered black Stetson, the ragged remains of what had been a splendid buckskin vest, faded blue waist overalls rammed into rusty boots, and saddle, bridle, bit, and spurs designed for use rather than for display.

For the rest of him, he was a sinewy figure a trifle above middle height, with a brown, high-cheekboned face, in which a gash-thin mouth and a pair of cold, pale blue eyes were the most outstanding features. Watching this man idly — he was certainly no figure to attract attention in that street — Clay was conscious of a mumbled word or two in the door of the dance-hall behind him.

He turned his head and saw Ritt Rales and Della standing there. Della was a little behind Rales and in such a position that one might have fancied that the hand which Rales held behind his back gripped her by the wrist. Clay, with blank-seeming glance, caught the merest ghost of a head-motion on the part of the girl. He checked himself only in time to keep from staring hard at her.

For the thought that came so flashingly was entirely too pleasant to credit. Before Rales had come, she had been talking of that extra man. She had said that he had not come to the county seat with Smiling and the others. Her unfinished sentence had led Clay to believe she intended to say that Smiling expected that extra man to come riding in. Well! Here *was* a man riding in! Was it possible that that tiny jerk of the head behind Rales's back had been intended to indicate this dusty, shabby cowboy?

On impulse, Clay lifted his hand as the cowboy came abreast of him.

Those pale eyes came to rest steadily upon Clay's face — after a flashing glance at the chief deputy's badge on Clay's shirt.

"Hello, Frisbee!" Clay called with a grin. "Long time no see you. Where you been?"

"I reckon you got the wrong man, Sheriff," the rider said evenly. "My name's not Frisbee and I don't remember you — and I got a right *good* memory, too."

"Ain't you the Buck Frisbee that was riding for the 77 outfit two years ago? The fellow that helped me round up that widow woman's geese, in Brazello, and herd them into the Dollar Bill Saloon?"

Clay's tone was one of amazement.

"Not me," the rider said briefly and without interest. He made as if to push on. But Clay was now frowning. He glanced suspiciously from the man's face to the 77 brand on the black horse's hip.

"Then wait a minute, you!" he said grimly. "There's something damn' funny here and

I'm going to get to the bottom of it. If you're not Frisbee, then who *are* you? Come down off that horse a minute. *We're* going to augur a li'l' bit. You know, I'm getting downright curious about you. And about what's bulging out your saddle pockets."

If the brown face retained its stony calm, into the pale eyes leaped a sudden light.

The man answered evenly:

"Fellow, you're swelling up to cover quite a considerable territory, even for a sheriff. My name is Templin and I have rode for quite a few outfits in this country. Down around Bear Paw and Jupiter and Arno I am right well known. I reckon I could even scratch around Gurney for a spell and find *somebody* that I have been on a cow-walk with, some time. I don't take it a bit kind, you swelling up like this, about the shirt and smoking tobacco that's bulging out my *alforjas*."

"If you're so well known as all that, then maybe it'll take no more than a minute or two to get things straight. Where have you been the last two-three days, anyhow? Uh —— How'd you leave everybody in — Porto?"

"Ain't been in Porto in a month of Sundays," Templin replied calmly.

But upon the smooth brown throat there

180

showed to Clay's strained gaze the telltale hammering of pulses. And he knew that, if here he didn't have the extra man of Smiling's gang, then he had someone else who needed heeling.

"Come down off that horse," he commanded with cold grimness. "Come on down, now!"

"You *asked* for it, didn't you?" Templin said in a thick kind of voice.

His left hand, which had been hanging limply down out of Clay's sight, slapped the butt of a gun on that side. Up over the horse's neck jumped the muzzle of the Colt.

"You asked for it!" he said again.

Clay's hooked thumb had been at his belt. Now his hand fell to the butt of his .44. The gun leaped out and as muzzle cleared the holster he let go the big hammer. Almost together the two pistols roared.

Clay's hat jumped. He felt his hair lift with the passage of that searching slug.

But he was too busy to note with more than faint interest any bullets that missed, however closely. For he was flipping back the hammer of the Colt and letting it go, flipping it back again.

Both Templin's hands went suddenly to the saddle horn. Under the tan of his face, a sickly pallor came. He tried to hold himself with right hand and bring up the pistol again with his left, but could not. Clay jumped across to rap the knuckles of Templin's hand with the barrel of his Colt. The pistol dropped and Clay hauled Templin from the saddle. He came down limply as a sack. As he lay huddled in the street, Clay jerked another gun from the waistband of Templin's overalls, where it had been hidden by the front of the buckskin vest.

"They'll get you for this! They'll get you plenty!" Templin croaked.

Clay jerked at the buckle of the nearest saddle-bag flap. There were two canvas bags. One that rustled; one that jingled dully. In the other saddle pocket was another, similar, bag. It held watches wrapped in torn bits of newspaper; rings and brooches and other odds and ends of jewelry.

There was one watch inscribed from the stage company to Driver Ed Jones, for saving a stage from robbery the year before.

Out of the corner of his eye, Clay saw Sye Stubbins, the marshal, almost at his elbow on the edge of the growing crowd.

"It's a damn' lie — and not important either — so don't say it!" Clay said savagely to Stubbins.

"Boy, I don't know what your reason was, but you certainly collected yourself an —

hard — case!" said Halliday, the grim storekeeper, who had moved nearer to look at the dead man, then up with marveling head-shake at Clay. "That's Dick Templin, and he was plenty bad medicine for anybody."

"Yeh? Well, he was one of the stage-robbers, too. Judging from the money and jewelry and all, he was packing just about everything the gang lifted off that stage, but . the bullion. That was too heavy for him."

Chapter X

"I be damned if *I* can figure that Old-Timer Committee!" Halliday snarled abruptly, as, with Chihuahua and Lum, he and Clay moved from stage-office to jail. He sat down in the sheriff's chair. "There's only three-four in Gurney that'd class as Old Settlers, and that Harrel, Powers, Comanche Smith, Bill Francis, and me we can't check up on. Lorn that owns the Star store, and Yowrie, his clerk, and Perkins that runs the eating-house by the stage-office — they're the only ones that'd do anything without telling us; or be low-down enough to gang Smoky. And they all claim *they* do'no' a thing about this committee."

"We'll heel them," Clay said indifferently, from the door. "Chihuahua, we'll likely take the Wyndhams out to the Ladder P tomorrow and augur with John Powell. We got plenty grub? I'm going out and ramble a spell. Can't stay still."

Presently, as he walked slowly toward the Palace, he felt that someone was trailing him. He stopped in a shadow until the man appeared. But it was only a shambling Mexican, who nodded to him. Clay shrugged and moved on. In the Palace doorway stood a huge Texan newcomer to Gurney, one Hemming. Beside him was his *compañero,* a weak-faced cowboy whom Clay knew only as "Stubby."

"Hi, Sheriff!" Hemming greeted Clay. "We got us a job, me'n' Stubby. It's going to be lots of fun, too: lots of fighting."

"Riding with Smiling, huh?" Clay said grimly. "Take good advice and don't. Smiling's day is drawing down close to sundown!"

"Yeh?" Smiling inquired from behind Hemming. "Maybe it ain't *my* day that's ending. You can chew on that a spell!"

He turned back to the saloon and the others followed. Clay moved on and presently turned off the main street. He was in semi-darkness. A shrill whistle sounded, somewhere in his rear. He spun about, half-drawing his pistol, but whirled back when a man wheeled out of the shadows and thickly demanded a match. Clay eyed him sharply, still wondering about that whistle. Then, from behind him, a lariat's loop dropped over his head and settled around his arms.

He whipped out his Colt then. He pivoted flashingly and ran straight toward the rope. But another loop dropped over him and he was jerked to a stop. A dark mass of figures swarmed out of the shadows. He fired — and fired again and again. He heard someone cry out. Then they smothered him, gagged him with a bandanna; swathed him with turns of the lariat. He was picked up bodily and put across a saddle, his hands lashed to one stirrup, his feet to the other. The horse moved off at a walk.

For what seemed endless time, he was carried so. Then the horse stopped and he was taken down. Men carried him into what seemed to be the shell of a ruined shed. A candle burned in the neck of a bottle. A man stood by it — a big man with hatbrim low over his eyes and a bandanna masking his face. Clay was dropped roughly on the ground by the wall, under the light. He was conscious of the creaking of saddle leather, the snorting and stamping of several horses, the rustle of chaps and small sounds of men, all around him. For that candle-light was a tiny glow, no more; it seemed only to accentuate the surrounding moonless dark.

"Set him up!" a low, weirdly mumbling voice commanded. Then: "Prisoner! The

All-Seeing Eye has been on you. The Old-Timer Committee has its ways of getting information. You have been watched. When our members were sure, you were tried. You were convicted. Tonight, the long hand of the Committee was put on your shoulder. You are about to hear sentence passed.

"Three! Take out that gag!"

A hand from the darkness twitched the bandanna from Clay's mouth. Then the weird, sinister voice went on:

"Prisoner of the Committee: You have been tried for violation of your oath of office; for secretly aiding the stage-robbers and other criminals while pretending to arrest them; for using your badge as a shield for your private murders; committing such murders as that of the late Dick Templin, under pretense of attempting the arrest of a criminal. You have been convicted. Now, have you anything to say before sentence is passed?"

"I have got plenty to say!" Clay cried desperately. For such charges as those intoned metallically by that unseen speaker, in these sinister surroundings, gave him an odd feeling of outraged indignation. "I have got just plenty to tell you stone-blind vigilantes. In the first place, anybody that says I side with stage-robbers or any other kind of outlaws is a God-damn' liar! And nobody but a nitwit would accuse *me* of doing anything but my damnedest to heel and hang this loose-holstered, long-riding outfit that The Territory has let hell around!"

"What proof have you to offer of your efforts to run down this gang? And what do you mean, when you speak of a gang?"

"You said something about an All-Seeing Eye. Well, if you had as much as one eye, and a nickel's worth of brains among the smear of you, you'd know that Smiling Badey and his outfit are responsible for the stage robbery and for such killings as the crippled beggar's. And that Ritt Rales, of the Palace, is siding with him. And that John Powell, of the Ladder P, aims to wipe out such little cowmen as the Wyndhams and the Howards one way or other. He's paying Smiling to do his killings for him. Such as his regular hands can't handily do."

"Talk! Nothing but talk. What evidence have you?"

"Evidence! What do you think I am?" Clay snarled, forgetting momentarily his desperate position in his disgust. "The sheriff's office has accounted for two stage-robbers and recovered the loot. Give us time and we'll clean up the whole mess that all of you have been living in and doing nothing about for all this time."

"You are simply making wild charges to save your own neck. The Committee privately investigated your charges against Smiling. It was decided that he could not have robbed the stage. He was at the ranch of Rales. Witnesses testified to that."

"Hen's milk!" Clay cried contemptuously. *"Rales!* He may fool you, but he never fooled me! Alibis-Cooked-Up-While-You-Wait Rales! He's on the list to get his horns knocked off. So are some more!"

"What does the Committee think of the prisoner's talk?" the voice inquired stonily — as if addressing the vaguely seen men in the dark.

" 'Hen's milk!' " a muffled voice repeated Clay's own contemptuous phrase, with an amused laugh. Others echoed the laugh.

"Then — having been duly tried and convicted, you are hereby sentenced to be hanged by the neck until you are dead. The sentence will be carried out immediately. Three, Four Five! You will take charge of the prisoner and prepare him for execution!"

Frantically, as hands lifted him and readjusted the lariat-turns to leave his feet free and his arms lashed to his sides, Clay was trying to find a way to beat this situation. Nothing that Halliday had said or implied about those sour old-timers — Lorn and Yowrie and Perkins — gave him any hope. He recalled all too vividly the two limp figures dangling from the crossbar of the old corral gate. These men were fully prepared to go the limit. Such beliefs as the speaker had voiced, as held by the "Committee," might be amazingly stupid, but that would make no difference, so long as they had him helpless here, and intended to act as if he were a criminal.

He strained desperately at the turns of manila about his arms. Instantly, a hard hand cuffed him on one side of the head and then the other.

"Cut out that damn' wiggling!" a voice snarled — muffled, unnatural, like the others Clay had heard. He guessed, then, that the explanation of those weird, unrecognizable tones was very simple — each man had a pebble on his tongue.

For answer — he was not a gentle soul, Clay! — he pivoted on one heel and kicked furiously. There was an agonized groan to tell that his box-toe had connected with someone's vulnerable and soft spot. Clay followed the kick with a pile-driver lunge of the head that caught a man jumping forward in the midriff, and sent him to the ground, groaning. Clay dropped on him, with the sincere intent to chew out his jugular or commit any other small acts of mayhem possible to him. He missed the man's throat, but he caught an ear between his teeth and bit furiously. But he was hauled off, kicking and butting, and held by two men until a horse was led up.

They put him in the saddle and a rope was put around his neck. The horse was led forward; others were mounted. They made a tight little cavalcade around him. The sky was black, but blacker still, against it, was the crossbar of the old corral gate. The led horse stopped under it. He heard a slight whizz; felt a jerk on the noose about his neck. The bight of the lariat had been cast over the crossbar.

His mind was racing frantically. Something to do . . . There must be something . . . This miserable horse-thieves' end could not come to him — Clay Borden — at the hands of this cowardly hit-from-the-dark crowd! It wasn't possible. He glared around at the dim shapes of the riders. The whole business seemed like a ghastly nightmare; it was utterly unreal — and yet it lifted the invisible hairs on his spine.

Then the noose scratched his neck. He knew that it *was* real. Horrible, but real. He had faced mere dying a good many times. With a gun in his hand, a chance, he could buck the prospect and grin. It was the idea of helpless strangulation that shook him.

"Ready?" that stonily even voice inquired of someone. "Then ——"

From the direction of the Palace Saloon — of town — came faint, but clear, a splatter of pistol-shots. At this distance it was a sound very like the rattle of gravel striking sharply upon a plank. The riders who were massed loosely around Clay turned in the saddle to listen and to stare.

The man who had thrown the lariat over the crossbar was reaching for it when the shot sounded. He turned with the others, his hand still outstretched. Clay saw his opportunity! He twisted his head flashingly and caught the vertical lariat bight between his teeth. So fervently that it was almost a prayer, he hoped that the horse under him was well-trained. He drove his heels into the animal's flanks as he leaned forward in the saddle. He stiffened his neck and ground his teeth down hard on the strands of the manila.

His horse shot forward. But it was no part of Clay's strategy to go racing away from town. Dragging twenty-five feet of trailing rope behind him, he would be ignominiously recaptured and returned. He leaned hard to the left in the saddle and so swung the horse to the left.

That maneuver gained him a precious fifteen seconds. For he made a horseshoe turn and charged back toward the crumbling corral wall, while the men behind him swung their animals frantically, hindered a good deal by cannoning into each other. He put his horse straight at a place in the wall that was a bare yard high, and the stubby pony took the jump with no more pause than was necessary for digging in at the take-off.

Clay did some more hoping as the little horse touched the ground outside the wall and went racing back toward the town. He prayed that the trailing lariat would not catch on anything. He bent low in the saddle and, after several attempts, managed to catch a *dale* of the rope around the saddle horn. Then he *did* drum frantically upon the horse's ribs!

The little beast went squattering around rubbish heaps, up the backs of buildings on this side of Gurney's main street, until Clay saw an opening between two store buildings. He leaned and sent the horse charging through this passage to the street.

At the furious pattering of the horse's

hoofs on the soft street, men outside whirled to stare. Those inside, and near enough to the front of the buildings to hear, jumped to door and window. Clay, low over the saddle horn, raced along the street to the jail. Sliding to a halt before the door, he yelled for Chihuahua and Lum; for the Wyndhams. Men were trotting after him from all directions. From inside old Jed Wyndham's suspicious voice challenged Clay.

"It's Borden! Step aside from the door, for I'm riding in!"

He suited action to word. The wise little horse entered the dark room without any hesitation.

"I'm all tied up. Cut me loose — quick! Get this rope off my neck, will you! Where's Chihuahua? Lum? Well, keep everybody out until I get loose!"

Ollie Wyndham, taciturn, very efficient, went like a puff of smoke to the doorway with a carbine across his arm. Old Jed, no less calm, loosed the noose from about Clay's neck and slid a knife under the turns of the lariat. As the bonds fell away, Clay half-slid, half-fell, from the saddle.

"And that's that! Or, anyway, it's part of that!" he said, very grimly.

In the forefront of those hurrying toward

the jail to see what had caused the furious charge, came Chihuahua and Lum. When they came inside the jail — now lit by the coal-oil wall lamp once more — Clay had kicked all the cut rope into a corner.

"Looking for you," he said to them, ignoring the others who crowded around the two. "Our friends, the Old-Timer Committee, are scallyhooting in our midst again. Let's go and take a look for the gents."

From the drawer of the desk he got Smoky's white-handled Colts and loaded them. The eyes of Chihuahua and Lum narrowed at this, and at sight of Clay's empty pistol holsters. The lank and sour Comanche Smith, with little Bill Francis, old Harrel, the banker, and the huge Powers, came forward now to ask grimly and very interestedly about this latest movement of the so-called Old Timers. With that crowd behind them, Clay was not willing to talk freely.

"They were somewhere in town, a few minutes back," was all the information he would give them.

"Then let's be looking for them," Harrel said quietly. "I would certainly admire to have a look at these stranglers."

But, comb the town as they did, a grim group with hands ready to weapon butts, they found no trace of the riders who had captured Clay. They stopped in the Palace for a night-cap, a suggestion of old Harrel's, which Clay thought not so innocently made as Harrel's indifferent manner indicated.

Standing at the big bar, with Ritt Rales behind it, was Smiling, with Yates, Prather, and various others of the saloon loafers whom Clay was about ready to declare members of the Smiling faction. Harrel drank, then delivered himself of sundry language, all in a tone clearly audible in the far corners even of the big barroom.

"We've been talking over this Old-Timer Committee business — Halliday, Powers, Smith, Sheehan, Francis and the rest of us that really *are* old settlers, and that admit we're old settlers without feeling it's necessary to say it from behind a mask or out of a dark corner! We don't just figure who the committee folks are. We'll find out, of course. But we aim to make it mighty plain, right now, we don't feel there's a bit of need for any such committee to be riding around Gurney.

"Hoof, hide, and tallow, all of us old-timers that move and work by daylight, we're standing solid behind the acting sheriff and his office. We have got nothing to do with this self-styled Old-Timer Committee. We want to announce right out in open meeting that they don't represent us, none the whatever!"

Back in the jail and pulling off his boots as he sat on the edge of his cot, Clay told the real story of the evening's events to the others, who were also preparing for bed.

"Me, I'm damned if I'm understand these Old-Timer Committee business!" Chihuahua said slowly. "Them notice they're give for them Ettison horse-thieves, it's talk about them crooked county official. *Bueno!* And everybody knows Smoky Cole, she's so damn' honest she will die hungry! And everybody but them damn' fool will know that *you,* Clay, are fight like the hell with them damn' thief, Smiling. Then, w'y will these old-timer fight with you? *Porque* the hell they're not go get Smiling? And them Yates and them Prather? And hang *them* to the corral gate? Me, I'm think she's damn' funny!"

The next morning after breakfast, Clay was possessed of a desire to see the corral gate by daylight. So the three of them, with the Wyndhams, started for the old corral. But old Jed Wyndham, who always reminded Clay of a gray wolf, the way he kept his head moving suspiciously to face all parts of the compass, like a scarred *lobo* sniffing the breeze for some danger, now grunted to Ollie, his silent son. Clay and the others, turning in that direction which Old Jed was facing, saw a grim quartet in battered Stetsons and faded overalls and worn boots, just getting down from their horses at the hitchrack of the Antelope Saloon.

"Neighbors of our," old Jed said curtly. "See you some more, Sheriff. We want to augur with them Howard boys a spell."

"*Pues,* me, I'm ride with them four Howards one time," Chihuahua grinned reminiscently. "Lit Taylor and me, trailing them Frenchy Leonard. They're live on Hell Creek, close by them Wyndhams' Triangle Bar outfit. *Amigos!* Me, if *I'm* John Powell, and I'm wish for to be them Big Casino in these damn' Territory — well, w'en I'm go to sleep at night, if I'm dream, I'm dream plenty about them four Howards."

They came to the corral gate and stood staring. There was a kind of gruesome fascination about that frame of cottonwood logs, even for one whose nerves troubled him no more than Clay's. Moodily, he recreated the scene of the night before, when his horse had stood beneath that crossbar. Almost, he could hear the rasp of the lariat-bight curling over the rough logs. For certainly it had been a near thing.

He had been saved by nothing but that splatter of shots — which reminded him that he had not yet learned the source of the shooting. Chihuahua shrugged. He and Lum had heard the shooting, too. Trotting that way to investigate, they had been able to find nobody who would admit to more than hearing the shooting.

It had sounded as if from the alley behind the Antelope Saloon. They had decided that it was some cowboy who had exuberantly shot off his pistol, then high-tailed discreetly and quickly. Clay nodded. He was staring at the tracks of horses, still plain in the sand beneath the crossbar.

Something that twinkled caught his eye. He bent and picked up a small, round locket, the sort which many men carried as charms on their watch-chains, which still had an inch of heavy, square-link, gold chain dangling from it. A worn, round-link chain explained the finding of the trinket there.

He opened it and saw that it was three-part — the two covers and a double-windowed center section. Through one of the tiny windows a little girl's face looked out. Through the other he could see a tiny lock of hair — golden hair — bound with blue silk thread. He wondered if he had discovered a clue. But neither Chihuahua nor Lum could make any more of it than he.

Chihuahua, studying the little girl's features very narrowly, shook his head. He had never seen her. Clay put it in his pocket and they went back toward town.

"Now, w'y will we have all these army?" Chihuahua wondered, as a cloud of dust lifted at the far end of the street, to show at least a dozen riders. They quickened their pace, but before they had moved very far, the body of horsemen had pulled in at the hitchrack before the Antelope and swung down with shrill, fierce cowboy yells. The riders ducked under the hitchrack and went with *clink-clump* of spurs and boot heels into the saloon. Then, from inside, a volley of yells announced their arrival at the bar.

Coming up to the hitchrack, Chihuahua moved out into the street to more easily inspect the brands of the "army's" horses. His turquoise-blue eyes were narrowed, his mouth lifting sardonically at the corners, under the spike-pointed black mustache.

"Something," he said very softly to Clay, "she is in them air. Fourteen horses and fourteen different brands. She's them gladiator comes for to fight and —"

John Powell and three swaggering cowboys came swinging down the street and turned into the Antelope without a look for the three men wearing stars, there by the hitchrack.

Clay moved over to the door of the Antelope, with Chihuahua and Lum at his heels. He looked in. The regular customers of the Antelope had given back before the press of the newcomers. They were a noisy, long-haired, daredevil-looking crew! Not for a long while — not since a certain cattle-war in southern Texas — had Clay seen so many salty-looking hard cases. John Powell stood beside a huge, red man talking earnestly. As Clay stared at these two, someone touched him on the arm. He turned to face Halliday.

"Boy!" said the storekeeper grimly. "I have been down toward Bear Paw on business and I'm telling you that, in all my days in this-here country, I don't know when I've seen so many gents riding the ridges — and not hunting out anybody to pass the time of day with! I bet I seen six different bunches of men and ary one of 'em packed enough hardware to start a store. I tell you — something's about to pop — loud!"

For answer Clay jerked a thumb silently at the horses at the hitchrack. Halliday, the veteran, looked once at the sweaty, dusty animals, nodded shadowily, then turned back to Clay.

"Like that!" was all he said.

Clay moved into the Antelope and up to John Powell. The Ladder P owner turned his head slowly and faced Clay.

"Want to talk to you, Powell," Clay said evenly — "off to ourselves."

"Trot along, and don't bother a busy man," Powell replied, in tone as even as Clay's own. "I haven't time for you today — or, perhaps, quite a number of days."

"Oh, yes, you've got plenty of time. For you're taking the time," Clay said, with face hardening. For the huge red man had laughed. "I know you're blind, and I'm beginning to believe that you're crazy blind. But I'm giving you this one last chance. Not only giving it to you, I'm just about forcing it down your stiff neck, if it's got to be handed to you that way!

"Now, don't be telling me about how much time you've got. I'm telling you that I want a private talk with you, and I'm going to have it, if I have to talk from the outside of a jail-cell — with you inside the cell!"

"You're quite a young bantam, aren't you?" John Powell said between his teeth.

"That's as may be — and it hasn't got a thing to do with what I'm talking about," Clay said, without interest, very shortly.

"Are these fellows anything to you?"

There came an odd light into John Powell's black eyes. In a man less dour, more human, it might have passed as an amused twinkle; but if there were anything of humor in John Powell's makeup, nobody in The Territory had ever detected it. He glanced at the noisy, drinking crowd beyond the big red man, then looked back at Clay.

"They're all Ladder P riders," he told Clay.

"Then all the more, we're going off to ourselves and augur a spell," Clay said flatly. "Come on!"

John Powell hesitated visibly. Then he seemed to note that Clay's thumbs were hooked in crossed shell belts, and that Clay's hands were very close to those notched white butts of Smoky Cole's .44s.

Chihuahua and Lum pushed up a little. They looked Powell long and earnestly in the face.

"I'll give you ten minutes," Powell conceded, and turned with Clay toward the bar-room door.

There was a little saloon across from the Antelope, a drinking-place not much patronized by either townsmen or riders from the big outfits of the country. Clay led the way across the street. He had grunted to

Chihuahua and that worthy, with an understanding grin, had disappeared. John Powell, Clay, and Lum Luckett sat down at a rough table in the back of the little barroom.

"You've started a good-sized fire in The Territory, Powell," Clay said abruptly, as soon as they sat down. "And don't think we don't know all about it. Or that we won't take all the necessary steps to stop it. And if you have nursed the idea you're too tall to be smacked, better buck that notion off, right now! The Territory went through one session with King Connell, when *he* wanted to be the Big Casino. He ——"

Chihuahua, with Jed Wyndham and Ollie, came into the room and walked back to the table. Powell seemed caught for a moment off his guard. He glared from the Wyndhams to Clay, then started to get up. But Clay lifted his hand imperatively. Powell seemed to catch himself. He relaxed where he sat. The Wyndhams pulled up chairs. Chihuahua squatted on the floor by the wall and twisted the points of his mustache. He looked for all the world like a great cat grooming itself.

"You have been having trouble — plain war — with the Wyndhams," Clay went on. "Now, I serve you warning, John Powell:

you're going to pull in your horns ——"

"*Am* I?" John Powell inquired with seeming amusement. "And if I don't? These fellows here, these two-by-four nesters, are squatting on my land, with their damn' little ragtag, bobtail herd drinking my water. They came in where they were not wanted and — those who do that take the consequences. Now, I'm through talking. I run the Ladder P outfit as suits me. No damned kid-sheriff is going to tell John Powell what to do! If you're well-advised, you'll confine yourself to the small business of policing Gurney. But don't come sticking your young and inquisitive nose into affairs that are too big for you. You'll get burned! I hire men who can protect my rights."

He got up and looked contemptuously at all of them.

"In other words," Old Jed Wyndham said grimly, but without any show of excitement, "it's fight, huh? All right, fellow — you have bought yourself a war! You have gone crazy, John Powell, on the idea you're going to be a regular king of all this Territory. Just because you come in a little ahead of the rest of us and squatted on free land, nobody else is going to be a two-spot in the deck, even."

He grinned mirthlessly.

"Well, you remind me of what I hear a talking fellow say, one time; about them that the gods would destroy they first turn crazy. You started all this trouble — stealing little men's stock and shooting at the little fellows and bringing in longhaired gunfighters to back your play.

"Well, it's right likely, to my notion, that you started more than you can handle — comfortable! I have got the idea that, when all the smoke blows away, no matter who else ain't here to know how things come out, you won't be. Them longhaired barroom warriors across at the Antelope — a lot of them will be chewing up the daisies. From the root-end, too! If you want war, you can be dadburned sure you're going to *get* it."

And that shabby, fierce old man somehow made the Ladder P owner look the smaller creature. He got slowly to his feet, glared for an instant at Powell, then with a summoning grunt to his son stalked toward the door of the saloon and disappeared. Powell followed, going with deliberate step and calm face.

Chihuahua whistled liquidly.

"Me, I'm think *all* the fighters in these damn' Territory she's not on them Ladder P payroll!" he said. "Well?"

Clay was thinking of Lorn and Yowrie and Perkins, the three old settlers whom Halliday had believed possible members of the mysterious Old-Timer Committee. If only he could discover upon one of them a watch-chain of square, heavy links; with a place for a locket-charm, but no charm . . .

"Wish you and Lum would sort of ride herd on those gladiators in the Antelope till I come back," he suggested.

He went to the general store of Lorn, the nearest of those suspected old settlers. He asked the sour old man the time. And from under his coat, Lorn produced a huge silver watch. It hung by a heavy rawhide string, so worn and greasy as to make Clay sure that it had been the old fellow's watch-holder for many a day. Yowrie, the clerk, had a watch-chain made of pierced red-gold nuggets. Perkins, of the eating-house, had a chain of gold links, but not of the same style and shape as that from which the locket had come. And, stare at them as he might, not one of the suspects showed any unease in his presence.

But, with affairs as they were in Gurney this morning, his failure was not large enough to occupy his thoughts for long. His head jerked sideways with the sound of a long, shrill, fiercely exuberant yell from somewhere around the Antelope; a yell in which many voices blended.

"Going to be trouble over that bunch of warriors Powell's imported," he told himself grimly. "Maybe trouble *with* them!"

CHAPTER XI

Clay, Chihuahua, and Lum "circled the herd" quietly and very watchfully. John Powell had disappeared, but his imported Tough Bunch remained, enjoying the whisky of the Antelope, the Palace, and other saloons, dancing with the — for cow-country ladies of pleasure — pretty girls of the Palace dance-hall. Gurney was used to cowboys on pleasure bent. But not for many a day had the county seat seen so hard a bunch as this.

Keeping pretty much together, they paraded from one saloon to the next. Clay and his companions watched them closely, but kept at a distance. For they knew — were they not of the reckless breed themselves? — that sight of their stars would rouse these heavily armed warriors as almost nothing else could do; incite them to foolish acts of defiance for defiance's sake. And if an open break could be avoided, they wanted to escape it.

The Tough Bunch took possession of the dance-hall. Ritt Rales answered their howling demands by sending in a bartender to the dance-hall bar out of hours. Della came darting out of a store down near Mrs. Sheehan's hotel as Clay was passing. The waist of the red silk dress she wore was badly torn.

"Did you really mean — what you said about — a ticket to Fort Worth and a letter to the lady that runs a hash joint?" she gasped.

"I have been trying to get a chance to see you without somebody seeing *me,* all morning," Clay assured her. "Stage'll be along inside a half-hour, I reckon. If you're ready then, I reckon it'll be better if you make it. Can happen?"

"If I can get back to my room without that crazy bunch catching me," she nodded. "Rales rousted us all out when they started yelling for dances. One of them got pretty rough with me and I clawed his face and broke away. I have been hiding here in this store, waiting for you to come by, the last twenty minutes."

"I'll drift down to the dance-hall and see if I can't start a little commotion. It'll attract their attention while you're getting your stuff together. You had better make it the back way. I'll go in the front door and that'll cover you."

The dance-hall was a perfect bedlam. The Powell gladiators were all drinking heavily. They staggered around the dance-hall floor, swinging the weary girls of the mechanical smiles awkwardly about. They bumped into each other and, very frequently, signified their complete enjoyment by choruses of shrill yells.

That huge red man with whom Powell had talked at the Antelope stood now at the dance-hall bar. Rodell, Clay knew his name was. He was a warrior! A bottle was on the bar at his elbow. In one hand he held a whisky glass, in the other a new horseshoe. He was trying to inveigle the bar-tender into a bet that he could not bend that horseshoe straight with his bare hands. The bar-tender was very much bored, but entirely too discreet to show it. He seemed to welcome Clay's arrival.

Clay moved toward Rodell, knowing that he was the straw boss of the bunch. Before he could reach the big red man, two of the bunch spied him. They came trotting with whoops of enthusiasm that turned all eyes that way.

"Look at what's wearing a chief deputy sheriff star!" they yelled. "Anybody ever see such a cute sheriff? Baby face! Baby eyes! No wonder this-here country had to send down for some grown-up men, if this is the kind of sheriff rides herd on things up here!"

As the two of them, approaching from different angles, were all but upon him and reaching out to catch his shoulders, Clay moved. He had been standing with expressionless face, watching them. Now he stepped backward and sideways, one step. They were both rather more than half-drunk and they could not stop themselves.

So they came cannoning into each other and their heads met with a thud audible for ten feet. They recoiled and glared, one at the other. Then each seemed to decide that the other had butted him viciously, treacherously, with malice aforethought. They rushed clumsily at each other. They flailed away with more good will than effect and Clay, with lift upward of one side of his tight mouth, continued down the bar to the big red Rodell.

"Howdy, son!" the big red man grinned at Clay.

"Howdy, son!" Clay returned very gravely. "Are you rodding this spread?"

"If I ain't, who is?" Rodell grunted belligerently. "Want to bet me I can't bend this horseshoe out into a straight bar using nothing but my hands? For twenty dollars?"

"Hell! If I was as big and ugly as *you*, I would do the trick with my teeth!" Clay told him — and grinned.

"You're a damn' cocky li'l' banty rooster! You want to kind of watch your step, sonny, or somebody'll be cutting your comb for you and then dropping you into the pot!"

"Well, if anybody does, I'll sure as hell crack his teeth when he tries to chew me! You know, down in my part of Texas they have a fine saying: 'The younger they are, often and often, the tougher they are!' You want to remember that."

"*You* ain't no Texas man — I mean, you ain't *from* Texas!" the big man cried incredulously. "Why, anybody ask' me, I would certainly have said you was out of some Sunday School."

"I *don't* like too much noise — in my town," Clay said, with thoughtful face, nodding. "That was why I stopped in to augur with you a minute. Gurney is right well used to outfits that're hard and outfits that — think they are. I reckon there's not a town this side of Cheyenne that'll stand for more hell-raising and call it boyish fun and frolicking. But — if she's quite a way to our limit, why, when you do get to that limit

—— Son! You have *got* to the quitting-off place' "

"Oh, we wouldn't bother you, milling around that limit you're talking about — probably!"

The two would-be tormentors of Clay had ceased their wild swinging now. One of them, swabbing a bleeding nose with his sleeve, looked with his one good eye around. He caught sight of Clay, who was half-turned away from him, standing as he was, watching Rodell. With an oath, the battler rushed Clay.

"You done that!" he snarled, and launched a round-house swing at Clay.

But Clay had not been so oblivious to the battlers as he had seemed. As a matter of fact, in this hostile environment he was as alert as any wolf. Now he stepped away from the bar and pivoted on his heel. He whipped over a smoking right hook with all the momentum of his turning body and rigid extensors behind it. A hard, if small, fist drove most terrifically to the side-jaw of the fellow, who, missing his own target, was beautifully off-balance.

It knocked the man into the bar, and Clay, stepping forward just enough to shift his feet, jolted a straight left into the already bleeding nose. It knocked the man's head back, but immediately he came forward until he was bent double. For Clay had put everything he owned into a terrific right which landed squarely in the midriff. For a split-second, Clay watched the collapse of the belligerent. Then he turned back to the scowling Rodell:

"I'm certainly glad you feel that way about it," he said — just as if there had been no interruption.

Then he turned and went out. He looked up the street and saw Della standing just outside of that store from which she had come a little while before. She waved to him. The stage had come in. The horses were being changed. Now, with a cloud of dust rising under the fresh team's hoofs, the Concord came out of the station down the street and rolled toward where they stood.

Clay caught Della's valise, and moved toward the edge of the store veranda. The girl put her hand on his arm imperatively.

"Nobody has been so sweet to me in — I don't know when!"

"Why, I owed you this — and plenty more!"

Clay grinned a little uncomfortably, fishing in his overalls pocket to bring out a roll of bills. "Hadn't been for you, Templin would've got to Smiling with that stuff in his saddle bags. And then ——"

He snapped his fingers and put the bills in her hand. Then he waved for the stage to stop. It pulled up with a great cloud of dust and under this partial cover, Della suddenly flung her arms around Clay's neck, to implant upon his surprised mouth what was perhaps the chastest kiss she had bestowed upon any man in recent years.

Clay could have done very well without it. For not even this dense dust-cloud was thick enough to entirely mask them from the view of those on the sidewalk — particularly from Barbara Kenedy, and a large, square-rigged variety of black-clad, very respectable woman, and Helen Powell. Stiffly, Clay helped Della board the stage and pushed her valise up to the boot.

"Luck to you!" he told her. *"Adiós!"*

Then he turned back quickly to the sidewalk. For out of the Palace, in a surging, whooping mass, now came the Powell Tough Bunch. One of them was spinning a rope. At sight of a Mexican, riding a burro and driving a second burro laden with mesquite roots, this rope-spinner emitted a shrill howl and spun his loop to increased size. Then he stepped forward and roped both burros and the Mexican. Others of the recruits caught hold of the lariat and helped him

haul in. Burros, Mexican, mesquite roots —
all piled up in the street. The Mexican
howled like a turpentined wolf from the
middle of the seething mass. Even Clay had
to grin. But then, abruptly, he sobered. For
Mrs. Kenedy was glaring at him.

"Look at that!" Mrs. Kenedy said — very
audibly. "Cowboys just taking the town!
And our sheriff, it seems, is too busy seeing
his painted lady-friends off to make 'em
behave 'emselves!"

Chihuahua and Lum came out of the Palace
and grinned at Clay. The Tough Bunch, they
said, had gone into the Antelope. The
Wyndhams had disappeared, after talking
long and earnestly with the four Howards.
Smiling and his immediate followers were
somewhere in town, but not with the Tough
Bunch.

"Well, so long's that bunch stays in the
Antelope, I reckon they're all right," Clay
told the pair. "Wonder where the Wyndhams
ghosted off to? Bet there's a good reason
behind that . . ."

They got to early afternoon without hearing anything from Powell's imported gunmen. Then Halliday burst into the office.

"Them bar-room gladiators is holding half
the town — from the Antelope on. Got

pickets out along the line. Liquoring up at the saloons, free. Walked into little Solly Greenberg's and fitted themselves out with new clothes all around — without paying. They're yelling that if the sheriff don't like it, he knows what he can do. Looks to me like nothing but a slap at you, Clay."

Clay reached for his Winchester. Chihuahua and Lum took theirs from the wall. They could hear shooting now, and when they reached the street they saw puffs of smoke coming from various shelters — and amazed citizens skipping for cover.

"Fifteen-sixteen. Too many for just you-all," Halliday grunted. "C'm'on down to Mis' Sheehan's. Harrel will be there."

"Go on, all of you," Clay said absently. "I'll be there in a minute."

Without waiting for their reply, he turned to cross the street. From the big freight wagon of Comanche Smith, standing team-less across from the Antelope, a rifle began to rattle. It sent slugs all around Clay, but he went on. If he were going to be hit, it was too late now to run. But he did snarl an oath that was a promise when a bullet glanced from a rock in the dust and barked his knuckles.

Inside the Halliday and Kenedy store, he found talkative citizens. These he ignored,

218

and drew a clerk to the rear and asked for dynamite. There were ten sticks there, but spoken for by the Spike E. Clay grunted impatiently.

"Hell with the Spike E! I want four sticks. Need 'em bad!"

He took them into the alley and arranged them to suit him. Then he went around and across to Mrs. Sheehan's where a dozen or more of the town's prominents were gathered.

"Now you're here," old Harrel snapped, "let's get going. By George! We'll show these-here *gunnies* they can't run Gurney!"

"Just a minute!" Clay drawled. The stinging of his knuckles did not serve to improve his temper. "You go busting down the street into 'em and they'll shoot the hell out of you! No use a bunch of good people getting drilled over them wasps."

"Maybe you think I never been shot at before!" Harrel said disgustedly. "Boy, I been shot at in more different languages —— Come on, men!"

"Is this a posse or a vigilance committee?" Clay inquired dryly. "If it's stranglers, it's nothing to me. If it's a posse, though, I have got a word to say about what it does ——"

"Listen, boy!" Harrel checked him tolerantly. "There is just one way to handle

wolves like them. It's to go gather 'em. So
——"

"I think it'll save a lot of trouble if they pay for the damage they have done, then hightail, without any shooting," Clay said mildly. "What do they owe you, Mr. Greenberg?"

"Three hundred dollars don't pay it! Overalls, you understand, they took! Shirts — boots — hats —— Oh, three-fifty, maybe."

On the veranda, by the rail, Mrs. Sheehan stared calculatingly at Clay. But the square-rigged Mrs. Kenedy beside her was as contemptuous-faced as old Harrel himself began to be. As for Barbara and Helen, Clay would not look directly at them.

"Going to write 'em a message?" Harrel inquired savagely.

"They'll have a message all right. But I'm taking it — for word of mouth's better. Now, I wish all of you would cut across and keep out of range till you plumb circle that Tough Bunch. Cover their horses. Get close as you can, but don't shoot! Not unless they break out shooting. If they come out the way I expect 'em to do, with their hands up, let 'em get on and get out!"

"You ain't going into the Antelope!" Halliday cried. "Why, boy, they'll plumb murder

220

you! It's you they're after."

"They won't bother me. Nah, Chihuahua! I'm lone-wolfing it. There'll be no trouble. I'm going to keep trouble from starting."

He stepped off the veranda. Someone behind him made an odd, gasping noise. The rifleman in the freight wagon opened up instantly. A bullet lashed the sand at his very feet; another and still another. Then a yell from the Antelope stopped the firing. When Clay came up to the wagon, a Winchester muzzle projected over the edge of the bed. He went up to it and called for Rodell, the warriors' leader. Rodell was in the Antelope, this sentry said.

"Why don't you ever try doing your shooting from the open?" Clay inquired — and stepped in flashingly, to the side of the rifle.

He jerked the amazed man out by the collar and smashed him in the jaw. "You God-damn' dry-gulcher!"

He drove in right and left to the chin with cold precision, left the man senseless there, and went across the street.

When he stepped into the Antelope, Rodell leaned on the bar, grinning as if he had expected the visit. He greeted Clay as "Baby-Face" and his men laughed.

"I just came in to remind you of what I said in the dance-hall. I told you, when you got to Gurney's limit — well, you're up there, right now!"

"Why, I believe I do recollect you saying something like that," Rodell nodded owlishly. "Well? What about it — Baby-Face?"

"Well, thinking it over — I hear that your side collected some money from John Powell, in advance. Hundred and fifty each, wasn't it? Now, you owe Greenberg the storekeeper five hundred. You owe the Antelope and the other saloons for drinks. There's sixteen of you, altogether — counting the imitation bad man I just batted cold in the street. Say, fifty apiece, to cover your debts, then — you get!"

There fell the stickiest of dead silences in the bar-room. Rodell's men gaped at this incredulously foolish boy-sheriff, then at their leader, to see just what he would do.

"You know, I've got a bellyful of you!" Rodell said thickly. "I *told* you that you was too damn' cocky a bantam ——"

"Before any nitwit starts any fireworks," Clay interrupted him, "le' me show you something interesting."

Hands slid down to pistols as he fished in a pants pocket.

"Dynamite!" a dozen hushed voices identified the greasy, paper-covered half-cylinder he produced.

"Recognize it, do you? Maybe you have seen one of these li'l' things before? In case you haven't, it's a match. I do hope nobody shoots at me. For I have got pieces of dynamite spread from head to heels, all over me. Shooting at me is plain suicide for everybody in here. Rodell! Fifty dollars out of each of you, I said. Then, your room and not your company."

Very calmly he pulled his right-hand gun. With the muzzle, he waved back the men too close to him. Then he squatted and put the gun on the floor beside him. He scratched his match and lit the fuse of the dynamite. He picked up his gun again and looked at Rodell.

"You don't *have* to believe a word I'm saying. You can bet I'll lose my nerve and jerk that fuse in time. If you want to. But ——"

His face was like a grim mask as he stared at the big red man.

"You came into town, a tough bunch. Nobody could stop *you!* You'd just take Gurney apart and anybody in the way would get tramped on. And you made remarks about kid-sheriffs. You're big, brave grown-up men, with real pistols and everything, you are. All right! Let's see if you're so tough! Let's see if you're a better man than the kid-sheriff! I don't intend to back

down from anybody in my bailiwick. You'd
better believe that, but you don't *have* to!
You can wait and see if I've got nerve
enough to stand being blown to hell — just
to take your windy bunch along!"

As he stood up straight again, to pinwheel
the right-hand gun in the air and catch the
white butt as it descended, there were
exactly three sounds in that big bar-room:
the *slap-slap-slap* of the white butt on his
palms; the sputtering of that fuse; and the
stertorous breathing of a dozen men staring
fascinatedly at the wisp of smoke rising.

Rodell's hand was on the butt of his pistol.
Contemptuously, he shrugged heavy shoulders and turned to the bar. But his men's
eyes roved from the burning fuse to Clay, to
Rodell — and back again. Longingly, they
fingered their own pistols when they looked
at Clay. Rodell whirled suddenly back, his
red face twisted.

"We'll bust out of this and massacree the
damn' town!" he snarled. "We'll shoot hell
out of anybody that's outside!"

"Try it," Clay invited him indifferently.
"Our folks are covering your horses. But,
even so, likely *some* of you could make
it . . ."

He hummed *Billy Venero* and began pin-
wheeling the Colt from right hand to left

hand and back again. The fuse burned on remorselessly, with that tiny sputtering sound.

"All right!" Rodell snarled helplessly. "You win. Put out that damn' fuse. It gives me the jiggers!"

He stepped forward and lifted his foot. The Colt butt slapped Clay's right palm. Hand and gun dropped, the big hammer sliding back. The gun roared and a bullet smacked the plank next to Rodell's boot. He recoiled with a furious oath.

"*I'll* take care of my dynamite," Clay said calmly. "Call in your wolves that are still outside. Shell out that eight hundred dollars. It's your business, of course, but — I *do* think I would sort of — hurry."

Rodell jumped for the street door and yelled. As the fuse entered its last inch, five men came running and crowded beside him in the doorway. They looked at the dynamite, then up at Clay, and back at Rodell.

"Never mind gaping around!" Rodell snarled at them. "This salty little fool of a banty rooster of a baby-faced sheriff, he has got us by the old ying-yang. Our horns is knocked off, and our necks is plumb bowed, right now! Shell out, you fellows! Fifty dollars apiece. Don't augur about it! Shell out — *pronto!*"

Clay bent and scratched a match. He scratched it with his left hand, though. He put his foot upon the end of the fuse and pressed out the creeping spark, but held the lighted match ready to relight it.

"Put that money down on the floor. Then walk out, with your hands in the air. Get astraddle of your horses and cut stick," he ordered Rodell. "I'd hurry a little, I think. Just in case you might change your minds, I'll light this again."

There was the jingle of gold on the floor near him. He put the match-flame to the fuse again, humming absently. At renewal of that sinister sputtering those grim warriors — who would have faced gunfire carelessly, grinning, even — broke for the street door, not forgetting to elevate their hands. Clay trailed them. He stood in the doorway, twirling his Colt by fore-finger in the trigger-guard, staring after them as they mounted and raced off. He was jerked about by a frantic yell from the bar-tender:

"Hey! Hey! Put that damn' fuse out! You forgot the dynamite!"

"No, I didn't exactly forget it," Clay told him.

He came loafing back, to stand staring as the flame ate up that last tiny remnant of fuse. The bar-tender, leaping for the back door, was recalled only by Clay's yell. He stared, that bar-tender, as the fuse came to the edge of the greasy paper and — nothing happened.

"My — soul!" gasped the man of drinks, "if you never bluffed that Tough Bunch!"

"It wasn't all bluff," Clay said slowly. "Not all!"

From a shirt pocket he pulled a half-inch of dynamite stick and held it out so that the end was visible. Apparently, the bar-tender knew dynamite when he saw it. For when Clay scratched a match as for application to this fragment, he lifted up his apron and hurled himself at the back door again. This time, he made no stop!

CHAPTER XII

His name was Wilson, and he was a rather distinguished gentleman, in appearance. He was from Bangor, Maine, on his first trip West, he told Clay, when at last he had tracked the acting sheriff down. He had been a passenger on the stage at the time of the robbery near Porto. He had lost his wallet, with money and papers; lost his watch and chain. His wallet he had just got back from the stage company's agent in Gurnew, having chanced to hear of Templin's death.

"But it was the watch and chain I had hoped to recover," he said. "The charm on the chain, rather. It contained my little girl's picture and a lock of her hair and — since she's dead, those are my only mementoes of her and ——"

Clay grunted as if he had been kicked in the stomach, while he stood gaping at Wilson. As he fished the locket from his vest, his mind was racing. He had no doubt that in his scuffle with that "Old-Timer" in the corral gate, the locket had been jerked from his victim's watch-chain. Then — then *that* particular member of the mysterious "committee" must have been one of the stage-robbers! Must have been! Smiling, Yates, or Prather!

Wilson took the locket with mumbled thanks, then stared at the set, white fury of Clay's face. For Clay was thinking what a damned fool he had looked, explaining with the sincerest motives all about Smiling and Company — to Smiling and Company. It fairly made him writhe. Wilson watched fascinatedly.

"Could you identify any of the robbers?" Clay asked him thickly.

"The man Templin whom you — killed. That buckskin vest he — he's wearing now was on his saddle horn. He held the horses and watched while the others lined us up. His horse moved and the vest almost fell. I saw it. But the others ——"

He described them as best he could. To Clay, listening sourly, it was Yates, Prather, and Gratt, with Smiling very cheerfully directing them. But this testimony was in no sense proof.

Wilson waited, then shrugged.

"I wish I *could* tell you more! For, while

the shooting of the driver and shotgun guard was more or less incidental to the halting of the stage, the murder of that inoffensive little drummer was done in cold blood. This cheerful cowboy who seemed to be leader told him he was too slow in finding his hidden money. He lifted his pistol deliberately. I watched in a kind of horrified fascination while his forefinger crooked and tightened and the hammer lifted a little at a time ———"

"*You what?*" Clay cried, jerked from his thoughts. "You saw the hammer go back *as* he pulled on the trigger? Not — not pulled back under his thumb? Be sure, now!"

"No! I recall it distinctly, every little detail. Even the battered corner of the hammer."

"If you're right! If *only* you're right . . ."

Swiftly, he showed Wilson the difference in operation between a single-action and a double-action — a "self-cocker" — and Wilson stuck stubbornly to his testimony. Clay grinned wolfishly.

"I don't want to scare you, but your life wouldn't be worth a plugged copper cent if Smiling Badey knew you had seen that. Mister! You stick right here. I'm going out to bring in some company. Smiling is the only desperado in these parts that uses self-cockers — .41s — one with a corner of the

230

hammer banged flat."

The Palace was his first thought. But neither Smiling nor any of his gang was there. The Antelope was equally barren. That bar-tender who had jumped for the back door when Clay pretended to light his piece of real dynamite was on watch at the far end of the long bar.

He grinned at Clay.

"Howdy, Sheriff! Glad to see you — if you ain't packing dynamite!"

Clay stood quietly until the attention he had attracted subsided. Then he looked at the bar-tender.

"Somebody," he said, with most confidential grin "has certainly got a chewed-up ear, *no es verdad!*"

"You see it, too?" the bar-tender said, and grinned. "He come in this morning, before that long-haired bunch took over the place. He was looking for an eye-opener. He had a bandanna under his hat hanging down on the right side, like his head was hot. But I see that ear with a rag over it. He said that he stumbled and fell against a plank that had a nail in it and jagged his ear something scandalous. I says to myself: 'Yeh, I *bet* you did!' "

"Where'd he go? I think I would like to hurrah him a little!"

"I don't know where he went — then. But yonder he comes, through the front door, right now."

Clay turned slowly. Prather stood in the street door, looking about the bar-room as if in search of someone. He had the bandanna under his hat, sagging to the right side. He came on in and stopped for a moment to talk to two hard-faced men who were more or less permanent residents of Gurney, even though they had no visible means of support except such gambling as they might do.

Clay moved. There was no doubt in his mind that it was Prather at whom he had lunged in the darkness at the old corral, his teeth clicking for the jugular vein. That same fury he had felt, with knowledge that Smiling and Company were at least members of the "Old-Timer Committee," shook him again. It was through a red and quivering haze that he saw the slinking, fox-faced redhead.

Prather turned slowly at sound of Clay's footsteps. Now, did his face change at sight of Clay? And, if so, was that change due to guilty conscience, or merely to his natural lack of ease in the presence of the sheriff? Clay wondered.

"Did I bite it clear off, Prather?" he asked

sardonically, taking a chance on a blind spot.

But Prather's face was only properly blank as he stared, not in Clay's eye, but on a level with Clay's compressed mouth.

"You? What are you talking about?"

Out of the corner of his eye, Clay saw the two hard-faced tinhorns moving a little, as if to rise.

"Just stay where you are," he advised them. "It'll likely save you trouble. Prather, you don't know how surprised you make me, talking this way! You mean to tell me that you've forgot our little sojourn down under the corral gate, so soon?"

"You haven't been drinking, have you?" Prather asked solicitously. "Still, if you haven't been, then it's funnier than ever!"

Then Clay, wondering what to do in this play of cross-purposes, let his eye wander up and down Prather's figure and he could have whooped his enthusiasm and his pleasure. The fool! The utter fool! He was still wearing Wilson's watch and chain. In Clay's mind there could be no doubt of it. For there was the square-link chain, within the first dozen links a large gold ring, obviously for the hanging of a pendant chain and charm — a locket.

He pushed his head back and surveyed

Prather from beneath lowered lids.

"Prather," he drawled, "if there's any little thing you're not comfortable without, I'll be glad to send and get it for you. In the boarding-house I'm running, it's my aim to make all my boarders just as comfortable as I can. Now, *is* there anything — a change of underwear, or a clean shirt, or — oh, — just anything you want to take with you?"

"What the hell are you talking about?" Prather snarled.

Again, out of the corner of his eye, Clay saw the two tinhorns move furtively. He whirled upon them:

"If one of you so much as bats an eye again, I'll knock his eye out for him!"

Then he whirled back again — and made a flashing two-handed draw of his pistols. For Prather had taken advantage of Clay's seeming preoccupation with the tinhorns, to reach inside his shirt for a "stingy" gun. He had it halfway out before Clay turned back. He groaned agonizedly with the landing of Clay's knee in his belly. He staggered and recovered, but only to crumple again with the crushing impact of a Colt barrel across his skull. Clay hardly waited to see him fall, for he had stepped in to the table, to the tinhorns again.

"I *told* you not to move!" he snarled.

He pushed the table over on them and, as they staggered, banged their heads with a gun barrel — as he had banged Prather's. Then he whirled back, seized Prather by the collar and dragged him over to the bar. Here he let him sag limply to the floor while he snapped his order for whisky.

"Whisky ain't apt to do *him* no good!" the bartender grinned. "He can't swallow."

"He don't have to swallow!" Clay assured him, taking the whisky. He squatted beside Prather and lifted the unconscious one's eyelids, then calmly poured the whisky into Prather's eyes.

The result was like an explosion. Prather had been on his way back to consciousness and, with the sting of the alcohol in his eyes, he recovered his senses — and his lungs.

"Now, now! Take it easy! A scratchy rope around your neck'll hurt a damn' sight more than a li'l' bit of Antelope whisky! It's the best liquor in town, anyhow. If I'd poured that poison Ritt Rales sells at the Palace into your eyes, you'd have a kick coming. Now, come along! Don't be so foolish next time as to go for a gun. Not to kill me with, fellow! You had much better let somebody else kill me, then slap leather. I said: Come on! You're headed for jail . . ."

"An' w'at's them charges?" Chihuahua

inquired when Clay brought Prather into the office. "She's rob them sick, cripple' Mex' woman, huh?"

"He's wearing your watch," Clay told Wilson. "Take it!"

"Like hell it's his watch!" Prather cried indignantly. "I had that watch for years. I got it ——"

Lum pulled the watch from Prather's pocket. It was a heavy, expensive, elaborately engraved time-piece, but without initials or other marks of identification. Evidently, Prather hinged his bravado upon knowledge of this fact.

"If it's yours," Wilson said quietly, "why has it my name, inside the inner dust lid?"

He opened the back, then pried up a second lid. He held it up. *L. M. Wilson, Bangor, Me.,* ran the engraved line. From between his shoulder blades, Chihuahua produced a ten-inch bowie. He began to whet it on his bootleg, cocking a hungry blue eye at Prather's red scalp, the while.

"Me, I'm think this will help Prather to get sick!" he said.

"I shouldn't be surprised if he believes he has an entire epidemic," Lum agreed pensively.

"My young and almost handsome friends," Clay said, smiling beatifically, "she's going to help more than Prather to get sick! For Prather's going to tell us — oh, so many interesting things, Right, Prather?"

"That so?" Prather cried — but his eyes wandered to the bright blade that went *whit-whit — whit-whit* on Chihuahua's boot. "I'm not telling a damn' thing!"

"Do you want to do the asking, Chihuahua?"

"Not alone!" Lum objected. "Something tells me that my assistance is practically indispensable. Gifted as Chihuahua is, he might miss a point. And when I was a member of Captain Smith's Ranger Company, the interrogation of redheaded sneak-thieves became almost my specialty. You would hardly believe stories I could tell you, Clay, of Prathers I have questioned; how they fairly wept with eagerness, after I had discoursed a while, and begged for permission to relate their histories. But you can help, Chihuahua! *You* can hand *me* the instruments . . ."

"Now, you-all better listen!" Prather told Clay angrily, but with a note of strain in his lifted voice. "You try any skulduggery on me and ——"

Chihuahua touched him with apparent gentleness beneath the left ear — using but two fingers. But Prather skated toward the door that opened on the jail corridor.

Somehow, Lum Luckett was standing there ready to receive him.

Lum leaned against Prather and drew the prisoner's right hand up into the middle of his back. While he held Prather by that wrist, and by his left arm, he addressed Prather soothingly, as one might address a drunken and argumentative friend, or a frightened child.

Prather suddenly began to kick and yell. Lum lifted him from the floor without appearance of exertion. Nor did his voice lose the gentle, reassuring note. "Now, now! You must not let your emotions govern you, Prather. Self-control — and, of course, *talking* — concentrate on these!"

Chihuahua's grin was feral. He approached the prisoner, to regard him fixedly. Lum's thick body shifted and Prather seemed to spin in air — like a fence post twirled from Lum to Chihuahua. Then he spun back under the impulse of Chihuihua's darting hand.

The trio vanished. Presently, Clay and Wilson heard the scream of a man in mortal terror. Again and again it rang through the jail. Wilson's round face blanched. The tip of his tongue came out to wet his lips. He looked furtively sidelong at Clay, who was staring serenely through the door.

"Hell to have a guilty conscience," Clay observed, out of the fullness of his knowledge. "Prather knows he's long overdue at a hanging, so if you wave a thick string at him, he squeals!"

Feet shuffled on the stair, many minutes later. The two in the office turned, and Wilson made a gasping sound. Between Chihuahua and Lum reeled the wreck of Prather. His face was the color of a fish belly; his mouth working like a crying woman's. But he staggered free of the grinning pair beside him and fairly flung himself at Clay.

"Keep those devils away! I'll tell you — I'll tell you! But don't let them hang me ——"

He and Smiling, Yates, Templin, and Gratt, had been the stage-robbers. Here in Gurney, a clerk in the stage-company office had sold Smiling information: lists of what the stages carried. Prather described the robbery: they had all fired at the stage, killing the driver; and Smiling had killed the drummer, "because he looked so damn' trifling."

"Who killed Bronzalez?" Clay asked quietly. "Ritt Rales or Smiling ordered it. But who actually shot him?"

"Dubose and Dort — the two you knocked over in the Antelope a while ago. Ritt sent 'em out when he saw you looking at Bronzalez. For Bronzalez knew when we rode in."

"Who-all made up that precious 'Old-Timer' gang?"

That, Prather said, was the idea of Rales and Smiling. They had organized their "committee" partly for amusement, but more for the mystification of the real old-timers of Gurney. They had hung the Ettisons because Smiling disliked them. The rank and file of the "committee" was composed of miscellaneous loafers from the Palace. Their "trials" had furnished them much amusement. Rales served as "Number One." He had once been a lawyer, Prather thought.

"What'd you expect to do for Powell?" Clay grunted suddenly. "You know damn' well there was killing in the wind!"

But of this connection, Prather knew little. He and Gratt had come up from Cananea riding together, only a month before. Too, Smiling had a way of keeping most of his real thoughts hidden behind that set smile of his. All Prather knew was that Powell had sent over to the Diamond River for Smiling, asking him to come to The Territory with "as many salty gunfighters" as he could enlist, for a "little war."

"So help me," Prather cried brokenly, "I ain't been in on a thing like that shooting on the Waxy! That was Smiling and Yates by 'emselves that called the Dutchman to his door, and shot him and his little boy to death. Smiling said Powell wanted him to discourage the Dutchman. And he says, he certainly was discouraged as anybody could be when he kicked over dead!"

He shrugged. He seemed to be recovering from his fear.

"Powell figured he was bossing Smiling, but I never figured that Smiling saw it like that. I don't know whether Powell paid over any money to Smiling. But, if he did, we never got any. We ask' Smiling for some — Gratt and me. He said he'd see about it. So the bunch of us went out and rounded up sixty-odd head of Ladder P stuff — prime steers, twos up. We drove 'em to Fort Lowe and sold 'em to a friend of Smiling's — the fellow that's got the fort beef contract. Smiling gave us all a hundred apiece. He says the money was just pay in advance from Powell."

He professed ignorance of the particular work intended for the Tough Bunch. It had been recruited from Arizona, Colorado, Texas, and Old Mexico. That was all he knew. Smiling, he thought, knew a good deal more. Yates might, too.

"Lock him up and we'll go collect Smiling and Company!" Clay told Lum, and grinned tightly.

He whipped out the white-handled .44s of Smoky Cole and inspected the loads, then spun them by the trigger guards and grinned at the gaping Wilson as he reholstered them.

"Prather is beginning to nurse the hope that we'll arrest Smiling dead," Lum told them, when he came back from the cells. "He has begun to do some thoughtful thinking. It occurs to him that Smiling may be displeased."

"Hell with Prather!" Clay said grimly. "Now, if we go charging down the street, hunting Smiling, he'll maybe open up his saddle bags and shake a war out of them. No use giving him the chance to kill off anybody. I'm going to borrow that Mexican boy from Halliday's store. I'll send him to scout around and find where Smiling is. And I'll have Halliday roust out some of his friends. You wait around here."

He made Halliday's by the back way. Briefly, he told of Prather's confession. Halliday's face was split by a warrior-grin.

"Good enough! If it's the showdown, that's just fine!"

He sent his Mexican errand boy to hunt Smiling; sent one of his clerks out with curt messages to Harrel, Powers, Comanche Smith, Merle Sheehan, Bill Francis, and other townsmen who could be trusted. Very quickly these men, to the number of a dozen, slid one by one into the store. Some walked stiffly, for they bore — as well-concealed in trouser legs or under their coats as might be possible — rifles, carbines, or shotguns.

Clay looked at them, and grinned hard-mouthed. For, if in appearance they were of just any size and age, they owned one thing in common, a grim eagerness to be at the business at hand. Then Lum Luckett and Chihuahua appeared, with the errand boy who had gone scouting Smiling's position.

"They are in the house of Malo Palomar," the boy reported nervously. "There are several Americans with Smiling and old Malo — who is well-named 'Bad'! I think that they have been drinking a good deal. One can hear them singing fifty yards away!"

"Do you think they saw you as you scouted?"

"I think none observed me, for I walked

by and I saw no one watching. If any did see me, he *should* have thought me but one who walked past without thought of those in the house."

"That house is a regular fort," Halliday drawled. "Not a speck of cover within thirty yards, ary side. People inside have got straight shooting at anybody that tries to cross the open between the next nearest house and Palomar's. But, if we can make the door, we'll have 'em where the hair's short!"

Clay shrugged fatalistically and led the way toward the rear of the store. They went along the back wall of those buildings fronting the main street, until they came to the edge of town. They picked up two Wagon Wheel cowboys of Chihuahua's acquaintance. Chihuahua grinned at these.

"*Por Dios!* She's like them old time, w'at?" he cried. "W'en we're have them fight in Gurney, always you fellow will pop up. You're remember them day here, when you're locked up for being most pig-drunk, and Lit Taylor and me, we're have to turn you loose, to help us fight them saloon bums w'at will take them prisoner from the jail? She's one *ni-ice* fight them time. But, *tal vez*, maybe today she's be one good fight, too! You're come along and maybe you're get killed. W'at the hell!"

Standing against the wall of the last house on this edge of town, Clay saw the square bulk of Malo Palomar's 'dobe just ahead of them. But they surveyed it across a bare expanse of ground, not thirty yards, but nearer fifty yards, wide. Here they settled their final arrangements.

'Folks call me a rustler;
My gal, she's a hustler!
She calls me her honey;
And gets all my money.

'But what care I?
I'll get me a gun by and by.
That means plenty of money
And then another honey!'

They could see the black rectangle against the gray-brown wall, the doorway from which came the old *buscadero* song. Except for the singing, it might have been a house asleep; a house empty — instead of a house that contained the most notorious killer of The Territory and at least a half-dozen thoroughly desperate henchmen.

They divided into four attacking parties, headed by Halliday, Harrel, Comanche Smith, and Clay. Three parties were to close up, each on a side of the house. Clay would attack from this, the front. The men there — and by some sort of "grapevine" telegraph news of what was afoot had spread in the town, and their numbers were steadily increasing — moved off under their leaders. Clay and his force waited for the others to take their positions.

The signal was to be a yell and a shot from Comanche Smith at the back of the house. At last the signal came and Clay, with Chihuahua, Lum, and the others, sprang out from the wall and sprinted toward that black and quiet doorway. A man appeared suddenly in it, stared, then ducked back.

They had covered approximately half the distance to the door when, as by magic, black rifle barrels came thrusting out of the apparently solid front wall. A very blast of fire greeted them. They hurled themselves down into the shelter of a little ridge fifty feet from the door. But one man dropped and came crawling after them; another dropped — and lay moveless.

"Loopholes," Chihuahua said grimly, shoving his carbine forward. "They're know w'at we're want. So ——"

From their slight shelter, they opened upon the loopholes. From the other sides of the house lifted a rattle and roar of firing to match their own. But it could be only by accident that the attackers could injure men so well-protected as Smiling's, sheltered in the thick-walled 'dobe.

Clay borrowed a white silk neckerchief from one of the Wagon Wheel cowboys, and tied it to his carbine. He waved it back and forth above the little ridge until firing from the house ceased. Smiling called from inside the partly open door, asking what was wanted.

"This is the sheriff!" Clay yelled in answer. "I want you and Yates. You might as well come out. If you do, you'll get a fair trial for the stage-robbery. If you don't — you might as well start carving your tombstones right there, and right now! For not one of you in that house will get out alive, except when you surrender!"

"Go to hell!" was Smiling's level answer. "Ain't enough of you damn' illegitimates in the whole damn' Territory to bluff us!"

"You men in there with Smiling!" Clay yelled. "This is your last chance. If he wants to stay there and collect a slug, that's all right with me. But if any of you others wants to come out, hands up, and save his skin, better come on now!"

On each side of the door was a square window, closed by a wooden shutter. These were high in the wall — perhaps set so in anticipation of just such an hour as this. For a moment after Clay's ultimatum, there hung over the whole scene a thick and heavy silence. Then what seemed to be an argument began at the door.

As Clay's side watched, the shutter of one front window leaned outward and dropped. A man appeared in the small square opening, scrambling through headfirst. He dived to the ground, landed on hands and knees, and jerked his hands into the air as he ran for the line of besiegers. From the door hurtled the lank, black-clad figure of Simon Dee, the county attorney.

Both Dee and the man from the window sprinted onward. From the house behind them there was no token that their flight was noted. They were on the very foot of the ridge which sheltered Clay and the others, when a pistol exploded in the doorway. Simon Dee spun about with a harsh cry and dropped, with his long arms thrashing limply. He never moved again.

Another shot came from the doorway. Dee's companion in flight plunged over the ridge into the little hollow beyond. He lay in a sprawling huddle. The bullet had gone in at the base of his neck and ranged a little upward to remove virtually all semblance of features from his face.

"Merry Christmas!" Smiling yelled mockingly from the house. "And remember there's plenty more for all you sons of dogs!"

One of the Wagon Wheel cowboys was scowling down at the dead man. He looked up at Clay.

"This is just nearly hell. It is that," he muttered. "Sheriff, it looks like we can't get *in,* and Smiling, he can't get *out.* Now, I know Smiling mighty well. I've played around with him — and with Frenchy Leonard, too, when they was nothing but cowboys a little on the rustle. Over at Tom's Bluff on the Diamond that was. I kind of hate to see him play the fool. I believe I can talk Smiling out of the notion of making Custer's last stand in the house."

"You'd be a plain, damn' fool, to try talking to that little rat, today!" Clay told him angrily. "No, we'll have to make that house too hot for 'em to stay inside it. A few chunks of dynamite — and we've got the dynamite, too! — will just about play hell with 'em. I reckon we'll try that."

"But," the cowboy objected reasonably, "you can't sling the dynamite from here. And it'll be plain suicide to try getting across that open, with men that can shoot like Smiling inside the house watching you.

And they've got their horses in that little 'dobe stable that joins onto the house.

"Now, come dark, they can make a run for it and some of 'em will get away, for this is going to be a dark night. But, if I go augur with Smiling a while — and tell him what you aim to do about the dynamite, too — I bet I can make him see the sense of coming out and standing trial."

He found no backers of his plan among them. But he was a one-idea'd soul. His brown young face set stubbornly.

"Maybe mention of the dynamite'll turn the trick, when otherwise he wouldn't listen," he told Clay. "And I admit I've got a soft feeling for Smiling. I've seen the elephant and heard the owl with him, many's the time. He took to swinging the long rope and the hungry loop, and I couldn't see that. But he's a mighty good fellow, in just a heap of ways. If we can get him out of that without his being shot into doll rags, I want to try it. And he ain't going to *hurt* me. Smiling's all right, if he likes you."

He ended the argument by unbuckling his belt and letting his pistol drop. Then he took back his white kerchief and stood up, waving it. No fire greeted him as he crossed the open to the door of the house. They watched him go inside, then settled down to wait.

Chapter XIII

After the disappearance of that Wagon Wheel puncher in the Palomar house, sullen quiet gripped the scene. On the edge of town behind Clay's party, men watched the battleground from the shelter of houses and stores. The saloons which had windows safely commanding the fight did a land-office business; bartenders came out from the bars with trays of drinks, to pass among the spectators.

Runners came to Clay from Halliday, Harrel, and Comanche Smith, to inquire why firing had stopped on his side. They went back and the attackers settled down to wait for the cowboy.

At last he appeared in the doorway. He had his back to those outside. He seemed to be arguing with someone. They could see his little gestures and hear the mumble of his voice.

"No use!" he called, when halfway to the

little ridge. "He ain't surrendering — none, a-tall! He ain't worried, he says. He'd like to see you getting up close enough to chunk dynamite into the house, he says. When he gets tired of squatting in there, him and the others'll pile on their horses and ride out. He says he wants to *see* somebody stop 'em! He says ——"

"Oh, Jim!" Smiling called from the doorway, and the cowboy turned. "Jim!"

"What do you want?" Jim asked hopefully.

"That's a louse-bound bunch you've took to running with — like I told you. So, *you'll* have to take what's coming to the rest of 'em."

Suddenly, Clay divined what was intended. He sprang up from behind the ridge, with a strangled cry to the Wagon Wheel man to jump — and jump quickly. But before the cowboy had more than begun to move, that deadly pistol barked in the doorway. A little puff of dust jumped from the cowboy's gray flannel shirt on his left breast. Clay caught him by the shoulder, but already he was dead. Again and again the pistol roared from the doorway. But Chihuahua had shoved his carbine forward. He rained lead around the puffs of smoke that came from the door. A bullet seared along Clay's back, from right shoulder-point to left hip. Others buzzed like spiteful wasps past him before he could drop back behind the ridge, pulling the cowboy's body after him.

"Now, I'm going after that dynamite!" Clay told the others grimly. "If The Territory *needed* anything to show people just what kind of lowdown skunk Smiling is, that killing ought to give 'em all the proof they want. It ought to shut up some of these folks that have been talking so much, about Smiling really being a good fellow, after all; just pushed into being an outlaw! Jim was willing to risk his neck for Smiling — and *he* got some of Smiling's brand of friendliness, now, didn't he!"

He looked quickly and shrewdly across that unsheltered stretch he must cover to get from the ridge, back to the buildings of the town.

"You-all give 'em hell, while I make a run for it," he grunted to Chihuahua.

From all four sides of the house, bullets pounded at the loopholes in the walls of the Palomar 'dobe. Clay sprang up from the little hollow and, running zigzag, raced for the nearest building.

As he appeared in the open, the firing from the house on this side became a frantic, drumming roar. Twice his hat seemed to lift up on his head and settle again. Time after time he felt the tiny, oddly gentle, touch of leaden slugs, picking like ghostly fingers at his clothing. But he reached the corner of a store unwounded. He sprang around it into the center of a group of men who gaped at him as at someone rising from the grave.

"My — soul!" cried the Antelope's bartender. "*I* wouldn't have bet five cents against a thousand dollars that you could make that run, with *that* outfit dusting you!"

Clay made no answer. Instead, he went at a fast trot up the street to the Halliday-Kenedy store. Here were women of the town, halted in their buying by the firing. They stared fascinatedly at Clay as he hurled himself through the door. Kenedy was out of town. Only two clerks were here.

"Has — has anybody been hurt?" Barbara Kenedy asked him. She came out of the group of women to stop before Clay.

"Three-four," Clay nodded grimly.

Then he turned to one of the clerks and said that he wanted all the dynamite in the place.

"But you! You're hurt!" Barbara said tensely. "Why — your clothes are simply shot to pieces!"

Sight of Helen Powell, quiet, rigid, white

of face, with dark eyes staring fixedly, brought to Clay sudden thought of John Powell.

For a wild instant he wondered if Powell could be hemmed in with Smiling and the others, in the Palomar house. Suppose the big, grim egotistical Ladder P owner had come quietly into town to confer with Smiling? Thoroughly as he disliked Powell, it was for him a shaking thought. For he knew, as he stared at her somberly, that he did not want John Powell killed. It was as if he were split in opposing halves.

One side of his brain said that it would be a fine deed, good for The Territory, if an exploding stick of dynamite could wipe out Powell as well as Smiling.

"For the man that hires a murderer is just a little worse than the man he hires!" this part of him charged remorselessly. "John Powell murdered that poor Dutchman and the little boy on Waxy Creek, using Smiling for a pistol. He's a *murderer,* the same as Smiling. And you hang murderers!"

But he could not be an inexorable judge — not altogether. The girl watching him was too pretty, too soft, too inexperienced in all the grim ways of this hard land that he knew so much about, to let him hold steadfastly to the rôle of "hanging judge."

When he turned with the clerk toward the shelves, he thought of her, not of the dynamite that within ten minutes might execute her father.

He had not fallen in love with her, he told himself. He would not let himself do a silly thing like that. He was a shrewd young man, accustomed to thinking about his problems. She was not his kind. The education John Powell had given her, the sort of life she had known until her return to the Ladder P, made her as different from him and most of the other people around her as if she were a girl of some foreign land. Practically, she *was* a foreigner! And that, he thought suddenly, explained her interest in Smiling. He was a creature strange to such a girl and so, interesting.

Realizing this, Clay realized how violently he had resented her apparent friendliness for the grinning killer, while treating *him* as if he were a creature untouchable. He had been jealous, not because he was in love with her, or had any thought that a cowboy would be permitted to fall in love with her, but because he was a better man in every way than Smiling, yet he was treated as if he were a worse man.

He turned — he could not help it — and

looked at her. She still stared fascinatedly at him.

"It's no fault of hers," he thought. "But she's certainly going to be pulled into the trouble that's in store for John Powell. And that's a shame, for *she* has no more idea about the truth of all this ——"

And sight of her, slim, very young, more than merely pretty, softened the harshness with which he had to regard John Powell. More . . . He looked at her and realized that he *had* thought of her, not as "the lady of the Ladder P," far above him and his kind, utterly different from any girl he had ever seen, unattainable, but as a girl to whom he might speak on the level of equality.

"You damn' fool!" he addressed himself caustically. "Oh, you poor damn' fool! We're just interesting animals to her — if we're interesting. Keep your eyes and your ideas to yourself, Clay Borden. This is The Territory, not Fairyland!"

He crossed impulsively to where she stood — so white and stiff — and asked about her father.

"What?" she said slowly. She seemed to have difficulty in forming words. "What — do you want with him?"

"Smiling and his gang are holed up in the Palomar house. They won't surrender. They have killed one of my possemen. And Smiling murdered two of his side — the county attorney and another man — and shot a cowboy, a good friend of his, too, in the back. So, if your father could persuade him to come out, it would save some of the men in there. I'm going to dynamite the house."

"I — I don't know where my father is. You're going to *kill* Smiling?"

"I don't know. I'm going to drive him out of that house, if he's alive after the dynamite goes off. Then it depends on him: I'm going to arrest him, or kill him if he resists. If I'm able to do it. And I mean by that, if *I'm* not dead."

She seemed about to say something more, but did not. Clay turned back to the clerk, who now stood nervously, holding the dynamite. Clay took the sticks and moved out the rear door. In the alley, squatting as he prepared the sticks carefully, he wondered how he was to get near enough to the house to throw the dynamite. He was in a grim and ugly mood. He was almost willing to accept the fact that, to get dynamite onto the Palomar roof he must take the slugs from the rifles inside. He could face the prospect, feeling as he did. It was the prospect of being killed before he could throw the dynamite, and so dying uselessly, that halted him.

Then a sparrow lit upon the ground beyond him. Absently, Clay stared at the "chee-chee." Then: "Got you, Smiling!" he snarled.

He left the dynamite there, to hurry back into the store. Here he amazed the clerk by demanding heavy rubber bands. He snatched a handful of them and went out again. From a tree he cut a large forked branch, then snipped two strings from the saddle on a horse standing behind the store. He went at a trot, back to the edge of town.

He yelled at Chihuahua and Lum. They opened up a hot fire on the house. Again Clay covered that deadly unsheltered open space at a zigzagging run. Again he got through untouched — but neither he nor any of the others could say how.

"What you got, Sheriff?" the surviving Wagon Wheel cowboy inquired. For Clay, squatting in the bottom of the little depression behind the ridge, busily whittled with his bowie knife at the forked stick. He merely grunted impatiently and went on with his work. Then the cowboy nodded:

"A nigger shooter!" he cried. "But — what you going to *do* with it? It's way too big to use ——"

For answer Clay picked up a pebble and

placed it in the leather pocket formed from a piece of his leggings, that now dangled between the bundles of rubber bands. He held the forked stick handle firmly and with difficulty pulled back the bands. The pebble described a flat arc in the air and dropped upon the roof of the house.

The next missile was not a pebble. Clay moved away from the others and slung a length of dynamite stick, with a short fuse lit. But the fuse was too short. In the air, at the very apex of its arc, the stick exploded. As if that heavy detonation were signal, all firing ceased for an instant, inside the house.

Chihuahua grinned rapturously.

"*Por dios!* Me, I'm know, like I'm looking through them window, w'at's happen in them house! Smiling, she's look at them ugly Eb Yates. Yates, she's look back at Smiling. *W'at the hell!* they're think. Will them Gurney posse now grow them little wing and fly in them air and drop them giant powder down our neck?"

The besiegers, also, had checked their fire with the dull explosion above the house. In the sullen silence that ensued, Clay scratched a match and set the flame to the fuse of the second length of dynamite. Then he placed it carefully on the leather pouch of his sling. He knelt on one knee — as many a time he had knelt to loose a horse-shoe caulk at a rabbit — and carefully stretched the rubbers. This fuse he had cut a trifle longer.

From watching the sputtering fuse nervously, those in the hollow turned, to crane their necks and watch the arc of flight. Over it went — and dropped on the roof of that little shed built against the house. For an instant, nothing occurred. Clay wondered if, by any chance, fuse and dynamite had become separated. Then, as if in answer to his mental doubts, there came a second explosion, duller, heavier than the first.

The shed seemed bodily to rise half a foot in air. But that was only the dust from the mud bricks lifting in wall-like sheets, to disintegrate swiftly and float away like smoke. Then the walls rocked and tilted and a section fell in. Clay loosed his third projectile. It fell short and exploded on the ground. But a fourth landed on the roof, a trifle closer to the house itself.

With the crash of it and the swaying of the whole house, Smiling's party leaped from the front door. But, eager as they were to leave the death-trap which was the house, and shaken as they may have been, they did not forget to elevate their hands as they jumped out! For they were plain targets for the rifles that ringed them in. One or two bullets did kick up sand around their feet. They yelled their surrender. The firing stopped.

The possemen leaped up from their various places of shelter and came trotting in a narrowing circle, weapons at the ready.

There were Smiling and Yates, with the hard-faced tinhorn Dubose — whom Prather had charged jointly with the murder of Bronzalez the beggar — and Hemming, the big Texan, with a bandanna around his left forearm, and Horton, who with Willis had played poker in the Palace with Smiling, Yates, and Prather, and helped in the lying alibi.

Yates and Dubose were sullen and tight of mouth; Horton appeared nervous; Hemming, holding his wounded arm, cursed in a furious monotone. Smiling only grinned at the savage ring of faces, as if the occasion were most usual, even casual. He still wore his holstered pistols — those self-cocking .41s with which Wilson had seen him kill the little drummer during the stage-robbery. And — he had dropped his hands; in his red-flecked eyes was a light that grew more and more calculating . . . Yates had dropped his hands, too. Horton and Dubose kept theirs at shoulder-level, while Hemming held his bandaged arm.

"You certainly showed yourself for a yellow-backed shoot-'em-from-behind murderer today, now, didn't you?" Clay snarled, ramming his face all but into Smiling's. "Damn' shame you couldn't get yourself blown to hell by that dynamite. But the Devil's got your name in the pot! You'll be landing in hell soon — right after you kick a while, hunting something to rest your feet on. *Get those hands up! Pronto!* Get 'em up — or I'll blow a hole through you that'll show that flyspeck you call a soul!"

"You have got mighty brave all of a sudden!" Smiling said in level, furious tone. "But I notice you waited till you got a whole bunch of guns behind you."

"Brave!" Clay cried contemptuously. "Brave! Who needs to be brave — if he keeps you in front of him! Now, if it was good and dark, and you could hide out and pop at me from behind, I'd be worried. That kind of killing suits you — and it suits Ritt Rales, and all the rest of the sneaking pack that's been riding around, calling itself an Old-Timer Committee!"

The crowd about gaped at this disclosure. Yates's sullen black eyes shuttled to Clay. Dubose, Horton, and Hemming betrayed their amazement at this show of knowledge by all-too-apparent head-jerks, then equally obvious attempts to look ignorant of the subject.

"I'm taking Smiling and Yates for stage-robbery, and murder in connection with that robbery; and for murder done here — the murder of Dee, and Wallis, and Grey, of the posse while resisting arrest; the murder of that poor, trusting fool, Jim Ellis — who tried to talk Smiling into saving his worthless skin. Where's Dort, Dubose? Dead, huh? That's fine! I want Dubose for the murder of that poor devil Bronzalez and for the murder of Grey. Horton, you're elected for resisting an officer and for murder ——"

"Murder?" cried Horton, interrupting Clay's recountal. "I never done no murder. I was inside there and you-all started shooting and ——"

"Murder in connection with the killing of Grey *and* the lynching of the Ettisons — and that charge goes against all of you except Hemming. He wasn't in the neighborhood. Neither was Stubby. And where *is* Stubby? Did we drill him, too? Well — if a man can't pick a trail for himself, he's got nobody but himself to blame if the trail somebody else picks for him leads to Boot Hill! I'll take you the same as Horton, Hemming — for resisting an officer. And for the killing of Grey."

Smiling's hands, held carelessly at his shoulder, now twitched the merest trifle. His red-flecked eyes swerved to Clay's empty hands, then up to his face. Imperceptibly, his shoulders seemed to stiffen, tense. Clay made no move to whip out a gun — though he did not miss the warning signals. Instead, his hands darted up to encircle Smiling's wrists. He hauled the killer's hands down. Instinctively, Smiling jerked, trying to free himself. But he found his straining in vain. The smallish hands that held his wrists were like steel clamps.

Further indignity awaited him. Standing with his chin rammed almost into Smiling's face, and his contemptuous stare meeting Smiling's smoldering black eyes, Clay grinned faintly.

He drew the killer's wrists together with a movement so smooth, so steady, that it seemed easy. The smile went from Smiling's lips — for the first time in the knowledge of any man there. Then Clay caught the tops of the leather cuffs that Smiling wore. He held them together with his left hand only while Smiling, the larger man, strained until his face reddened and beads of sweat burst out upon his forehead.

From a pocket of his leggings, Clay took a

pair of handcuffs. He snapped the circlets on Smiling's wrists.

Then only did he pull the deadly self-cockers from Smiling's holsters.

"And *you* have been going around calling yourself a wolf!" he said scornfully. "You look more poodle to me!"

"I'll put *you* — kicking like a hen with her head off — if it's the last thing I ever do!" Smiling assured him in a choked, thick voice. "I'll gut-shoot you and let you put in a couple hours dying and ——"

"Said that bold, bad little fellow, Smiling, one sunny afternoon in Gurney!" Clay scoffed.

He caught Smiling by the shoulder and spun him deftly into Lum, who caught him with one big hand and forced a pained grunt from him by the grip he took on his arm.

"Jail with 'em!" Clay grinned. "After they're all hung, I reckon we'll have to burn sulphur in the cells, to clear the smell out of 'em. Prather's waiting there for you-all. Take 'em down, fellows. I'm going to look at the house."

Then he whispered to Chihuahua, suggesting that the crooked clerk of the stage-company would be a valuable addition to their prisoners. Chihuahua's grin was catlike as he nodded and turned away.

Clay found not only Dort and Stubby dead inside the 'dobe; Malo Palomar, too, lay curled under a loop-hole, with a Winchester under him and a bullet neatly through his forehead. And, fishing around the littered, dirty house, Clay found the pistols taken from him by the spurious "Old-Timers."

"I think I'll add Mr. Ritt Rales to our bag," he told himself, as he pushed the Colts affectionately into the waistband of his trousers. "He just seems to naturally belong with 'em . . ."

But Ritt Rales was not to be found in Gurney. The bartenders at the Palace said Rales had ridden out before the battle started at Palomar's — to his ranch, probably. He had not said.

Coming outside, Clay stood on the sidewalk to stare grimly, almost blindly, up and down. He wondered if it would be best to trail Rales and bring him in. But it would be dark soon, and it had been a very full day — even for a young man as tough as Clay. Besides, there was yonder procession, moving so certainly toward the sheriff's office . . .

Clay trailed the four women and they had barely entered the door before he followed them inside, Mrs. Kenedy, with both Barbara and Helen Powell and also a middle-aged Mexican woman. Clay glanced curiously at the latter; she was paler than most of her class; she yet bore the traces of unusual prettiness. Just now, she was red-eyed as from crying.

"Here is the acting sheriff, now, ma'am," said Lum, with obvious relief. "Clay, Mrs. Kenedy has something to discuss with you."

"Are they all right, up above?" Clay asked stonily. "Then all of you — Shorty Wiggins, too — had better get supper. I'll ride herd till you come back."

As he turned to Mrs. Kenedy — ignoring the others — the three deputies went out, heading for a restaurant. The women sat down in the chairs he indicated silently.

"This is Maria Gonzales, Pedro's mother," Mrs. Kenedy said grimly. "You know, 'Bronzalez' the beggar. That's Pedro. Maria has worked for me, off and on, for years. She's a good woman, even if he was a love-child and —— Well, what I was going to say is, Maria's a good woman. You can believe anything she tells you. And she's got something to say."

"What is it, señora?" Clay asked Maria in Spanish.

"You have in jail here the man yet alive of

the two who murdered my son. But — do you know who used these two as his hands? Who ordered them to murder my Pedro?"

"Yes. Of a certainty," Clay told her calmly. "Rales and Smiling. They feared he would tell me at what time Smiling and the other thieves and murderers had really come into town."

"Rales, yes — but not Smiling. Not that boy! No, no! Smiling is too happy, too generous, to have had my son murdered. Why, he had given Pedro a handful of silver but a little while before!"

"It was Rales and Smiling," Clay said again in the even voice he had used from the beginning. "Smiling *is* happy — when everything moves to please him. He *is* generous — with tiny bits of that which he has stolen from someone else. That Wagon Wheel *vaquero* whom he shot in the back today — Jim Ellis — Smiling once gave him a horse with saddle, bridle — everything. That was at Tom's Bluff on the Diamond. And why should Smiling *not* give Ellis this outfit, if he felt generous? He needed but to go out and steal himself another!"

Mrs. Kenedy had been translating for Helen's benefit. Now, she — like Maria Gonzalez — glared at Clay's contemptuous face.

Barbara Kenedy frowned uncertainly. Helen — but Clay could not tell, from her steady regard of him, what she felt or thought.

"You're blaming Smiling for that stage-robbery — and for the driver's killing, and the drummer's — because you don't like him!" Mrs. Kenedy cried indignantly. "It's the old story: Give a dog a bad name and you might as well hang him. I bet you'll never prove what you're charging him with!"

"Don't bet," Clay counseled, with a lift of one mouth-corner. "For you'll certainly lose your money."

Then his quick temper snapped the control he had held upon his tongue.

"This is the *oddest* country I have ever been in!" he cried angrily. "*You* and your like, Mrs. Kenedy, calling yourselves good citizens, have the *quaintest* ways of proving your claims! It seems you're just running over with sympathy for every two-legged polecat around, but you've got nothing but abuse for possemen and others that the murderers like Smiling may kill, and for the officers who try to clean up the mess this country is in!"

He checked himself abruptly.

"Señora! What evidence have you that Rales ordered your son killed?"

"My nephew, Antonio, is a porter in the Palace. He was in one of the poker rooms when you were there; the time when you looked too long, too hard, at my Pedro. He heard Rales order Dubose and Dort to kill Pedro — and kill you, also, if you stepped outside before Pedro's murder was done. Antonio had no time to warn Pedro; no opportunity to do anything. He will testify in the court. But, señor! You must not breathe a word of Antonio's knowledge! Otherwise, he will go as my son has gone! Promise!"

Clay nodded — inwardly well-pleased. For he had wanted better testimony than that of Prather. Besides, nobody could say how Prather would feel about talking when time came for testimony. This cousin of Pedro Gonzalez was an ace in the hole.

"Happen to strike you as being just a little odd, Mrs. Kenedy," he drawled, "that Smiling's friend Rales would want the beggar murdered, to keep him from telling me what time Smiling and his gang rode in — *if* they hadn't been up to some devilment? Especially when one of Smiling's own gang confessed that they did the robbery? And especially — too — when we have got in a cell the crooked clerk from the stage-company office, and *he* has confessed to selling Smiling the information about the treasure safe and the kind of passengers?"

"Give a dog a bad name ——" Mrs. Kenedy repeated stubbornly.

Clay could not help it. Furious as this helplessness made him, he still must turn his eyes furtively to Helen Powell's face. She was staring at him with an odd expression. Of uncertainty? Of dawning belief in what he said? He had only an instant to wonder — and to say again, what he had said in the store, that she was the *loveliest* girl he had ever seen; and the lovelier, perhaps, because utterly unattainable. For him.

Then she looked away.

After they had gone, Clay took Smoky's white-handled pistols from his holsters. He unloaded them, dropped the cartridges on the table, and put them away. He was about to reload his own when he heard a light, quiet step outside the door. Flashingly, he considered the effect of his being caught by anyone unfriendly — and there were plenty such in Gurney, he thought — with pistols obviously empty. He swept the cartridges into the drawer and rammed the pistols into the holsters. And through the door came — Pecos Pawl.

"Howdy!" Pecos said calmly — as if there had never been a time of playing poker and drawing pistols at Poplar Station. "Hear you got Smiling in your ho-tel. Mind if I talk to him?"

"No-o. Reckon not. At the proper time . . . *That'll* be just before he stretches the kinks out of a new rope."

"*You'll* never win against Smiling," Pecos told him tolerantly. "You might's well act sensible. What's all this helling around going to buy you, anyway? Nothing! Why'n't you ——"

His yellow eyes had been roving. Now, they came to rest on Clay's right-hand Colt, and narrowed incredulously, then shifted to inspect minutely the left-hand gun. Both Colts were showing pretty prominently above the holster-tops.

"Why'n't you — you —"

But, very evidently, Pecos Pawl's mind was not on whatever suggestion he had been about to make.

Clay got up abruptly. If this killer had noted the lack of any brazen glint at the cylinder-ends of his pistols, *something* would happen! He grinned at Pawl.

"Well, nobody has made me any kind of useful proposition," he grunted. "Wait a minute! Let's see how the boys are doing up above."

He was across the office and in the doorway leading to the jail stairway before Pecos had more than begun some sort of objection. There was a shelf, beyond that door. Boxes of shells were on it. With fingers that fairly twinkled, Clay jerked one shell from a full box, pushed it into his right-hand gun and spun the cylinder. He had just reholstered the pistol when Pawl was behind him in the door.

"Them three deputies of yourn are certainly hungry," Pawl grinned at Clay — as if to inform him that he knew the others were gone; knew Clay was alone. "So —— You know I've got a score to settle with you, Baby-Face! And — right now — I'm going to wipe her plumb clean!"

Very deliberately he put a hand on his own Colt. His thick lips twisted in a tigerish grin, as his fingers tightened on the checked black stock. The Colt began to rise in the holster, slowly — for he seemed to be prolonging the motion to enjoy Clay's expression.

Clay whipped out his right-hand pistol and, with hammer held under his thumb, he aimed it at Pecos's waistband. Pecos only grinned and continued to draw his own Colt.

"Go ahead! Shoot!" he laughed. "Go on! That's one hog-leg I ain't worried about. I'm going to blow a whole damn' gate in you, and then, we'll let Smiling and the boys out and ———"

"Drop that gun!" Clay snarled at him. "Drop it or — *this* time — I'll kill you, Pawl!"

Pecos continued to level his Colt, his grin widening.

"All right, then . . ."

Clay let the hammer go and with the roar of the .44 Pecos staggered. Clay lunged at him and struck his wrist. The Colt dropped — to be raked away by Clay's toe.

"I be damned!" Pecos mumbled. His face wore a surprised expression. "If he never shot me with an empty gun!"

He clawed at the door-facing and began to slide down it.

Chapter XIV

Clay waked with wolfish possession of all his faculties. He stiffened, on the cot in the back room, when his hand closed upon a pistol butt. He stared through the darkness toward the sound of that hammering upon the street door. Chihuahua — who had the watch — went by him like a shadow. Clay waited. He heard the mumble of voices, then the opening of the door. Clay got up and went into the office, with Lum trailing him.

"I'm Sally Sumerlin — from Arroyo Seco Ranch!" the slender girl beside Chihuahua panted. "They're a-killing off my folks, Sheriff! Shooting into the house — the sneaking, lowdown bushwhackers! Must be twenty or thirty of 'em outside, a-ringing the cabin around. Don't know how I ever got through, with them a-shooting at me. They barked my arm, but it's nothing to matter."

"What started it?" Clay demanded.

She shrugged: "We was all asleep when somebody come pounding on the door. I reckon I dozed off again, then Ma shook me awake. Everybody was shooting. Ma says to me to drop out of the window and scoot for Gurney and bring help!"

Within a brief half-hour, Clay, Chihuahua, and Lum sat their horses on the northern edge of the county seat. With them were such efficient stalwarts as Halliday, Kenedy, Comanche Smith, Merle Sheehan, the huge blacksmith Powers, and seven others of the same caliber.

"Ready? Then, let's go!" Clay grunted.

It was a long fifteen miles to the poverty-stricken homestead of Sumerlin on Arroyo Seco.

But when still some distance from it, they heard the dull, flat sound of firing. Clay pulled in to state the situation to the posse:

"Likely, there's a considerable smear down yonder. There was sixteen in that Tough Bunch and, if Powell sent other hardcase cowboys with 'em, we're maybe bucking twenty to thirty. But — it's a lowdown job they're on — shooting at a house with women in it. They know it. They won't be courting witnesses. So, if we ram in the hooks and charge down, I figure they'll

278

maybe cut stick."

The others nodded grimly. So, a hundred yards from the ring of flashing rifles that encircled the cabin, the posse spread out fanwise. Then, raising a wild yell, they poured fiercely down the slope, toward the blazing corral and stable.

The fire outside the cabin halted for an instant, but, when the posse opened up, the attackers began to blaze away at them. A man close to Clay cried out as he toppled from his horse. From their positions on the ground the Ladder P men — Clay had no doubt that they were Powell's "gladiators" — jumped up. They showed as a dark single rank, retreating with rifles at hips. There was plenty of lead singing through the flame-spangled darkness! For the Sumerlins took advantage of this new visibility of the enemy to rain bullets at the black mass of men afoot.

The attackers made their horses beyond the cabin. Some fell and got up to limp or crawl onward. Others did not get up. The horses were stung by stray bullets. They were kicking and plunging. Some jerked free and ran away.

"Let 'em go — for the minute!" Clay grunted.

He raised his voice to yell his identity to

those in the cabin and, when the door opened, he pushed in. It was a two-room 'dobe, with pallets spread around the walls. On two of the thin blanket-heaps lay figures that needed but a glance to show that they were men — dead men. On a third "shake-down" a boy of no more than thirteen hugged a Winchester .45-90 almost twice as long as he was. His face was white and pain-twisted, but his grim, dark eyes were steady.

The two dead men were cousin and nephew of old Sumerlin who with his brother and his wife were the only defend-ers still on their feet. And Mrs. Sumerlin had been shooting with a rag around a bullet-hole in her left arm. Sumerlin was a gaunt, narrow-shouldered, narrow-faced man, red-stubbled, with narrow ice-blue eyes, a great hooked nose and mouth like the white mark of a crayon. His brother was younger, but very much the same iron type.

From under a great iron kettle — that had splashes of lead upon it — Mrs. Sumerlin got her six-months-old baby. It was a warrior-family! Even the baby was quiet, staring around without alarm.

Sumerlin added little to what Sally had told them in town. The Ladder P men had tried to draw him outside. Failing, they had fired through the door, then besieged the place.

"Jill — my cousin that's dead, there — he clumb onto the roof and he shot one of them fellows at the door plumb through from head to heel, like as if he was skewering a shote!"

"Ladder P killers, of course?" Clay asked him.

"Well," Sumerlin began, then hesitated oddly. "I wouldn't go so far as to say they was, and likewise, I wouldn't even say they wasn't."

As Clay stared, puzzling this queer reticence, repression, old Jed Wyndham and his silent son Ollie came pushing in. Clay would have sworn that some sort of signal — message or warning — flashed between these two grim nesters, who were so much alike.

Jed shook his head at Clay's question. He " 'lowed there must have been a right smart bunch of the scoundrels." Beyond that cautious conjecture, he would not go.

Outside, Clay found that the posse had collected five men of the Tough Bunch and two cowboys none could identify. That man who had fallen from his horse beside Clay was the posse's only real casualty, and he was not dead. Two had wounds, but not sufficiently serious to prevent such as these from going on.

"Ladder P, all right!" Clay grunted to Chihuahua and Lum. "No doubt, either, that Sumerlin and Jed know it. I reckon if we tell 'em we're more or less on the little men's side ——"

"*Pues,* I'm think that if we're tell them Wyndhams and them Sumerlins all these thing, w'y, we must ride like the hell! For they're sneak off most *awful* very damn' quiet!"

"The devil!" Clay cried irritably. "Then let's trail the Tough Bunch. If John Powell imported that kind of gang for this sort of dirty work, either he'll bump into a snag or I'll meet a slug of somebody's lead. Can you cut their trail, before daylight?"

While Chihuahua was hunting the trail, the others of the posse agreed that this Tough Bunch had to be heeled. Chihuahua called presently from beyond the smoldering ruin of the corral. The trail, he grunted from the saddle, led toward Wyndham's.

It was good daylight before they made the 'dobe cabin of these Hell Creekers. Not one head of stock had they seen on all the range; the cabin was a ruin of mud brick, gutted by fire. Lum departed to scout the water holes. He came after the posse, spurring furiously, to report no stock visible.

It was the same at the Howard Brothers' place. The same at the somewhat extensive homestead of Napoleon Buisson. Except for one dead and unknown cowboy, sprawled in the greasewood near Buisson's trail, there was no sign anywhere of a fight between the raiders and any of the small ranchers.

"When we find the Wyndhams, the Sumerlins, the Howards, and the Buisson outfit" — Clay told the posse, with sudden inspiration — "we will find the Ladder P killers. *That's* what Wyndham came to see Sumerlin about! The little fellows are pulling their side together, to buck the Ladder P!"

With handsome black head a little on one side and his jaws parted to take the strain from his eardrums, Chihuahua listened intently. Then he turned to the others whom he had guided, and the turquoise-blue eyes were shining with the battle-light.

"Them Tough Bunch, they're fight by Walker's. W'at the hell!"

He reined his calico down the rough trail from the "high roll" toward Walker's. A half-mile from the Walker house, Chihuahua pulled in. It was possible, now, with the aid of glasses, to get a pretty fair idea of the fight.

Walker and a grown son lived alone in this

house and there were far too many puffs of smoke coming from the walls and windows to be accounted for by any two men — unless, as Lum Luckett remarked pensively, each had as many arms as a millipede and was as agile in their use.

The house was on a side hill — a low-lying structure of cottonwood logs, partly formed in an excavation in the hill. The attacking party encircled it. Those on the hill above the house fired down and sent their bullets slanting at the dirt roof of the house.

"I bet the Wyndhams and Howards and Buissons are in there, with the Walkers," Halliday grunted, staring down the slope to the battleground. "And they're certainly putting up a pretty fight, too! See that fellow trying to get at the woodpile for a shot into that end window? Man, they parted his hair for him plumb proper!"

"Fourteen of us," Clay mused. "Suppose we split — half going around to come down the hill on top of those sidewinders that are shooting into the roof, the rest to hit from the front?"

So it was done. Halliday, Harrel, Medbury the restaurant man, little Bill Francis, and three others, dashed to the right, to ascend the little hill above the house. For twenty minutes Clay and the others were interested observers of the hot fight in the yard below them. There was a pile of mesquite roots — that from behind which Halliday had seen an attacker killed — which was an important objective of the attackers. It was large enough to afford good shelter for three or four men, and close enough to permit a very dangerous fire upon its end.

Time after time, as Clay's party watched, attempts were made to reach the woodpile. Each time that three or four of the Tough Bunch and Ladder P cowboys tried to make a run for the mesquite roots the defenders opened on them so blazingly that they dropped flat to the ground, and either crawled back to their original cover — or did not crawl again.

But, at last, all the attacking force on this side loosed a very blast of bullets that shredded into the cottonwood logs. Four men rushed the woodpile, but one of the runners dropped flat and lay moveless; another dropped, but scrambled, dragging a smashed leg under him, back to his own side. Two men, heads down, sprinted on. Plainly visible to those who watched from the greasewood on the hill above, they squatted behind the shelter of the mesquite roots and busied themselves at something which they had on the ground between them.

They were no more than twenty-five feet from the cabin end, now. Suddenly one stood up, with what looked to be a large, yellowish ball in his hand. This he hurled toward the cabin. It struck the logs and burst into a blaze. Another, and still another, he hurled.

"Time to horn in!" Clay grunted. "Harrel's outfit has had time to top those bushwhackers on the hillside."

They spread out in their fan-formation, as they had done the night before at Sumerlin's. At a walk, a trot, a lope, then at the pounding gallop, down the hill they came hell-bent, rifles lifted above heads, yelling like so many Comanches. And — again as on the night before at Sumerlin's — the attackers ceased firing; but only to begin again, with the riders on the wild-eyed horses for targets.

"They know who we are, all right!" Old Comanche Smith yelled at Clay. "And me, for one, no damn' bushwhacker is going to shoot at me, without me shooting back at him!"

And that seemed to be the sentiment of the whole posse. Without waiting for any suggestion from Clay, they returned the fire of the Ladder P men. Then, from the hillside above those men of the Powell faction who shot into the roof, came a blast of firing from Halliday, Harrel, and their men.

As sullenly the ring of besiegers retreated, firing at the charging posse, there ensued one of the fiercest battles even the blood-soaked Territory had ever known. Saddles were emptied among the possemen; horses galloped away riderless.

That grim, fierce line of men with savage, intent brown faces, now taken by fire from front and flank, was bullet-lashed precisely like a row of cornstalks under a hailstorm.

Men crashed forward or merely collapsed where they stood with cheeks against brown Winchester stocks. From the house the defending ranchers rained their lead into the Ladder P line. The posse no longer galloped forward. They were on the ground now, firing over the saddle or under their horses' bellies.

Down from their position on the hillside, pursued by bullets of Halliday and old Harrel, the other section of the Ladder P men were also on the run. All were retreating — moving toward the clump of horses at the corral. With a final ragged volley they mounted, leaving dead and wounded men about the ranch yard.

"No sense to letting them ride off!" Old Comanche Smith yelled fiercely, dabbing a bullet-skinned cheek with the back of his gnarled hand.

Clay put the spurs to Azulero and at the risk of his life dashed toward the mounting Ladder P men, yelling at them to surrender.

Their answer was a hail of lead that fanned the air around him. A bullet glanced off the fork of his saddle. Another nicked his carbine-stock. Still another slapped the Stetson from his head. Then, as the others of the posse mounted and charged to his support, the Ladder P men — a very ragged and slim remnant of the original forces — whirled and put spurs to their mounts.

Out of the house poured the defending party. They, too, went for their horses — which were in the log shed. So, within five minutes, there were three parties not very widely separated, racing hell-for-leather on a course that led vaguely northwestward — the Ladder P men, Clay's posse, and the little ranchers.

Clay was well in the van of the pursuers, and Azulero's speed easily widened the distance between him and his nearest fol- lower — Chihuahua on the calico. A big black horse was gradually dropping behind the fugitives ahead of Clay. Clay could not be sure, but he had a feeling that John Powell rode that black. When the horse stumbled, fell to his knees, and hurled his rider over his head, there was no doubt. It *was* Powell.

A big man turned from the press of the other riders and rode back to Powell. He checked his horse and opened fire on Clay with a Winchester. Clay pulled Azulero to a quick stop and the drum of his firing rose above the thud of hoofs behind him. The big rider fell sideways from the saddle. Clay rammed the hooks to Azulero and raced across to where Powell was now sitting up dazedly. From the ground, the man who had fallen from the horse under Clay's bullet suddenly whipped up a Colt, fired it twice and missed widely. The pistol dropped from his hand and he groped vaguely for it, but could not muster strength to pick it up. It was that big red man, Rodell, straw boss of the imported gunmen.

"I reckon you was right — about being from Texas," he mumbled, with a stiff grin up at Clay. "And about — the younger they are — the tougher they are!"

His eyes closed. Clay looked quietly at Powell, who had scrambled to his feet and stood staring sullenly, almost stupidly, at the oncoming riders. It occurred to Clay that if the bunch from the Walker house came up with Powell, the formality would be brief: a rope, John Powell's neck, and the nearest cottonwood . . . And if his posse were to overtake the bushwhacking Ladder P men, they could not be bothered with such a prisoner as Powell. So he spurred Azulero over to Rodell's horse, caught the reins and led it back quickly to Powell.

"Get on and get out!" he counseled the Ladder P owner grimly. "That gang back there, that you have been trying to murder is not likely to stand on much ceremony if they come up with you. And damned if *I* blame 'em any!"

Gratitude seemed a quality utterly lacking in John Powell. Without a word of thanks, without a glance at Rodell, he snatched the reins and hurled himself into the saddle, to race westward as the posse approached.

"Come on!" Clay yelled to these. "We can gather Powell any time. It's his bushwackers we want to heel, right now!"

Chapter XV

Within a quarter-mile Azulero began to limp. Somewhere, the blue horse had strained a foreleg. Clay cursed wearily and looked forward over the trail they were following, then back at the men clustered about him.

"Heeling those killers before they do any more murder is the important thing," he told them. "And — much as I hate to admit it — you're likely to do right well without me. So you-all go ahead. Walker had some horses caught up in that fenced pasture. I'll ride back and get one of 'em and try to catch you. Luck!"

Slowly, with the blue horse limping more and more perceptibly, he rode the back trail. He made the last mile on foot, with his leggings hung over the saddle, hobbling uncomfortably on high heels.

The fenced pasture at Walker's was hardly more than a large corral. Three horses were in it and one long-legged black pleased Clay. He took down his rope and shook out a loop. But some time was used in working the black into a corner where the snaky flip upward of the loop settled over his slim head. By the time he had shifted his saddle, Clay was in thoroughly bad humor.

Very much he disliked the prospect of leaving Azulero here. Then it came to him that a good deal hinged upon whether or not he saw the blue horse again. If he recovered Azulero, it would be because his plans succeeded, and John Powell's grandiose schemes miscarried. For if the Ladder P came to dominate this section of The Territory, Walker would hardly have a pasture fence, or be alive to consider the lack!

But there was no time for consideration of the matter. He slapped the blue horse with rough affection and rode out of the pasture gate. When he had fastened it behind him, he roweled the black into a racing gallop and back-tracked the distance to that point where he had left the posse.

The trail swerved presently, going toward rougher country, and stonier. He pulled in after a little while, to scowl at the fainter hoofprints. More and more difficult the trailing became, even to a cowboy used to tracking stray stock for miles. He came out on the road between Gurney and the Ladder P, not sure that he was on the posse's trail.

While he sat there, two riders bobbed over the crest of a ridge half-mile away. He got out his glasses and waited until they reappeared upon another rise.

"Helen, and Barbara Kenedy!" he said aloud. "Hell and hell! They can't go on to the Ladder P, not today, with the Tough Bunch likely to hole up there, and the posse ringing 'em around. But how to stop 'em ____"

He kneed the black forward and went at the gallop to where the girls, observing him, had pulled in. Barbara Kenedy sat her horse with a pistol at her side. She regarded him with blankness of face that he found odder, even, than Helen Powell's intent stare.

"Ladder P bound?" he asked them, and Helen nodded.

"We are," Barbara said evenly. "And we don't need company. Where's the posse?"

Clay waved vaguely toward the country beyond, and explained his shift of horses. Barbara nodded and lifted her reins. Helen looked sidelong at the storekeeper's daughter.

"Wait a minute!" Clay checked Barbara. "There's apt to be trouble — fighting —

293

between here and the Ladder P. That Tough Bunch you saw in Gurney is out, with two posses after 'em. We've had two brushes with 'em. You girls can't go on this way. Gurney's the best place for you ——"

"Why better than my own home?" Helen demanded, speaking for the first time. "My father ——"

Barbara watched him and he knew that she was intently staring at his face. He hesitated, hunting for a way to say that John Powell was not at the Ladder P house — nor would he get there unhurt except by luck. He turned upon her.

"Ride off a way with me, Barbara," he said irritably. "I want to tell you something. I —— "

"I'll ride off!" Helen offered stiffly.

She spurred her horse so viciously that it lunged forward with startled grunt. Clay pushed up beside Barbara.

"I'm taking you for a sensible person," he told her.

"Oh, kind sir, you flatter me! Also, you make a grave mistake. Never consider a girl as a sensible person. Even if it's true, she doesn't regard it as complimentary."

"I swear, I don't know what to make of you! You've always acted the part of a nice girl, and one knowing pretty well what's going on in the country. Now —— You've got to go back to Gurney, both of you. If you have to know, John Powell and his cowboys and the Tough Bunch have been trying to kill off the little fellows — the Sumerlins and Howards and Wyndhams and Buissons. We've got 'em on the run, now. We've rubbed out some few of 'em. And if I hadn't caught a horse for her father, John Powell would be dead this minute. Now, will you help me turn her back, away from what may be ahead of her? Barbara ——"

"Don't *Barbara* me!" she said angrily. "Whatever I do will be done because I want to do it, not because you ask me! You're like every other jackfool in high heels — you fall in love with the first pretty little helpless thing who comes along. No matter how she treats you ——"

"What are you talking about?" he cried. "You're not trying to tell me you think I'm in love with her? Of all the idiotic ideas — Barbara! I swear I was fooled about you. I thought you had the levelest head — even Smiling, I thought, didn't fool you with that grin of his and — and now you're talking like any other nitwit ——"

"Nitwit nothing! I'm not nitwit enough to believe that you didn't tumble head-over-heels in love with Helen Powell the minute you saw her — the day you killed that black steer on the Ladder P! And you think you have a chance with her? With John Powell's daughter? You're funny! Funnier, even, than Smiling — who has the same idea. For Smiling will take any way he can think of to get what he wants, and he can think of several that might very well work, to make John Powell glad to let him marry the Ladder P heiress ——"

"Smiling may think of a lot of ways to do a lot of things," Clay assured her grimly, "but he's not likely to get out of my jail to work any of his chemes ——"

"Get out? *Get* out? He *is* out! He was out on bond furnished by Ritt Rales, almost before you were out of sight! Do you think — you young simpleton — that nobody's ever been arrested in Gurney before? That Ritt Rales and his kind don't know the kind of justice of the peace they put into office? Smiling and the whole bunch are walking the street! But about Helen — I'll tell her to turn back ——"

"Thanks," Clay said, almost mechanically. For he was still trying to make himself understand that Smiling had beat him, with the help of Ritt Rales. "Why, thanks. And ——"

He shook his head, as if the physical

movement would clear the bewilderment he felt.

"And I'll ride back with you. There are plenty in the posse to handle Powell's Ladder P bushwhackers. And *I* am needed in Gurney, if Smiling and his gang are loose."

"But you're not going to walk into the middle of that bunch alone?" Barbara cried. "Clay! They'll kill you on sight! It's foolishness! You don't have to ride back with us — I'm perfectly capable. You go get the others if you're bent on carrying out your feud with Smiling ——"

"Feud?" he repeated, honestly puzzled. "This is not a feud — not exactly. It may have been something like that in the beginning, but it's a lot more than that now. I'm working for Smoky Cole. I'm trying to do what he'd do — make more than Smiling understand that some kinds of murder will bring a rope, in The Territory. My personal grudge against him has got no bearing on that."

"But you do have a grudge — just as I said!" She caught him up quickly. "And the funny thing is, you're wrong in that belief of yours. Helen thinks Smiling is an interesting animal. Just as she thinks you are the handsomest animal she's ever seen. You're silly to get yourself killed because you are jealous of him. Clay, doesn't it occur to you that some others in the neighborhood are — well, just possibly better friends of yours than — than Helen Powell ever could be? And that if you set your sights too high, you stand a good chance of missing *everything?*"

He turned back, frowning, without gesturing Helen to come down from the ridge upon which she sat her horse.

"If you could talk plain English, it would certainly be appreciated," he suggested. "The only aim I'm taking right now is at Smiling Badey — and, too, at John Powell. If you are still harping on that silly notion, of my being in love with — with *her,* yonder, buck the notion off! Because ——"

He pulled tobacco and papers from a pocket of his shirt and began almost blindly to make a cigarette.

"Maybe I did think that she was about the loveliest girl I'd ever seen," he said slowly, rather as if thinking aloud. "Maybe I still think so — being honest and not trying to tell you that I can't see where she is prettier. Maybe I always will think that. But I know well enough what she is, and what I am. I don't believe in fairy tales! I'm nothing but an uneducated saddle tramp. She'll own the Ladder P one day — she and her husband. She ——"

"And now you're talking like another kind of idiot!" Barbara interrupted waspishly. "You're a better man than she will get — very probably. If she marries one of her own kind and brings him to the Ladder P to manage it, somebody like you will eventually own the outfit! For you're the kind to go up. Saddle tramp you have been; but when you pinned on that star, you began to grow up. You can do anything you want to do, in The Territory. Own your own outfit; get yourself in politics; anything!"

"Then — then what are you driving at?" Clay demanded. "First, you tell me it's funny for me to look at her; next, you say I'm as good as she is —— What *do* you mean?"

"I'm done answering riddles," she said huskily. "It wouldn't be any use, at all, to tell you. Not a bit. I — can tell that. I can tell it by the way you — look at me!"

At first, the three of them rode together on the Gurney trail. And they rode silently. Then Barbara spurred ahead and Clay and Helen Powell followed, stirrup-to-stirrup.

"I hope that you and Barbara finished the important conference — satisfactorily?" Helen inquired after a time.

"She's the oddest girl I ever saw — and I had three aggravating sisters."

"She's very fond of you. Perhaps that explains her oddities. She thinks you take unnecessary risks ———"

Clay made a grunting sound, entirely contemptuous.

"If *you're* suggesting the same thing she was ———"

"You don't mean she suggested your marrying her?" Helen cried, with glance at Barbara, and at him. "She didn't!"

"Of course not! As a matter of fact, she ———"

He regarded her maliciously, and grinned.

"She was insisting that I fell in love with you the day I first saw you. And explaining several things to me that she really didn't need to tell me."

"Such as?" the girl prompted him. She was beautifully flushed and the stare trained upon Barbara's back was narrow-eyed. "What did she suggest — or, rather, explain?"

"Well, the fact that you're a sort of stranger in our midst, examining the wild animals that live in our part of the geography book. Saying that one is interesting, another is handsome — as animals go, of course. And that if one of the natives *should* be so silly as to misunderstand the way you looked at him, it would be just too bad —

for him."

"She didn't say such a thing! She — she never would say any such thing!"

Very calmly Clay turned in the saddle to study her. He found himself thoroughly enjoying her evident discomfort. So he made an expansive gesture — spoke very reasonably.

"Why shouldn't she? It's true! That's what I meant, when I said that her explaining wasn't necessary. I knew what you thought of Smiling Badey, and of me and all my kind."

"Why do you so hate Smiling?" she demanded abruptly.

"Hate him? Well, probably because we're two different kinds of men. Up and down, I've seen quite a few like him — born killers, cowards at heart most of 'em, naturally mean. I am not bragging when I say that I feel myself better than they are. Not when I say that I've tangled with some of 'em and haven't come off second-best, any more than I expect to with Smiling, when we meet again. But there was more than just that general feeling, in this case."

He grinned at her.

"I am troubled by my face, you see. It is a durable kind of face; doesn't take marks as much as other men's. So, where I am not known, mistakes are often made. It was that way in Poplar Station some time back, with a man named Pawl, a man who rode with Smiling and the other thieves of that gang."

"That was the man you — killed in the sheriff's office?"

"That was the man — a sidewinder rattlesnake in the form of a human being. Just as deadly. In Poplar Station ——"

He told her the story of the poker game and of the loss of his winnings.

They were on the last turn of the trail, almost overlooking Gurney, when he was done with the story. Barbara waited for them on the shelving road.

"And so, here I am, wearing a star," Clay told Helen. "I want you to understand that I harbor no such notions as Barbara thought. But — I would like for you to understand that I can see a lot of points of difference between myself and the like of Smiling, Pecos Pawl, and the rest of that outfit. If *you* could see those differences, it would somehow please me."

"And Barbara? *She* sees them?"

He stared at her, but her face was expressionless.

"I imagine she does," he said. "If it matters."

They came up to Barbara and she led the

way downslope without speaking. They entered Gurney — a place almost deserted, very quiet, with absence of so many townsmen. Before the Kenedy gate Clay swung down and moved toward the girls. He held their stirrups — first Barbara's, then Helen's. He took their horses to the corral behind the store, when they had gone into the house. When he came back to the black horse, a yell from across the street pivoted him to face, diagonally, the group of men standing outside the Palace Saloon.

"Smiling, Hemming, Yates, and two or three of the Palace bums," he muttered. "Quite a welcoming committee. I would give all the pay I'm ever likely to collect from the county to have Chihuahua and Lum siding me right now. For that is a precious bunch of wolves . . ."

"Clay!" Barbara Kenedy called from the house. "Clay! Wait a minute!"

She came running down the walk to the gate and he turned toward her. Over at the Palace Hemming's bull voice lifted:

"That's the way to do it, Sheriff! Borrow one of her aprons and a sunbonnet. Maybe, then, you won't be knowed!"

"What's it?" Clay asked Barbara. "I'm in a hurry ——"

"A hurry to get yourself killed! If you start

across that street you'll be dead before you get halfway to them! Do *you* know anything about that bunch to make you believe that they care how they kill you?"

He shifted position a trifle so that he could look again at the men before Ritt Rale's place. The group was larger now. Barbara tugged imperatively at his sleeve.

"Idiot! What good will it do to play the Boy Hero and get yourself shot into doll rags? Nobody thinks you're afraid of that pack. Don't be a show-off. Come on in here."

"You know," he said with a sudden tight grin, "that is ex-act-ly what I'll do . . ."

A derisive yell lifted across the street, when he led the black through the Kenedy gate. But with no change in his humorless smile, Clay took the black around the house. There he stopped to regard Barbara with head a little on one side:

"Thanks! You were absolutely right about my going across the street. There's a better way. I just thought of it. And I do appreciate your waking me up to it."

She frowned suspiciously. Helen Powell appeared at the back door.

She stared at them, then ran to where they stood.

"I'm glad you made him see reason!" she

told Barbara.

"I'm not sure I have," Barbara answered acidly. "I've a well-founded notion that I just turned him from one form of lunacy to some other — probably just as bad."

"You're not going to face all those men, by yourself?" Helen cried. "I thought ——"

"The way I'm going to face them," Clay drawled, "the chief danger will be to Smiling and Company, not to me. I am not a bit braver than need be, and I know I am no centipede. One pair of arms is all I own. So all this pulling me out of the street — about as if I was four years old and heading for the well — pleasant as it is, is not necessary. I ——"

Mrs. Kenedy called shrilly from the house; called Barbara. The girl answered, still staring at Clay. And:

"You're not going to play the idiot?" she demanded.

"Absolutely not! I'm going up the street along the back walls, where they won't even see me if I can help it."

She nodded, but her expression had little of conviction. She went into the house. Helen stood close to Clay.

"What *are* you going to do? Barbara should have seen you crossing your fingers, mentally. I saw it!"

"Goodness, me! Don't tell me you watch the interesting animals so close as all that!"

"Don't be silly! Do you think I want you to walk away from here and get killed? Isn't anything serious to you? And I wish you'd stop talking about me as if I walked about telling everyone how much superior I am because I went to school in Philadelphia and my father owns the Ladder P. I never said any such thing; I don't believe Barbara gave you to believe anything like that. She's too — too decent. *You're* the one who puts the wall between you and — and other people! Even my father doesn't!"

Clay stared. The stammering voice, the flushed face, the suspiciously bright eyes — he would not believe what he came slowly to think they meant. His own voice shook, though he tried to speak lightly.

"I'm sorry, but — after all, you are the daughter of the biggest man in all The Territory. And your father would explain just what that means ——"

"That's not so! The only thing he said against you was that you're a young idiot, swelled up with your first dose of office-holding. He said you'd get over that. More! He said that when you did come down from your high, world-reforming perch, to the place where practical men could talk common sense and have you understand them, he had a job for you!"

He was staring bewilderedly when Barbara came out of the house. He was in no mood for more cross-examinations. He swung into the saddle hurriedly and looked at them both.

"Be seeing you!" he said and spurred the black into a run. To himself he mumbled: "I'll be damned! John Powell offering a deputy sheriff a job!"

He did exactly what he told Barbara he intended. He rode up the rear line of the buildings on this side of Gurney's main street, then looked out from the corner of the jail. The group was gone from before the Palace — returned to the bar, he thought. He went across the street with the black fairly doubling himself, and pulled in to swing to the ground and jerk the carbine from its scabbard. He left the horse with reins trailing and once more kept to the back walls of stores, saloons, and other buildings.

At the back door of the Palace he listened, but heard only the murmur of voices from the bar-room. He slid inside with the Winchester at full cock and crossed the back room soundlessly. Now Smiling's voice carried to him distinctly:

"— And dump him right alongside that illegitimate, Prather. Then we'll go down to Kenedy's, like I said."

"San Isidro, huh?" a man cried. "With enough Ladder P steers to pay the ticket!"

Clay looked cautiously inside. Smiling, Yates, and Hemming were at the bar, with beyond them four or five of the usual Palace crowd. Not a man in the place was a respectable townsman, so far as he could determine. He stepped through the door and got his back to the wall.

"Reach!" he snarled at the bar-room generally. "Every one of you — reach!"

Yates was nearest him and he whirled drawing his pistol. Clay shifted the carbine muzzle to the left and fired. Yates came forward, shooting into the floor as he fell. Hemming and Smiling lifted their hands. So did the men beyond them — even the doughy-faced bar-tender.

"Step away from the bar, Hemming — and you others! Line up across the room. Stay where you are, Smiling. You men! Begin with Hemming and drop your artillery on the floor. If you're addicted to hideouts, now's a good time to break the habit. Every gun on the floor!"

Hemming drew the pistol from his holster very carefully and stooped to put it down.

He hesitated, then got from the waistband of his overalls, under his shirt, a second, shorter, Colt. When it was beside the first, he straightened, to glare at Clay. Man by man, five prisoners unburdened themselves of one or two pistols. The bar-tender contributed the house shotgun and two Colts from beneath the bar. He came laggingly out to gather the discarded weapons and carry them to Ritt Rales's big safe that stood open behind the bar. The door slammed on them; the bar-tender spun the combination knob, then rejoined the others.

Clay shifted the Winchester to his left hand, dropping his right to his side. He crossed the room to Smiling, still standing with fixed grin at the bar, hands upon it.

"Back over against that wall, all of you!" he commanded the disarmed group. When the shuffle of feet had ceased, he faced the gunman's red-flecked eyes, and laughed harshly. "A gunslick! You — calling yourself a gunslick!"

"You'll find out!" Smiling assured him. "Be damn' sure of that. You've run over your time. You ——"

Clay began to work the lever of the Winchester, lifting it so the muzzle covered Smiling. He unloaded it and dropped the shells into a pocket of his leggings, then dropped the carbine on the floor.

"A gunslick!" he said again. "What's keeping those hands so high? You know, Smiling, one day a lot of men will begin to think what I've known for a long time — that you play the sure shots. Look at you, now! You won't even pull with me!"

His left hand darted up, pushed Smiling's head back. Smiling's fingers clenched. His elbows jerked. But he looked at Clay's right hand, hanging close to Colt butt. Clay slapped him in the face and Smiling gave ground. Then, while silence hung over the bar-room, Clay forced the other back foot by foot, slapping him methodically, almost rhythmically.

Smiling's face was dark with congested blood. The grin was a snarl, now. But clawing hands stayed away from the handles of his pistols. And Clay addressed him venomously, by every savage term of contempt the cow-country knows. At last Smiling was pushed out onto the sidewalk.

Men were on the street now; in doorways, before store or saloon or office, staring toward the Palace as if drawn to the scene by the shot which had killed Yates.

Some of these, Clay realized, must be friends of Halliday, Merle Sheehan, Kenedy, and the other stalwarts of Gurney, if perhaps not of the same grim disposition which sent the others riding with posses and mixing in battles.

But one swift, comprehensive glance was all he gave them. If some partisan of Rales and Smiling shot at him from the side, that could not be helped. Success of his plan to thoroughly discredit this boy killer depended upon concentration, now. He had pushed Smiling off-balance and every second that passed added to his domination. He knew this instinctively; knew that only some sort of ratlike desperation would send Smiling's hand to a pistol. And he would draw and kill Smiling if the gunman tried to draw. He knew that, also. But he did not want to kill Smiling; not now.

So he gave Smiling no opportunity to consider the degree of this disgrace. He slapped him into the street and in its center suddenly paused.

"A rat! Just a rat!" he said contemptuously — and so clearly that every watcher could hear. "Except that a rat's said to fight when he's cornered, and you won't! Do you always have to get a gang of sneaks at your back before you can shoot somebody from behind a rock? Can't I find any way to make you fight?"

The darting left hand came forward to

311

jerk a gun from one of Smiling's holsters. Clay tossed it behind him, pulled the second Colt and sent it whirling. Then he closed his hands and Gurney watched them fascinatedly while Smiling was beaten to the dust, jerked to his feet and pounded remorselessly down again. Smiling sprawled in the street. His arms and legs jerked feebly, as if his back were broken. Clay turned and looked all around. He faced honest townsmen whose amazed expressions were twisting into pleased grins; eyed some men who began to look most uncomfortable; stared long at Hemming and the Palace loafers, who were framed by the Palace door.

But it was a stocky, frowning Mexican youth who held his attention longest. Antonio, cousin of that imbecile-beggar Bronzalez, looked moodily at the battered, bloody figure of the man who had ordered his cousin's murder. Catching Clay's eyes on him, he stiffened. His brown face blanked. He turned and went shuffling away.

Into the street, now, from the road across the Diablos, horsemen came at the trot. Clay stared, then grinned, recognizing Chihuahua, Lum, Halliday, and Old Comanche Smith. The posse turned his way, staring at the huddle in the dust. Clay walked out to the calico's head. Chihuahua's blue eyes flashed to Smiling, narrowed, shuttled back to his friend.

"You're — kill him at last, hah?" he said softly.

Then Smiling moved, rolling over and propping himself on a hand. Chihuahua swore snarlingly and whipped out a Colt — Clay checked him with a word and they watched — all the posse staring — while the deflated, discredited gunman staggered to his feet. Smiling did not turn toward the Palace. He seemed not to see the riders. Swerving from left to right, staggering like a drunken man, he went down the street.

"You just beat him about to death, huh?" Halliday said disapprovingly. "Clay, that was God-damn' foolishness! That kind is deadly till its tail stops wiggling — like any other brand of snake. You know what you done? You just the same as killed two-three men. He'll have to kill some nitwit to get back his place in the hard cases. Yes, sir! You meant right, no doubt, to shame him before everybody. But what you done was kill some men you never laid eyes on ——"

"No-o," Clay disagreed. "I think you're wrong, Halliday!"

"He's right as hell!" Old Comanche Smith said viciously. "I seen it happen time and again. You poke a pin in the circus balloon that's strutting around any town, and he has got to run out after and kill somebody to get back where he was."

Merle Sheehan and others of the old-timers nodded agreement. But Clay, watching the wavering progress of his enemy toward the Mexican end of Gurney, shook his head.

"No! What I have done is kill Smiling. I have showed him to the people around as owning a skunk-wide yellow streak. Now, some two-by-four hard case with a shiny, new pistol will slap leather with him and ——"

He stopped, leaning a little forward. Smiling was fifty yards away, now. He staggered less in his walk. Out from the sidewalk a stocky figure moved, going toward him. While Clay watched, Antonio, the one-time porter of the Palace, stepped in front of Smiling. The two short figures were moveless for as much as ten seconds. Then Antonio stepped back. His white-sleeved arm jerked. He swung something wide ——

"A cleaver!" Clay said in awed voice. "A butcher's cleaver! He — *amor de dios!* Look at that!"

Smiling's head jumped upward a foot, turned sluggishly in air and struck the dust

314

while yet his body was erect. Clay shivered, then whirled to Chihuahua and caught the cantle of his saddle. He went up behind on the calico and Chihuahua spurred down the street to pull in, sliding the paint horse to a dust-wreathed halt. Clay dropped off.

He looked once at Antonio, who stood with the cleaver sagging at his side, staring vacantly down. Then the sight of a brown belt, strapped about the tanned skin of Smiling's belly, drew his eyes. He bent and moved the flapping shirt-tail farther, while he unbuckled the money belt.

"He was a coward," Antonio said thickly, almost dully, in Spanish. "I laugh to think of the days when I was afraid of him. But after you showed me — and all these others — that he was a coward, I knew that I would kill him as easily as I have stamped upon a snake. I surrender to you, for trial."

They gathered in the sheriff's office to take stock — Chihuahua and Lum, Halliday, Comanche Smith, and Clay. Grim Old Comanche, even, was repressed. For Smiling and Yates were now lying in the vacant store beyond the Palace and these were the men who had moved them out of saloon and street.

"So," Halliday said thoughtfully, ending his report of the posse's doing, "such of that

Tough Bunch as won't be permanent in the county are splitting the breeze away. And John Powell will be needing to hire him some more riders to go on with Ladder P work."

"And Powell?" Clay inquired tonelessly. "He got away from you all right?"

They nodded. Chihuahua grinned suddenly:

"Me, I'm wonder w'ere's Jed Wyndham and them other nester. We're riding hard, but ——"

He shrugged. Clay lifted a shoulder and let it sag.

"Probably they're looking over the Ladder P to decide what they ought to be — what's it Wyndham calls getting stock from Powell? *Recovering!* They'll probably recover enough to even up for what they've lost. Can't blame 'em. But, all in all, as I sit here looking around, it seems to me that my final report on conditions will be short and encouraging."

"And — just what is the implication, my young friend?" Lum Luckett inquired. "Why the necessity at this particular moment, for a *final* report?"

Halliday, Chihuahua, and Comanche stared at them both. Clay fumbled beneath his shirt to find the buckles of that money belt which he had taken from Smiling. He looped it snakily on the table and opened pockets of it. Bills and gold spilled before the watchers. He grinned faintly:

"When I left Poplar Station to head this way, I figured that Smiling owed me nine hundred and eighty dollars which one of his shoulder-strikers had taken off me. I found twelve hundred and some dollars in this belt he was wearing. I'm not bothering the county to straighten this little matter. I'll call the extra my interest. Now ———"

He replaced the money and buckled on the belt before turning to Halliday. He surveyed that puzzled gentleman for an instant, then reached to the badge upon his shirt. He unpinned it and pushed it across the table.

"You're a county commissioner, Halliday. You swore me in. So — I'm handing back your star and resigning. We have got John Powell on the run. Smiling and Company are" — he snapped his fingers eloquently — "and Ritt Rales, when he comes back to town, can be convicted of something or other. Bronzalez's murder, for instance. Antonio ———"

"Sí, señor! What is you wish?"

Antonio came into the office. His square face was blank.

"I was about to say," Clay told him, "that you are a witness to the conspiracy to murder your cousin. You will testify against him ——"

"But, señor," Antonio said softly, "I cannot do that — now. For Ritt Rales came to Gurney a while ago. I — saw him. He saw me also. He was a very bad man, señor — señores all! He would have killed me, I am sure, because of what I might say in the court. If he had *known* that I had heard him order my cousin's death, I am certain that he would have killed me. He saw me, Antonio. Upon his pistol he put his hand. *Ay de mi!* If I had not shot him before he shot me, I would now be dead, señores all!"

He leaned stolidly against the door-frame and shook his head. They stared at him, then at each other.

"Good riddance!" Comanche Smith exploded. "But about this resigning, Clay ——"

"I'm going home and dump a thousand dollars in my mother's lap," Clay told them carefully. "That's all I came over for — to collect what Smiling owed me."

"Wide — Green — Land — of-Goshen!" Halliday grunted. "If that is all brought you over, Smiling would have been owl-wise to send you the money. Remind me, Co-

318

manche, never to owe a Texas boy above a few dollars! You won't change your mind, Clay? You really aim to quit us?"

Clay nodded. He avoided Chihuahua and Lum with his stare about the office. They said nothing. Halliday nodded at the last and he and Comanche filed out, to go about their regular business. Lum rose and stood behind Clay. He rubbed that young man's hair with hard knuckles. Clay snarled and Chihuahua, grinning, reached down to catch an ankle and tilt Clay's chair so that he leaned against Lum.

"So young!" Chihuahua sighed. "So young for to be so fi-ne liar, w'at, Lum?"

"The point which grieves me most," Lum said with equal melancholy, "is the reiteration of the financial angle. Who ever knew a cowboy to speak of money? The question being purely rhetorical, no answer is required. But, Clay, my young and transparent companion, never think that this commercial, this mercenary, red herring you draw across the trail leads either Chihuahua or me an inch from the truth. It's — the girl. *No es verdad,* Carlos José de Guerra y Morales? *'Sta la niña y nada mas!*"

"*La niña,*" Chihuahua agreed, nodding. "So, this *tontito* — this young idiot — she will run like hell away."

"All right!" Clay said flatly. "If you two longnoses have got to know all about it, it *is* the girl who's running me out of The Territory. Here's one Texas saddle lobo with good sense; too much sense, anyhow, to stick his head in where a brick can land on it. I'm not in love with the girl — but I could fall so far in love that there'd be no pulling myself out — ever! I'm not going to do it."

"*Pues,* me, I'm not say she's not best," Chihuahua admitted. "But — she's one ver' lovely girl, them Helen Powell. You're come back. You're hear about them Rowdy River water? Once you're drink it, you'll never stay away . . ."

"I'll take whisky!" Clay told him — and his tone was grim.

Chapter XVI

The western sky was cloudless, and now, as the three friends walked from the courthouse toward Mrs. Sheehan's dining-room along a quiet street, Clay watched mechanically the miracle of a Territory sunset.

One huge sheet of palest salmon faced him, as evenly tinted as if colored by a single gigantic brush stroke. The Diablos were not solid mountains. They became for an instant a ground-hugging roll of smoke, so gray a blue and so dappled by shining patches of reflected sunlight that they appeared translucent.

"I have watched a thousand sunsets," Lum said slowly, as if speaking to himself. "Each was different. Now, do you suppose that somewhere out of sight there is a stage manager such as that one I watched in Kansas City last year? *He* was a busy man, with his bag of tricks, and his signals for more of the yellow light and change of the thingumajig there and another place. But his best sunset was an utterly insignificant red ball with streaks of pinky light around it. *That ——*"

The golden hue dulled and was instantly so blue that only the silvered outlines of the Diablo peaks against it, shining saw teeth, divided mountains and sky. Along the street lights shone through windows and doors, making gilt patterns upon the sidewalks. Clay stared broodingly.

"You know," he said slowly, "there's one fine thing about making up your mind. Even if what you're bound to do is not anywhere near what you'd like to do. It's — well, it's a good deal like standing around a restaurant and not having money in your pocket to buy all the fancy items on the menu. You dig your nickel out of the seams of your pocket and take a loaf of bread and go out under a hackberry tree and sit down. And it turns out a pretty good *comida,* after all . . ."

"A philosopher!" Lum cried admiringly. "Nothing less!"

"And w'at's these philosopher-animal?" Chihuahua demanded. "Me, I'm shoot many thing. But no philosopher."

"A philosopher, in this specific instance, is a young man of — well, of Clay's general similitude. He loves a girl, but she is far above him in worldly station. She realizes not that beneath his tattered flannel shirt may beat a heart of gold. Nay, nay, Pauline! Not she! Instead, she is lured by the glitter of superficial accomplishments. So our Young Hero — Philosopher to you, Mister de Guerra — reconciles himself to his fate. Upon his noble steed he throws the caparisons of travel and hies him forth to slaughter dragons and — ah-h-h!"

"Dragons and — w'at?"

"That 'ah!' was not explanatory, but exclamatory." Lum grunted, hopping while he rubbed the shin that Clay had kicked. "It signified one philosopher reverting to cowboy."

"You're ride out, tomorrow, for Walker's, huh?" Chihuahua asked Clay. "For Azulero. And then you're travel for Texas. But — Clay, you're never cut out for to be them granger and follow them plow and look two mules in the tail. *Nunca! Jamás!* You're one fi-ine cowman, Long Al Kendrick's tell me and Lum on them Bar B. You're come back! These damn' Territory, she's like you fine, Clay. W'y will you not take up some ranch and build up like John Powell's Ladder P? And be them *político* and, maybe, them Governor? She's not so hard."

"I'm coming back!" Clay confessed. "I've

seen a lot of country. But there's none of it spread out behind Azulero and me that really pulls — the way The Territory pulls me. I'll be back, and I'll hunt up you two abandoned souls and give you the benefit of associating with me again. Of course, by that time Lum will probably be managing the B K Doughnut Factory and wearing one of Barbara's checked aprons. But that's all right. Water finds its own level, they say. So if a just-fair-to-middling cowboy gets to be a *good* doughnutmaker ——"

He sprang ahead of them and raced across Mrs. Sheehan's porch and so into the hotel hall.

They ate very cheerfully. Clay found himself not in the least unhappy about leaving Gurney. That oddity he had commented of finding peace of mind in any sort of decision was very plain to him. He would not forget Helen Powell, but neither would he go up and down making a life work of nursing disappointment. He had too much pride for any such silly weakness as that. He was a good man — he knew it, now. He would make The Territory feel his hand. He ——

Barbara Kenedy materialized at his shoulder and he stared, jerked from his thoughts, hazy plans.

"You're wanted, Clay," she said quietly.

"Come along. Quickly, for there's not much time."

He got up automatically. The others stood, too. But she shook her head at them.

"Just Clay. It's a — very personal matter. He may be back soon. Or —— Come on, boy!"

Outside, he recovered his voice. He asked her what was wanted and in a flat tone she told him that John Powell was dying in her house.

"Only he knows how many miles he rode after he was shot. But he had things to do and so he simply refused to die until he had got here to Gurney to see Helen. Typically John Powell! Now, he insists that he has to talk to you. So — I trot like a little doll on a string to find you, and you trot to talk to him like another puppet. Until he's in the ground — and perhaps for years after he's dead — certain ones will be dancing to his last jerk on the string!"

"But what does he want with me? Oh, I suppose he hasn't heard that I resigned my star. He wants to tell the acting sheriff who shot him and be sure that something's done. Typically John Powell! Never had a friend; never forgot an enemy. But he ought to tell his story to Chihuahua and Lum."

She said nothing. They turned in at the

Kenedy gate and went with elbows brushing up the walk. The sitting-room was lighted; so was a bedroom off it.

John Powell's long body, his Indian-like face, were an incongruous spectacle against the bright frills of Barbara's room. There was a flush upon his high cheekbones, giving them the look of burnished copper. His narrow, dark eyes were as steady, as sardonic, as Clay had ever seen them.

"Come over here," he commanded evenly. "I have no strength to waste in yelling."

Clay looked at Helen, who sat beside the bed with a glass in her hand. She was pale, very grave, but dry-eyed. He could understand that. To her John Powell must be a comparative stranger; at most, no nearer than some cousin or uncle seen but recently. And he had appeared as cold and hard toward her as toward the rest of his world.

Moving to the side of the bed to look down at Powell, Clay faced her. She did not speak to him, or make any other sign of recognition. And that stiffened him. He waited for Powell to say what he had to say. And he felt no slightest pity for the dying man. John Powell had done as nearly what he wanted to do as had been possible. He had ordered the murder of men, the theft of their property, the ruin of their lives, without the faintest sign of hesitation.

"Serves the devil right," Clay thought.

"That horse of Rodell's was a good one," Powell told him. "I got clear of everybody. But Jed Wyndham guessed the way I would go and he was waiting for me. And so John Powell is beat at the last by an ignorant nester and a dime's worth of Winchester cartridges — John Powell!"

"No-o," Clay disagreed. "John Powell was beat because of his own ignorance. You have always over-estimated yourself and underestimated other men. Jed Wyndham was not an educated man in your way. But you forgot that you were playing *his* game, not yours, when you started shooting. You should have lawed the little fellows out of their property. Shooting is a two-handed game."

Powell's eyes narrowed and brightened, as he faced the younger man's contempt. A corner of his thin mouth lifted.

"Young! You are very young! But I have to turn to you because out of the men available you come nearest fitting. I'm not going to waste time, arguing with you about morality. The world is a place where the strong eats the weak. I had plans that would have made, not merely the Ladder P, but the whole Territory, what now it will not be

327

within fifteen years, if ever! But that is off the board, now. For I was the only one who could have done the work. I called you in to tell you what part you play, in salvaging what may be from the wreck. Give me a drink, Helen!"

White-faced, looking almost like a sleep-walker, Helen leaned to put the glass to his mouth. He drank with gasping noises and settled again on the pillow. Helen straightened and continued to sit staring straight ahead of her.

"One of my plans," Powell continued in the flat, strained monotone that told, as almost nothing else about him did, the effort of will he exercised, "concerns the Helen Grove Powell Memorial Ward. It has existed for years — since shortly after the death of my wife. I — have few soft places, as The Territory knows. This was the idea of Helen's mother. I created it. I have supported it. I intend that it shall continue."

He motioned, and again Helen put the glass to his hard mouth and he swallowed chokingly.

"There are several ways by which I could provide for money to be paid the Memorial. But most of them would necessitate joint management of the Ladder P, in Helen's behalf and that of the Memorial

Fund. Or sale of the Ladder P. Probably either would mean destruction of my work, eventually. And I want the Ladder P to go on — twenty-five years of my work and thought are in it — and now my blood as well as my sweat. I will *not* have that go for nothing! I — I —— But never mind that! The important thing is this — my decision:

"I have provided in a will now being drawn up by Judge Blankenship, my attorney, for the payment to the Memorial Fund of certain sums out of net income. They are not large. Efficient management of the ranch will easily reduce them to the net income from about an eighth part of the property. The joker in the deck is that term 'efficient management' — and that is what I am trying to provide!"

Clay stared frowningly from Powell to Helen. The thought that was forming seemed upon examination too incredible for belief. Powell saw his puzzled face and grinned sardonically.

"Yes! Exactly! Out of the men I can draw upon, I choose the idealistic young deputy sheriff who has thrust himself into my affairs with more persistence — and, I must admit, more success — than anyone has done in a quarter-century. It happens that I took the trouble to look over your back trail.

The idea was to see what might be used against you. But I find that you have some talent for management, even some experience as foreman on the Bar B and behind that. *So* I choose you to step into my shoes and keep the Ladder P a going cow-outfit!"

"I —— Well, this is ——" Clay began stumblingly. "You know about how any man with ideas would look at a chance to run the biggest outfit in the country. But — I think I can promise to — to make it a day-and-night job ——"

"I'm providing the incentive to assure that," Powell said in an odd tone. He looked at Helen's pale, mask-like face and a corner of his thin mouth lifted. "Providing, also, for security and continuance of the Ladder P management under you . . . I have already spoken to Helen about it. She — agrees with me. I am not providing for a salary or a per centum of profits to be taken by the manager, except in a particular manner. What I *am* providing for is a half of the net income — after the Memorial Fund is cared for. I am willing to give Helen and her husband three-fourths the Ladder P — the legal terminology may be a trifle at variance with this, but it amounts to the same thing. To Helen and her husband . . . If you want the management of the Ladder P, you will marry her here, while I am still alive to see."

Clay stared stupidly at the coppery mask upon the white pillow. Then his eyes shifted to the girl. She did not look at him. Apparently, she had not even heard.

"Naturally," Powell's level voice cut in upon his bewildered thought of this unbelievable proposal, "I have devoted a good deal of thought to Helen's eventual marriage. Because the Ladder P is more important than any silly considerations of romance; and juvenile likes or dislikes. I could pick an Eastern son-in-law — rather, let her choose one, now — with all the airs and graces that *I* brought into this country. But for my purposes you are the ideal type — an ambitious and honest frontier type. So ____"

"Knowing how you feel about — about us — about me," Clay said slowly, hesitantly, to the quiet girl, "are you willing to do this? Willing to marry your ranch manager?"

"Knowing how I feel, I am willing," she answered, and her tone was as flat, even, as John Powell's.

"But you don't know much about me!" Clay persisted. He was surprised at his own calmness. "My people are Texas farmers. My sisters are married to cowmen and

farmers. I am in no sense an educated man
——"

"Helen's grandfather was a Pennsylvania farmer," Powell put in. "He made fortunate speculations and so I went to college and even into the sacred precincts of a bank. Books! Anything you need from books you can get. You have education in your own field. If *I* say so, be sure you have! Now
——"

"All right!" Clay drawled, and there was a metallic tone about his acceptance. "One Texas saddle tramp is the new ramrod of the Ladder P. Oh! It's going to be run on a different plan, Powell. Years from now, maybe, The Territory may even forget that the P stood most often for Potshot — at little men. It's always been my notion that a big brand wouldn't just have to go broke, being honest."

"Call Judge Blankenship," Powell commanded the room in general. "He should be done with that will. And he's a justice of the peace."

Clay had never really considered the formalities of a wedding. His own, least of all. But he found himself a trifle surprised that so little was entailed, in a ceremony he had always believed so important to the pair concerned. John Powell produced by some legerdemain a gold band ring which had been in some pocket. Clay found the room crowded without knowledge of how Chihuahua, Lum, Barbara Kenedy and her mother, the Sheehans, Halliday, had got there. He made responses mechanically; slipped the ring upon Helen's limp finger.

"Now, kiss the bride," old Blankenship commanded him.

Helen's face was flushed, now, but as expressionless as when she sat beside John Powell's bed. He brushed her chin lightly with tight mouth and straightened. Then they were separated. Barbara Kenedy's face was as smileless as Helen's. The two moved toward Powell's bed. Clay looked stonily that way.

Powell called Blankenship. His voice was low, strained. He seemed a smaller man, somehow, Clay thought. As if he had been robbed of something that had swelled his chest. Suddenly, the room was unbearable. Clay turned abruptly and went out. He stood in the moonlit yard, at that corner of the Kenedy house where he had talked to the girls before going to face Smiling. He heard no sound, but Chihuahua's soft drawl remarked the brilliance of the moonlight and went on to speak of the Wyndhams and Howards and Buissons and other little men.

"I'll make up to 'em as best I can for what they've lost," Clay said. "If you and Lum will stick with me ——"

"Me, I'm ride with you all right," Chihuahua assured him. "But Lum — she's bite by them ambition, too. She will be acting sheriff and chief deputy w'en Smoky's come back. Barbara Kenedy will be the brand these ambition wear. But me — w'at the hell! W'ere will I find more than w'en I'm range boss of them Ladder P? We're have trouble until these red time of your — father-in-law, she's wipe away. She's not so bad, now, w'en all them scoundrel w'at we're put in jail, they're gone — hightailing or dead. But —— You're not happy, my friend?"

"I'm wondering why the hell I did it!" Clay cried with sudden savagery. "Barbara said that some of us would be dancing to his God-damn' string pulling after he was dead! And I'm one of the dollies that'll dance! Why did I let him put me here? He reached out and got me just as he'd get a prize bull or a stallion to help the Ladder P. And — for a few minutes I had a notion — and by the time I realized it was damn' foolishness, it was too late to do anything!"

"You're — you're *not* love her?" Chihuahua demanded incredulously. "W'y ——"

"That's the trouble! I'm crazy about her — I have been from the beginning, but I wouldn't admit it. And now ——"

"Chihuahua," Helen Powell said imperiously from behind them, "will you — run along, please?"

She came to stand before Clay, looking up at him silently. He watched, very stiff and uncomfortable.

"You asked me, in there, if — feeling as I did about you — I were willing to marry my ranch manager. And I answered you that — knowing how I feel — I was. I could have said more, but nobody asked me; not my father, nor you. I could have said that, feeling as I do, as I have for a good while, I was *happy* — or would have been, if I had thought you cared ——"

"Cared?" Clay said huskily. "I had the wild thought for a minute — that you might unbend a little and lean my way — and then I looked at you ——"

She was very close to him, suddenly. Her face came up.

"That wasn't much of a kiss, in there. I think I could show you how — if you needed showing ——"

"If I needed showing!" he said. "But I don't!"